'He's mine!' Os   neck. 'He's mine

Grandpa thought rapidly. This was a horse that had arrived as though the sea god Manannán himself had sent it; a horse that wouldn't let Grandpa, with all his years of horse-lore, command it yet allowed a little boy of seven whom it had never seen before mount and ride it.

'He has a strange name,' Grandpa said smiling to himself as he thought of the perfect name.

'He's my horse!' Ossie said, half talking to himself, still running his hand along his mount's neck. 'What's he called?'

'He's called Tir na n-Og.'

'Why is he called that?'

'Because he came from a land under the sea,' Grandpa said. His eyes focused in the distance and he added softly, 'He came from a place where it is always summer and where no one grows old . . .'

Ossie's eyes filled with delight. He knew his grandfather's storytelling voice. 'Will you tell us the story, Grandpa?'

Into the West

Mary Ryan

HEADLINE

Copyright © 1992/1993 Littlebird Venture 3

The right of Mary Ryan to be identified as the Author of
the Work has been asserted by her in accordance with the
Copyright, Designs and Patents Act 1988.

First published in 1992
by HEADLINE BOOK PUBLISHING PLC

10 9 8 7 6 5 4 3 2

All rights reserved. No part of this publication may be
reproduced, stored in a retrieval system, or transmitted,
in any form or by any means without the prior written
permission of the publisher, nor be otherwise circulated
in any form of binding or cover other than that in which
it is published and without a similar condition being
imposed on the subsequent purchaser.

All characters in this publication are fictitious
and any resemblance to real persons, living or dead,
is purely coincidental.

ISBN 0 7472 4160 0

Typeset by Keyboard Services, Luton

Printed and bound in Great Britain by
HarperCollins Manufacturing, Glasgow

HEADLINE BOOK PUBLISHING PLC
Headline House
79 Great Titchfield Street
London W1P 7FN

Into the West

Chapter One

The sea was calm. It surged gently, but broke on the shore in ragged lines of fury. The moonlight silvered the water, outlined the dark mountains of the hinterland. There was no sound but the sea, surging, receding, surging again. There was a breeze, but it was almost silent and full of salt.

The horse came at full gallop round the bay, a white horse, mane flying, hooves pounding. It tore through the surf, head up, white tail flowing. In the moonlight it seemed part of the tableau, the silver sea, the sand, the white spume of the breakers.

Grandpa Ward heard it. He drifted out of sleep and heard the hooves. At first his sleepy mind filled with stories of what plunging hooves in the night could mean: horses were the messengers of the Sidhe, the fairy people; or it could be the Pooka, a black horse with eyes of fire, a harbinger of death.

As his mind cleared he realised that the thundering hooves were below him, down on the beach under the cliff. He listened, all senses alert, his body rigid in his narrow caravan bed. Then he made the sign of the cross in the darkness. He worried about his own horse, old Dan; the Pooka might attack him and poor

Dan was hobbled and couldn't run from it.

At dawn Grandpa Ward emerged from the caravan; he knew the Pooka couldn't touch him once it was daylight. He checked on Dan who was still on his hobble, quietly grazing in a circle. Then he crept to the edge of the cliff and looked down on the bay.

Galloping through the surf was a white horse. He watched it. It was beautiful, it held its head proudly and there was spirit in the lashing of its tail. Its spine was straight; it was young and wild and free. The look of a horse that has never been broken, Grandpa thought. Where do you come from? He watched the white horse for some time, feeling a fierce kinship and envy. The morning light shifted across the bay and touched the panorama of mountains, bluer and bluer in the distance, the heather and the grey rocks. The dawn cry of seabirds rose above the murmur of the sea and the turmoil of the breakers.

Grandpa got his bucket and sickle and picked his way down to the beach. He was looking for mussels and carragheen moss. He found them in abundance, filled his bucket and kept a wary eye on the white horse. It threw its head upwards when it saw him, reared, whinnied, stopped and stared. For a moment man and horse took each other's measure. Grandpa's spine tingled.

Then he went back to the caravan, picking his way carefully on the rocks. He gave Dan his breakfast, offering him some of the mangles he'd pulled a while back. Dan seemed unaware of the close presence of the other horse, which was strange, but he was seventeen years old and getting on. Getting on like meself, Grandpa thought as he ate his own breakfast of buttermilk and brown bread. When Dan had eaten the mangles and drunk his fill from the bucket of water, his master harnessed him to the caravan, climbed on to the seat, slapped the reins against his rump and the caravan trundled away.

Grandpa Ward was sixty-six years old. He was thin, spry, weathered, with a shrewd old face, etched and crinkled with lines, kind eyes and a beard which had once been brown but was now almost entirely white. He was older than his years, a travelling man, a tinker, who had lived his life in barrel-topped caravans, moving with his tribe from location to location, setting up camp on wide stretches of the 'long acre' on the side of the road, or sometimes in the shadow of a mountain, or on a bit of commonage within hearing of the sea. The camp fires would crackle, washed clothes would be spread on the bushes to dry, the skewbald and piebald and chestnut ponies would graze, the children scream in play, while the adults looked to the sky and tasted the wind for tomorrow's weather.

Grandpa knew every good halting place in the length and breadth of the country, recalled them with nostalgia, smelling often in memory the smoke from the wood fires, the delicate aroma of potatoes roasted in the ashes, the scent of spring after a hard winter. It had been a life of freedom and hardship and fierce tribal loyalties, all lost to him now. His family were no longer wandering people. His son-in-law, John Riley, otherwise known as Papa Riley, had joined the settled community and lived with his two young sons in a flat in a great tower on the north side of Dublin.

Grandpa loved his grandsons, twelve-year-old Tito and seven-year-old Ossie, and he mourned for his dead daughter Mary. But he seldom stayed with his son-in-law, hating the concrete hellhole he and the children inhabited fourteen floors up, with its distant view of the Wicklow hills and freedom, preferring instead to roam at will. When he wasn't on the road, he stayed in the travellers' encampment near the Towers of Ballymun. He had left his own tribe when his daughter died and his son-in-law defected to the settled world, and he knew that he faced an uncertain and possibly solitary old age. The travellers were not free, as once they were; the roads were no longer open to them; the pressures of the modern world demanded that they stay in their encampments or that they join the settled community. Grandpa dismissed all this; he would roam until the day he died.

He lived by occasional horse-dealing and scrap-dealing. He liked to use his hands and was a skilled craftsman, a maker of tin pots and pans, a repairer of old tin vessels of all descriptions. He remembered the old people's talk about the days when the tinkers were welcomed, the days before newspapers, radio or television, when it was they who brought the news to the countryside as they sat in the farmers' kitchens plying their trade. But most of all Grandpa was a storyteller, a dreamer, a reluctant seer, his soul searching the secrets in the wind. He read the cards at fairs for all comers, was a tipster at race courses, but was prudent enough to make sure he was gone before the big race started.

Now he turned his back on the sea and sought the road. Dan quickened his pace, feeling the reins sharp on his rump, the voice of his master crying 'H'up.' He knew that the road lay east and that there would be resting places along the way and that he could take the journey at an easy pace. He and Grandpa had been together for a long time and knew each other well.

Grandpa lay back against the half-door of his caravan, watching the road through almost closed eyes. He forced himself to think of the load of scrap back in Dublin, of the farmers' houses he would call at, of where he would camp that night, forced himself to recall each snare that he had set. But his brain was in turmoil. All he could see in his mind's eye was a breathtaking panorama of blues and whites and a beautiful horse charging through the breakers as though it were part of the wildness and mystery of the waves.

Suddenly Dan whinnied and flattened his ears. The caravan jolted in the traces as the old horse came to an abrupt stop. Grandpa Ward opened his eyes. Blocking the road at the next bend was the white horse. There was no mistaking the arrogant stance, the toss of the head, the flowing tail. He watched the animal, fascinated, waiting for it to move. It had not passed them on the road. It must have moved across country, as though with the deliberate purpose of blocking their path. It stood, with no apparent intention of getting out of the way, and its calm, dark eyes stared at Grandpa.

The old man got down from the caravan. 'Who are

you at all, at all?' he muttered under his breath as he slowly approached, only half aware of a thin shiver of fear crawling through the roots of his hair. The horse did not move.

Grandpa reached out to touch him, ran both his warm calloused hands slowly down the animal's left foreleg, sliding his thumb slowly past the coarse 'chestnut', until he reached the fetlock. 'Sound as a bell,' he muttered, 'sound as a bell, my beauty!' In his mind mercenary principles suddenly asserted themselves; he saw himself taking this horse with him, thought of the price it would fetch, scanned his mind for likely customers. Then he picked up the leg and stared at the hoof. The frog was still clotted with sand, held in by the shoe. 'You're no wild horse; you've been recently shod!' he exclaimed out loud. 'Maybe there's a reward for whoever catches you.' And then he stared again at the shoe and drew his breath in sharply. 'But how'd they get the shoe on without using nails?' he whispered and looked up at the horse. It regarded him warily from large black eyes and did not answer.

'Modern technology again, I suppose,' Grandpa answered himself with thin distaste. He reached into the caravan for a halter, but as he tried to slip it on to the horse it threw up its head, snorted, rolled its eyes. Grandpa whispered to it, gentling it. 'It's all right, it's all right. Will you hold your whist a minute now,' but the white horse would not be haltered and reared again in outrage as Grandpa tried once more to assert dominion.

I'm too old for this, the old man thought as he

retreated out of reach of the flailing hooves and climbed back on to his caravan. 'Catching the likes of you is a job for the young. I'll be on my way, my beauty, and let you go yours!' He slapped the reins on to Dan's rump and the caravan started to roll, moving past the white horse on to the clear open road ahead. 'Let you go about your business now, and good luck to you,' Grandpa said out loud in parting.

One person who would have been able for the horse was his son-in-law Papa Riley, he thought, the one time 'king' of the tinkers, killing himself with grief over Mary. She had been dead for seven years and still he mourned with the first fury of his bereavement, as though his sorrow sustained and fed on itself. Grandpa thought of his two grandsons, motherless, tribeless; Tito and little Ossie, lost in the way of life of the settled people, mitching school, having the benefit of neither one way of life nor of the other. Ossie had asthma; sometimes his breathing stopped and he turned blue. Tito knew how to 'steam' him, make him sit over a basin of hot water and cover his head with a towel until the vapour eased his tubes and he could breathe more easily. Tito at twelve was surrogate mother; a strange job for a lad, his grandfather mused, a strange, hard, cruel class of a job for a kid.

Grandpa felt Ossie's passionate yearning for his mother, saw the way he would watch women holding children by the hand as they went by on the street, the way he would follow the interplay between child and parent with a white face, like someone, banished for ever, looking in on Eden. And he would stare, riveted, at television pictures showing mothers reading to their children or cuddling them, his eyes big and dreaming in his small face.

Once, after some such children's programme, Ossie asked his grandfather, 'Did she love me?'

'She loved you!'

'If she loved me why did she go away?'

'She had no choice, God took her. Ask God about it.' Grandpa schooled himself as he said this, holding back the emotion which threatened to overwhelm him. How often had he not asked the same question. 'Why? Why Mary?' But his grief was just as much for Ossie and for Tito as for his daughter; her children were so desperately alone, waiting every night for their father's return only to have him brush by them and fling himself down on his bed, drunk and useless.

Ossie had burst into silent tears, his little face screwed up in anguish. 'Will God let her come back? I want her to come back.'

Grandpa took the child in his arms. 'Whist now, whist. She cannot come back, but you will go to her.'

Ossie's tears stopped and his face brightened. He stared up into his grandfather's face. 'When?'

Grandpa sighed. 'When you die, child. When you go to where she is.'

But Ossie only cried the harder. Then he ran to the balcony overlooking the crashed cars, the rubbish, the travellers' encampment and the distant whispering mountains, and screamed into the wind which whipped and sang eerily round the tower: 'Mammy! Mammy! I want to see you, Mammy. I want to see you.' He paused and, standing rigidly, raised his face to the sky and screamed with all his strength, '*Mary . . .*'

Grandpa felt the hairs rise on the nape of his neck as he heard the thin howl of pain and longing. Ossie had screamed his mother's name to the wind. What if the mountains heard it, sent it far off? The child's voice was wild and fierce and was picked up and carried away by a cold gust which rattled the door of the balcony and brought Grandpa running. The old man took Ossie's hand, pulled him in, shut the balcony door and tried to comfort him, offering him a boiled sweet he found at the bottom of his pocket.

'Whist now, child,' he murmured, afraid the boy would hear how hard his old heart was thumping. But Ossie seemed suddenly dazed and exhausted.

More recently he had taken to pointing out photographs of women in scraps of newspapers. 'Grandpa, was she like her?'

And he would answer, 'More beautiful than that, much more beautiful than that.'

Ossie never mentioned his mother to his father. Grandpa knew why – the sudden terrible tension in Papa Riley's face and, later, the comatose figure in the bed, the bottle of whiskey or red biddy beside him. Big, strong Papa Riley was turning into a sot.

The children have neither mother nor father, Grandpa thought, and became angry as he always did when he thought of the bleakness of their lives.

He stopped his caravan near the spot where he had set the last snare, climbed down and saw immediately that the white horse had followed him. It was there on the road, about fifty feet behind the caravan. He tried to approach it, but it moved back from him, so he crossed the stone wall into the field to find his snare, muttering under his breath, 'You're one queer hoor of a horse.' He found the snare, which contained a rabbit, still alive, but only barely so. Glad that he had got to it before the fox, he wrung its neck, brought it back to the caravan and began to gut and skin it. As he worked he whistled, keeping an eye at the same time on the strange white animal just a matter of yards away, which grazed the long grass of the roadside and occasionally looked up at him.

'Jaysus,' Grandpa muttered, 'I don't know whether I'm comin' or goin'.' There was something unnatural about what was happening; it made him very nervous. He approached the horse again, flailing his arms. 'Clear off outta this and go back to wherever you belong,' he shouted but the horse just danced away from him, watched him quietly and then returned to its grazing.

Grandpa lit a fire, cooked his rabbit on a spit, ate it with relish; then he washed his hands and face in a stream and wiped his hands on his jacket to dry them. He stroked Dan's velvety nose before climbing back on to the seat and moving off. As he did so, he shouted back at the white horse, 'Be off about your business now and don't be followin' me!'

The white horse stood still, watching the caravan move away down the road, and then it shook its mane and trotted after it.

All the way across the country, the white horse followed. At night Grandpa lay awake in his narrow bed, trying to make sense of it. The horse was real enough; hadn't he felt it with his own hands? It was no Pooka, but all the same there were old stories about people watched by the Sidhe being followed by a white horse. He gibbered at the idea that the Little People might be watching him. He was an old man now, old for a traveller; his time could not be that far off.

He knew a lot about fairies. They inhabited their own kingdom known as the 'Realm'; they were immortal, had insubstantial bodies, could appear and disappear at will. He had met many a traveller who had seen them; they manifested themselves only to the poor and innocent, to those who lacked certainty as to the parameters of reality. But few mortals were equal to the passions of the Little People; once in their power, death was the only escape. There had been great exceptions to this in the past: Oisin had been the lover of a fairy woman until he returned to the land of mortals and died. Oisin had gone with her to Tir na n-Og, the land of the eternally young, the land of heart's desire, far out to the west under the sea. Grandpa pondered the ways of the Sidhe. He feared them; the last thing he wanted was one of their horses latching on to him.

Then it occurred to him that he had it all wrong, that the white horse was merely lonely. A wild horse would have been part of a herd, and it would not have been shod. But here was this creature with no obvious owner. Had it escaped from a horsebox perhaps? Maybe the owner was scouring the country; maybe there would be a reward? He toyed with the idea of calling into a garda station, and rejected it with alacrity. Travelling people steered clear of the police.

So, except for one or two further attempts to catch it, he ignored the white horse for the most part. Every morning when he woke up he expected it to be gone and every morning it was still there, grazing near old Dan. The latter, who by rights should have gone for the stranger with his big yellow teeth and given it something to think about, seemed strangely oblivious of its presence. And the young horse never troubled the old one.

'You're well-behaved anyway,' Grandpa thought. 'But are you half-broken or what, that you won't let me near you?' He had tried everything, cajolements, sugar, curses, but the horse would let him come within an inch or two and then dance away out of reach. For all this recalcitrance, it followed Grandpa's every move and no matter what ploys the old man used to throw it off the scent, no matter how many wrong turns he took to double back on his tracks, the strange animal was there the next time he looked round.

For the first time in his life Grandpa was glad when he saw the Towers of Ballymun above the horizon. They rose, all seven of them, solid and huge and inhuman, like great concrete hives, or like those termite hills in far-off countries he had once seen on television. 'They stick people in them!' he used to mutter. 'Real people!' but today he was silent, aware of the mystery he was unwillingly trailing behind him. The airport was not far off and he heard the sound of a jet, but paid it little heed.

There was the sudden clatter of furious hooves; the white horse shot past the caravan, turned and reared.

Dan whinnied, halted in the traces. Grandpa heard the scream of the jet engine almost above his head and ducked instinctively as the enormous aeroplane crossed the road some small distance ahead of them. The noise seemed to fill the world. The huge underside of the plane was silver, like a great fish. Grandpa felt the warm blast from the jets, the rush of hot air, and experienced, as he always did when he saw aeroplanes at close quarters, the sense of nature's secrets having been uncouthly plundered. His ears rang with the power of the thing; his humanity, which belonged to the earth and the wind and the wild open spaces, was awed and marginalised and angry.

He watched the rearing white horse ahead. 'Bloody fool doesn't know about them planes,' he thought. When the plane had gone, soaring into the sky, the horse trotted back quietly to its self-appointed place behind the caravan.

'It's almost as though he was trying to protect us,' Grandpa thought. 'Jesus, Mary and Holy Saint Joseph, but I've picked up a queer class of a beast!'

He flicked the reins on Dan's rump. He wanted to get to the Towers as quickly as possible. He wanted to see his grandchildren and his son-in-law and be with his own. He looked up at the sky. It was overcast, but there was no rain in the breeze. The city began to enclose him, roads of terraced houses, busy traffic hurtling by, the frenetic modern world he usually tried to steer clear of. He was glad of it now.

Chapter Two

Papa Riley was dressed in an old black leather overcoat, a black polo-neck shirt, brown trousers and cracked shoes. He stumbled across the 'wasteland', a scrap dump in the shadow of the tower where he lived, heading for the travellers' encampment at its boundary. He was over six feet tall and built to match, with very black hair, dark blue eyes and a long, sensitive mouth. He was unshaven and slightly drunk, a condition which was now habitual. Behind him, Tito and Ossie tried to keep up, running a little to match the long strides of their father. They were thin, anxious-looking kids, wearing old anoraks. The older boy had freckles, a grave face and a way of constantly looking out for his little brother. The younger boy had a soft, petulant face, in which his emergence from babyhood and his desire to be a tough guy were at odds. When he opened his mouth you could see from the gaps that he was losing his milk teeth.

Papa turned to them, stopped, looked down into his sons' upturned faces, licked his finger and slicked their hair. 'I'm not your father. The other man is your father. Do you understand?'

The two boys nodded. They always nodded when

Papa delivered himself of a decree. Papa was law. Tito nodded with understanding. Ossie nodded with incomprehension. He knew Papa was his father. Any other prospect filled him with an insecurity which drained the life out of him, made him feel invisible, like someone who didn't really exist.

'Now what's your name?' Papa demanded.

'Murphy,' said Tito.

Papa turned to little Ossie, staring up at him with his mother's eyes. 'And what's your name?'

'Riley! Ossie Riley!' Ossie said this defiantly, with the air of one who wasn't going to be bamboozled.

Papa sighed in exasperation, gritted his teeth and stared into his little son's face. 'Are you trying to put me in jail or what? Now, what's your name again?'

Papa did not understand that he was striking at the roots of Ossie's precarious sense of security. He did not know that the child lay awake at night, talking to the mother he never knew. He did not know that sometimes the little boy felt like a grain of sand in a storm; that only a stubborn, defensive courage stood between him and the nothingness he felt was waiting to overwhelm him. Papa had never acknowledged the emotional needs of his children because he could not cope with his own.

Ossie glanced at Tito, always his mentor, who had moved behind his father's back and was silently mouthing the name 'Murphy', pouting out his lips in a slow phonetic mime.

'Moorphee,' said Ossie.

Papa's face softened. 'Murphy. The most common

name in all Ireland. Can't you bloody well say it and not forget it?'

Ossie's face registered total bewilderment. He knew his name was not Murphy. His name was Riley. He felt that names were important. He did not understand why his father wanted him to change his name. It was like losing his identity, his family. It made him afraid. If he wasn't a Riley then he was no one. His dismay translated itself into physical distress. He began to breathe rapidly, the shallow, tortured breaths of an asthmatic.

Papa pursed his lips. 'Now don't start the funny breathing. Just say your name to the man!'

Tito looked at his small brother's face and said urgently, 'Your name is Murphy. Do you understand?'

Ossie nodded.

'I'm not your father,' Papa added. 'The man you met this morning is your father. Now do you get it?'

Ossie nodded. He didn't get it; he didn't want any other father, but he stared into his father's stern face and he nodded.

'I wish Grandpa would come back,' he confided to Tito as they continued on their way. Their father was striding on ahead, out of earshot. 'I don't want to be a Murphy!'

'Don't be such an eejit!' Tito said, his face a study of elder brother wisdom. 'It's only pretending; it's a kind of game. If you say you're Murphy, that ould fellow we met this morning will get money.'

'Where will he get the money?' Ossie demanded.

'Why would anyone give him money if I say I'm a Murphy? It's stupid!'

'The bloody Government will give him money if you say you're Murphy. Isn't that enough for you?'

Ossie shook his head. 'When will they give him the money?'

'At the encampment, where we're going with Papa,' Tito said. 'There's some man coming from the welfare. You have to tell the man. Then they'll give him the money.'

Ossie brightened. 'Will they give us money too? Will they give us money for saying we're Murphys?'

'No.'

'Why not?'

Tito groaned. 'Why should they?'

Ossie spelt it out. 'If they give him money because we say we're Murphys, why won't they give us money for saying we're Murphys?'

Tito felt that his brain had begun to spin. 'Will you stop asking questions and just do what you're told!'

Ossie was distracted by a mongrel running from the direction of the encampment with something hanging out of its mouth. A young girl was giving chase. 'Stop him. He's stolen the sausages! He's robbed the tea on us!'

Ossie ran. Tito whooped like a red Indian. They cornered the dog eventually, but the sausages had, predictably, disappeared.

'Me Ma'll kill me!' the girl said. She aimed a kick at the dog, but he dodged her and ran sniggering away.

The girl glared after it. 'I'll be murdered. I left the door open!'

She had mousy hair cut short; her teeth were a little crowded in her mouth and her face was sprinkled with pale freckles. She was dressed in jeans and an anorak. She looked at the two boys belligerently as though daring them to laugh.

Tito always avoided girls on principle, in case he caught 'Sissy Disease', but he stared at this one with interest. She was different. She gave him the impression that if it came to a fight, she wouldn't be behind the door; she looked like the kind of girl who'd knock your teeth out first and negotiate afterwards.

'Tell your Ma you don't know anything,' Tito advised.

The girl gave him a pitying look and walked away.

The thought of the sausages reminded Ossie that he was hungry. He looked at the shop they had just passed and then at his brother. 'I'm starving. Tito, I'm starving.'

Tito took a fifty pence piece from his pocket. He had found it that morning in the lift and he handed it over with a sigh. 'Get some crisps – and a bar of chocolate,' he shouted after his brother as Ossie headed for the shop.

When Ossie caught up with his brother and father, Papa looked at the bag of crisps and the bar of chocolate in his hand. 'Where did you get the money for that?'

'I found it,' Tito said. 'I found it this morning in the lift.'

'Be careful about finding money,' Papa said. He gestured to the tower behind him. 'They'll say you stole it. Because you come from travelling people they'll say you stole it.'

'I didn't steal it!' Tito said indignantly.

'I know.' His father placed his hand gently on his son's head. 'I'm just telling you to be careful.'

Tito nodded and followed his father and brother, munching hungrily, shoving the crisps into his mouth as fast as he could stuff them.

The travellers' encampment was full of ramshackle caravans, rusty old cars, stray dogs and roughshod children. They played and shouted and ran around like dervishes. Some of them had a dirty yellow ball and were kicking it, others were vaulting over a pole, landing on the ragged mattress waiting to receive them. Ponies were hobbled on the edge of the encampment and were grazing what was left of the short trampled grass between the rubbish and puddles. The towers threw long shadows across the ground, and the myriad windows of the myriad flats stared out on the travellers and their comings and goings.

Papa stayed at the perimeter. He saw the man in the shiny black shoes and the suit picking his way along the muddy path to the Murphy establishment. He saw Murphy come down the caravan step to talk to him. Mrs Murphy, a red-haired, plump woman in an old pink cardigan, ran out after him and took the man's arm, thrusting her plight at him immediately – all these children and a hard winter behind them. Her husband stood beside her and tried to get a word in.

The man in the suit had a folder and he consulted it as he addressed the Murphys. 'So what exactly do you want from the Department of Social Welfare?'

'An address, sir.'

'You want accommodation?'

Mr Murphy looked woebegone. 'Just a roof over our heads, sir.'

'For the winter that's coming, sir,' Mrs Murphy interjected.

The man in the suit looked around. All he could see were children. 'How many children do you have?'

The Murphy parents exchanged glances. 'About fifteen, sir,' Mrs Murphy said with the air of a woman who had given up conducting head counts.

'About fifteen, sir . . . roughly . . .' her husband added, with the air of a man who left these mundane matters to his wife.

The man in the suit wanted to go back to his office. It was cold and his new shoes were dirty. Milling around him were children of varying ages and sizes and genders. How could anyone have had all these children? But he knew the travellers had large families, that such a large family was feasible. What wasn't feasible was that they should fail to know how many kids they had.

'You don't know how many children you have?'

'I'll have to count them, sir,' Mr Murphy said helpfully. He raised his voice and shouted, 'Boys and girls! Boys and girls!'

Papa Riley, watching from the shadow of the caravan at the edge of the site, thrust his children forward. Tito knew what was expected and Ossie followed him. Their father stood and watched them run to the Murphys. Tito was fine, he thought, a bit thin, but Ossie was frail-looking and too small for his age. For a moment he thought guiltily about his performance as a father. He seldom cooked meals for them; he brought them back fish and chips from time to time or he would give them money and let them buy bread and milk and sausages and eggs and maybe some bananas, and Tito would do the cooking. Sometimes he burnt the food, burnt the pans, and that old biddy Mrs Whelan from next door would complain that the fumes were getting into her flat. She was so fussy about her effing flat you'd think it was bloody Buckingham Palace. And that scutty little yoke of a dog she had – Fu-Fu or Poo-Poo or something. Yap, yap, yap. He longed to plant his boot up its arse.

But Papa knew that sometimes he did not give his children money for food; that he drank every penny he had and left them to fend for themselves. Papa did not like thinking about this. He did not like the waves of self-reproach which engulfed him. But it was easy not to think, easy to forget everything. All he needed was a bottle by the neck; then the world contracted and the past became a blur and the future didn't matter anyway.

Murphy started to count the children. The man in the suit conducted his own count. As they counted, Papa, who was watching with wry amusement, glanced at the entrance to the camp and saw Grandpa Ward arrive in his caravan, turning in from the road, a white horse behind him. His mouth stiffened. The old codger was back, with a new horse by the looks of things, and now he would have to listen to how badly he, Papa, was bringing up the children and how they should take to the road again.

The voices of Murphy and his interrogator came across to him. 'Fourteen,' Murphy said and was nudged by his wife. 'Sorry, fifteen with the baby.'

The man in the suit raised his eyebrows and made a note. 'How many boys and how many girls?' he demanded.

Murphy and wife looked uncertain. 'I never counted them that way, sir,' Mrs Murphy told him.

The man from the welfare sighed. He surveyed the sea of faces. 'Hands up who are girls.'

The hands went up. The count was taken. Some of the 'girls' looked like boys, but he reckoned they ought to know whether they were or not.

'Hands up the boys,' the man said.

Four hands went up, Tito and Ossie's among them. Ossie's went up last. He had to be nudged to comply; his face registered stubborn, childish exasperation.

The man in the suit saw him, saw his reluctance. 'And what's your name, little man?'

Ossie was silent, then he began to breathe heavily. He felt as though time stood still. Panic waited for him, the panic of not wanting to say what he had to say and the panic of not being able to breathe as he wanted to breathe.

'Murphy,' he said on a sudden exhalation of breath.

'And what's your first name?'

Ossie stared at him aghast. No one had told him what his first name was supposed to be. Was it supposed to be something different too? He looked at Tito in desperation, but Tito was aware of the eyes of the stranger on him and stayed silent.

'Mister,' Ossie blurted crossly, 'Mister Murphy!'

The man in the suit laughed. The Murphys laughed. The children picked up the laughter and laughed too. Ossie set his mouth. The man smiled at the child, noting the small soft face, wide eyes and petulant little boy's grimace.

'Well Mr Murphy,' he said conspiratorially, leaning towards Ossie, 'I'm going to put you in a nice warm bedroom,' and he pointed to the towers behind them, 'right up there. Would you like that?'

Ossie glanced back at the towers and made a face. Murphy moved forward quickly.

'I need the address to claim the assistance, sir.'

The man wrote something on a form. 'Just take this to the welfare office. You'll be entitled to a large allowance with fifteen children.' He made as though to hand the form to Murphy, but Mrs Murphy intercepted it with the speed of a striking cobra.

'Thanks, sir; we'll do that, sir.' She glanced triumphantly at her husband, folded the form and put it in her bosom.

Murphy drew a silent sigh of relief. He looked over at Papa Riley as the man turned away and winked at him.

'Thank you, sir, thank you kindly, sir,' he said obsequiously to the welfare man, grinning behind his back in the knowledge that he had him well codded.

24

The fourteen children to whom he had laid claim were allowed to return to whatever they had been doing.

Ossie and Tito stared at the towers for a moment, imagining the Murphys as neighbours, and then looked after the departing man. The children began to disperse back to their games. Tito and Ossie, about to return to their father, saw that Grandpa was back. He had unhitched Dan and was tethering him to a tree. They ran towards him, whooping with delight, already basking in the sense of family and safety they felt whenever he was around. Grandpa held out his arms and hugged them.

While Grandpa was greeting his grandchildren, Murphy walked across the camp to Papa and grinned at him.

'Thank you, thank you, Papa. Looks like we'll be neighbours so.'

Papa stared at the florid man in front of him. He registered nothing, certainly not pleasure at this intelligence. He was thinking of the empty flat next door and how they'd probably give it to the Murphys and then he'd never have a minute's peace.

'I'll hang out the flags,' he said drily.

Murphy did not answer. Something flickered in his eyes for a moment but he bit his lip and turned away.

Papa looked over to his children as he heard Ossie shouting, 'Have you come to live with us, Grandpa?' and he saw Grandpa Ward look up at the tower and turn back to Ossie's hopeful face.

'No, Ossie. It's too high for me up there!'

Papa walked over to his father-in-law. He did so reluctantly; Mary's father made him feel inadequate

25

without even opening his mouth. But he couldn't walk off without a word to him; the old man represented his only link with the past. He saw his sons patting old Dan, saw them stare uncertainly at the new white horse which stood quietly nearby, wrenching scant mouthfuls from what was left of the grass.

Grandpa looked at his son-in-law, and Papa gazed levelly back. There passed between the two men something of reproach on the one hand and defensiveness on the other. Papa moved with a show of confidence towards what he assumed to be Grandpa's new white horse, raised his hand to stroke its nose, but the horse jerked back from him and would not let him touch it.

'Lost your gift, eh, Papa?' the old man sneered. He smelt the drink, saw the uneven gait of his son-in-law and, because of the children, hated him for it.

Papa ignored the provocation.

'Where did you get him?'

Grandpa looked at the horse. 'What you should be asking is where did he get me.'

'Can we ride old Dan?' Tito asked. The children loved Dan and knew him well. Papa turned to his elder son, saw the freckles, the eager hazel eyes, the boyish delight. Tito didn't smile that often; he tended to gravity, to desperate efforts to understand the grown-up world so that he could find his way in it.

'It's your Grandpa's horse, not mine,' he said tersely.

Tito and Ossie turned to their grandfather. 'Can we, Grandpa?' Tito asked eagerly.

'Please,' Ossie said. 'Please, Grandpa.'

Grandpa smiled at them. He looked at Dan who was glad to be out of harness. He looked at the white horse which had followed him all the way from the Atlantic Ocean and which had only once allowed him to touch it. Standing there, it was an unknown quantity.

He regarded his grandchildren, resented the constrained tenor of their lives, the claustrophobic future, sensed the desire in them for freedom.

'You can if you're able,' he said.

Tito ran to Dan, untethered him and jumped on his back.

'Let me up,' Ossie called. 'I want to go up.'

'One at a time,' Tito said firmly as he rode off, bouncing up and down happily, leaning forward as Dan broke into a canter.

The other children came milling with shouts and laughter, and quickly improvised fences from bits of packing cases and old wooden planks. Ossie watched his brother's horsemanship with envy, saw the eyes of his father and grandfather watching him too. He looked at the white horse and found that it was looking at him. He approached it softly, put up his small hand to stroke its nose. The horse did not move. He stroked its chest. The horse looked down at him from dark eyes and nuzzled against him.

'Watch him, Ossie!' Grandpa called in sudden alarm. 'He might be a bad one!' Ossie didn't seem to hear. He disappeared, came back with a bucket and a bridle from Grandpa's caravan. He turned the bucket upside beside the white horse, stood on it and slipped the bridle over the horse's head, buckling it swiftly, and then he jumped lightly on to the animal's back.

Grandpa watched with consternation and disbelief. Every sinew in him was poised to move should the white horse show either skittishness or viciousness. But there was Ossie, like a little prince, kicking this strange animal and moving him forward as though he were riding the best schooled horse in the world. The horse danced, moving under his little rider in equine joy, and Ossie crowed with delight.

Grandpa felt the old shiver climb slowly up his backbone, tingle in the hair at the nape of his neck.

Ossie glanced triumphantly at his grandfather and saw without particularly remarking it that the old man seemed very tense, that his eyes were narrowed and that he stood very still.

'Begod!' Grandpa shouted in a cracked voice, trying to put the moment of premonition behind him. 'You must have the gift, Ossie. He must like you!'

Ossie beamed. He nodded, smiling down at his grandfather and said with the simplicity of his seven years, 'He likes me because I like him!' He kicked the horse again, steered him towards the playing field beside the camp. His face was flushed with excitement.

'Be careful!' Grandpa called, but Ossie was gone; the horse cantered gently round the field with him, and the set of its head and the muted spirit of its stride reminded Grandpa of so many stories. I'm getting old, he thought. A fanciful old man. He's only a bloody horse.

Meanwhile Tito and some of the Murphy children

were encouraging old Dan over an improvised jump.
Tito made the black horse stand on its hind legs. The
children stared up at it, awed to see it fully extended
over them, forelegs raised, hind legs stretched, belly
straining. For a moment, framed as he was against the
huge towers which caught the late afternoon sunlight,
it didn't look like old Dan at all, but some great beast
from another age. Birdie Murphy, one of the real
Murphy children, the same girl who had earlier
chased the sausage-stealing dog and given Tito a
moment's pause, sat watching on a piebald pony
belonging to her father. Her six-year-old brother,
Conor, clung to her back. Birdie was twelve, a
dedicated tomboy, fighting desperation at the prospect of her imminent and inescapable journey into
womanhood.

'How many kids is really in your family?' Tito
asked her and Birdie laughed.

'The four of us,' she said. 'Me and Angela and
Conor and the baby.'

'Not fifteen?'

'Jaysus, no!' Birdie detested children. She was surrounded by them, not just her own siblings – Angela
who was ten, Conor who was six, and the baby who
was fourteen months – but other people's children as
well. She was always being deputised to mind them.
She had long since decided that she was never going
to have any, that she was never going to get married.
When she grew up, she wanted to be a man. Life was
simpler if you were a man. You had a bit of fun and
you weren't always stuck with bloody kids and you
didn't have to have babies and people were careful

before they belted you. If anyone belted her she'd break his head. She had told her father that once, when he had given her a clip round the ear: 'I'll break your head, y'ould bully,' she had screamed. 'The minute I grow up I'll break your head!' but all she got for her pains was another clip, much worse than the last. 'Mind your mouth, miss!' This had made her cry and forced her to consider the merits of diplomacy. Later her mother had said to her, 'Haven't you an ounce of sense to be vexin' your father!'

Tito smiled at Birdie. He wanted to laugh, remembering the man from the welfare with the shiny shoes and the way they had codded him. 'The welfare man thought you had fifteen!'

Birdie gave a short chirp of a laugh. 'I know. Wasn't he the right ould eejit?' She shuddered. 'Can you imagine fifteen kids in our caravan?'

Tito laughed. He liked Birdie.

'Did you get into trouble over the sausages?' he asked.

Birdie pursed her mouth. 'Yeah . . .' But she did not elaborate.

Tito saw the brooding look in her eyes. He considered young Conor behind her, clinging like a limpet, his sticky fingers clenched round her waist.

'Race you down the field?' he said.

Birdie laughed and Tito steered old Dan towards the playing field and took off, followed by Birdie and Conor on their father's horse.

The white horse, with Ossie still mounted on it, turned its head and regarded the other ponies as they cantered past and then it turned quietly to follow them. Ossie, his eyes brilliant, laughed and called to his brother, and then looked back at Grandpa with a triumphant expression. Grandpa stood impassively and watched. Around him were the sounds of supper, the clink of crockery, the murmur of family voices through open caravan doors; there was also the wail of crying children, the barking of dogs and the steady rhythm of hooves in the adjacent playing field. The autumn nights were drawing in and the afternoon light was already darkening into dusk; the central camp fire had been stoked and yellow tongues of flame darted up through the smoke.

Grandpa's head was full of memories of evenings like this. He kept his back turned to the towers and his face towards the mountains and pretended that the old days were back again, that he was young again; he remembered the taste of youth and his belief in the future. He remembered his daughter Mary playing with a doll he had made for her. Maggie, her mother, had made a blue dress for it, with frills and a white collar. The little girl had sat and played with it in the caravan on an evening much like this, an evening with pink streaks on the horizon and the smell of wood smoke. He could have scoured the world then for Tito or Ossie and never found them; they were waiting for their turn on the stage of life. But Mary was gone and Maggie was gone and the time had passed, sneaking by him on tiptoe like a thief in the night.

Chapter Three

Grandpa watched the children for a while and then, satisfied that they were safe enough, followed his son-in-law to the car dump near the encampment. It was here that Papa Riley conducted his business, buying the occasional crashed car, selling parts, and accepting damaged cars for repair.

Papa was deep in conversation with a customer beside a damaged car – broken windscreen, dents, buckled bumper hanging on drunkenly. The customer was frowning, his face a study of angry desperation.

'Can you take all the bumps out of her?'

'It'll cost,' Papa said, raising his right hand and showing four fingers. 'I'll need a float.'

'It's a wreck!' the customer said in disgust. He put his hand in his pocket and dug out a wad of notes, peeled them off into Papa's hand.

'A wreck like myself,' Papa muttered. He took the money, pocketed it, looked at his customer. 'Leave it with me.'

The customer left, glancing back at his vehicle as though trying to reconstruct it in his mind to its former respectability.

Grandpa watched the transaction and when the customer had gone, he strolled up to his son-in-law and regarded him from quizzical old eyes.

'Kids look great,' he said nonchalantly. He knew this was not true, but it was a conversation opener; it would not be politic to tell Papa that the kids looked like proper little orphans.

'So they are.'

Grandpa was silent. He heard the shouts from the field; the children were erecting fences. He smelt the scents of cooking. He sensed rather than saw the great tower block beside him, thrusting its tons of reinforced concrete up into the sky.

'They'd be happier on the road,' he said.

Papa ignored this remark. He had made up his mind that his children would be brought up as part of the settled community; they would be literate, they would be a match for the modern world; they would never be 'green monkeys' among the majority. He thought this happy state of affairs would be achieved simply by living among settled people and sending his children to their schools.

'Are you coming for a drink?' he demanded gruffly.

Grandpa didn't answer the question. He was not going to let Papa off the hook so lightly. He understood Papa's new perspective, but it was a mirage. The children could be literate even if they were travellers, and the life they were living in the concrete termite mound beside him wouldn't equip them for anything. He thought of the journey he had just completed, from the wild Atlantic seaboard, across the most beautiful country God ever made, with the wind and rain and plentiful pickings from nature, a wild rabbit roasted on a spit, mushrooms picked on September mornings with the dew still on them, hazelnuts gathered in great basketfuls in autumn when the leaves were a riot of russets and gold. His grandchildren were being denied their inheritance.

'We're travellers,' Grandpa said stubbornly, looking up at the towers. 'We don't belong with the settled people in their concrete prisons.'

Papa turned away abruptly, as though he hadn't heard. 'I'll see you tomorrow so,' he said.

'I'll be gone before you're up,' Grandpa cried bitterly, angry once more that his attempts to change things were again frustrated. In the last few years he had tried everything, argument, blandishments, pleas and warnings, but it had always ended with anger and bitterness.

Papa turned, his face expressionless, his manner indifferent. 'Well, I'll see you when I see you.'

'You might never see me again!' Grandpa shouted after him.

Papa stopped in his tracks. He had heard this before, this old man's threat.

'You're a fallen man, Papa,' Grandpa flung the words after him as a kind of coup de grâce. 'This is not the way Mary would have raised them!'

Papa froze. His face hardened, his blue eyes narrowed. He turned back to the old man, his expression full of cold fury. How dare the old codger rake up her memory to serve his own purpose.

35

'God rest her,' Grandpa whispered.

Their eyes locked. Neither spoke for a moment and then Grandpa said in a voice full of passionate pleading, 'Come with me, Papa. Call the boys and jump up on the back and we'll go – to the west. Back to the old life.' He looked around him at the squalor, the inhuman, inhospitable towers, the urban detritus, the broken cars, the graffiti. Papa's eyes followed his, looked over at the playing field where the children were still on the horses, shouting and laughing.

'We're staying here,' he said. 'I'll not have my boys running around the country with the arse out of their trousers. The old ways are dead. They sound great, but they're nothing but hardship!' His eyes assumed a faraway focus and his voice became hard. 'Nothing but hardship and suffering!'

Grandpa brought his eyes back to the towers. 'Welcome to the modern world,' he said sarcastically. 'This is a grand substitute sure enough. This is a much better life for them all right. No hardship, no suffering, here!'

The two men stared at each other. Papa felt the pull of the old life rise up in him, felt the yearning for the taste of the rain in the wind and the sight of the road winding ahead and the steady clopping of the horses and Mary's voice as she crooned Tito to sleep. But he had killed Mary, as surely as if he had taken a knife and let her red blood out to stream and puddle in the night.

The longing for a drink rose in him. He hated this old man before him, who conjured everything he longed for and had lost. He hunched his shoulders and turned.

'Don't let me keep you from the drink!' Grandpa said bitterly behind him. Papa didn't answer. His tall figure disappeared round the side of the tower block.

Grandpa went back to the field. The children were jumping over small fences, which they raised higher as each round ended and a new one began. Grandpa thought that he had never seen Ossie so happy or so animated. He had seen him transported once before, on that last birthday, when he had screamed his mother's name to the November wind, but that had been a different kind of animation and one which still sent shivers up Grandpa's spine. To see Ossie as he was now, shouting, his breathing normal, sent a glow through his heart. The old man looked to the distant mountains, now dark blue in the gathering dusk, and back to the towers and then to the happy scene in the field where old Dan and the white horse entertained his grandchildren.

The bonfire in the centre of the encampment was now burning merrily; people had added old planks from packing cases, fallen branches, rubber tyres, and the smoke rose in a grey-blue pall into the evening sky. The smell of burning wood and rubber filled the air and the orange flames crackled and reached upwards, higher and higher, throwing shadows across the ground and the faces of everyone in the vicinity. In the field the children paused, looked over at the bonfire.

'I bet no one can jump that fire,' Tito said to the others.

Young Angela Murphy shook her head scornfully. 'No one could jump that!'

Birdie, who still believed in meeting challenge with ferocity, or at least in being seen to do so, shouted, 'I could!' and turned her horse in the direction of the encampment. The horse quickened its pace, threw back its head as it surged into a canter.

'Let me down, let me down,' her little brother Conor wailed.

Birdie reined in the horse, her mouth pursed at the insufferable cowardice of little brothers. When Conor had slipped to the ground, she kicked her mount to a gallop and thundered down the encampment towards the fire. Adults moved back to give her leeway, some of them gesturing in annoyance and alarm, all of them ready to react, but curious also as to the outcome of what was being attempted.

Birdie kicked furiously as she approached the flames, leant forward intently, but a shiver of fright went through her as she saw the fire looming before her. At the last moment her horse shied and ran sideways away from the flames. Birdie's strong young thighs gripped the shying horse, pulled him up as he danced with fear towards the caravans.

Grandpa was suddenly afraid of what was about to happen. He heard Tito's shout, high and wild, 'Go, boy!' and then he saw his elder grandson charging down the encampment on old Dan, straight towards the yellow flames. He felt his stomach tighten, his chest constrict in sudden terror for his grandchild and fear for his horse. But Dan, although normally obedient and accommodating, reacted at last to the awe of fire in his horse's soul, and shied violently, almost throwing Tito over his head into the flames. Tito held on and Dan came to a stop, his flanks quivering, his coat covered in sweat.

Grandpa sighed with relief. These children needed a strong hand, but where would they get it with a sot for a father and no mother? If they would only all come back with him on the road!

His thoughts were arrested by the sight of Ossie, small and fragile on the back of the strange white animal, galloping towards the fire. Ossie looked nervous. Grandpa tried to shout, but the words died in his throat. He ran forward to stop this mad attempt, to catch the wild brute before it hurt his grandson, but he was too late. He heard Ossie's sudden command to the horse – 'Go on!' – and the horse surged effortlessly forward and cleared the fire with ease and grace, landing perfectly and trotting gently to a standstill with its triumphant rider still safely aboard. Everyone fell silent. Seen through the heat haze and firelight, white horse and rider seemed a single being, Ossie for all the world like a young prince of the Sidhe from the Realm.

Grandpa felt his heart flutter as it returned to a semblance of normality. He looked up at the little eager face, illuminated by the firelight.

'He's mine!' Ossie said wildly, stroking the horse's neck. 'He's mine. What's his name?'

Grandpa thought rapidly. This was a horse that had arrived as though the sea god Manannán himself had sent it; a horse that wouldn't let Grandpa, with all his years of horse-lore, command it, yet allowed a little boy of seven whom it had never seen before mount and ride it.

'He has a strange name,' Grandpa said, smiling to himself as he thought of the perfect name.

'He's my horse!' Ossie said, half talking to himself, still running his hand along his mount's neck. 'What's he called?'

'He's called Tir na n-Og.'

Ossie's face crinkled in incomprehension. 'What's that?'

'It's Irish.'

'What does it mean?'

Grandpa looked into the wide eyes of the child. 'It means the land of eternal youth.'

Ossie was silent, pondering this. His lips were drawn together; he frowned. 'Why is he called that?'

'Because he came from a land under the sea,' Grandpa said. His eyes focused in the distance and he added softly, 'He came from a place where it is always summer and where no one grows old . . .'

Ossie's eyes filled with delight. He knew his grandfather's storytelling voice. 'Will you tell us the story, Grandpa?'

Later, round the fire, the group listened. There were women with babies asleep in their arms, some elderly people, and a number of children, among whom were Tito and Ossie and the Murphy children. Ossie was still on the back of the white horse, from where he had refused to be dislodged. They all listened spellbound to the old man tell the story, their eyes soft and shining with fantasy and firelight and memory. Most of the older ones had heard the tale before.

Grandpa did not stay seated for his story. He stood and paced and lost himself in the drama of what he had to relate. When he paused for effect, as he often did, his audience enjoined him to 'Go on, go on. Don't stop.' He told the story of Oisin who met the fairy princess Niamh Cinn Óir, Niamh of the Golden Hair, and went away with her on her white horse to Tir na n-Og. But one day, after a thousand years, he wanted to come home, to see his friends and his native land once more.

'So the princess gave him her most precious great white horse and told him he'd be safe as long as he stayed on the horse. He came to the shores of Ireland but, by God, how things had changed! He'd forgotten he was gone a thousand years. All his old friends were dead and gone. Even the grand castle where he had lived was in ruins and covered in weeds and brambles. And even the people who were alive looked miserable and half dead to him. One day he saw a group of the poor devils trying to shift a big rock. He rode over and leaned forward to give it a push, and by God the girth broke and down fell Oisin off the white horse. It was most terrible to see. He lay there shivering and turning into an old man, with his fingernails and hair three feet long . . .'

Grandpa paused, looked round at the spellbound faces, the intense wide eyes of the children, the listening faces of their elders, the smile on the old people's mouths.

'And it didn't stop there. Remember, he was over a thousand years old. He just got older and older until he turned into bone and then to dust . . . Dust he became, all for getting off the horse . . .'

Grandpa bent down, picked up some warm ash from the edge of the fire and then leant towards Ossie. He held out his flattened hand in front of the little boy's face and blew on it. Ash blew from the palm. Ossie drew a sharp breath.

'He should have stayed put,' Tito said earnestly, wishing he could go back in time and whisper a word of advice into Oisin's ear.

'And the Princess and Oisin never argued?' Birdie Murphy whispered, her tough incredulity at odds with the secret yearnings of her heart. People who didn't argue and fight and take the odd drop too much were too good to be true.

Grandpa looked at her, this little hoyden who would have ridden a horse over a blazing bonfire. 'Never!' he said definitively. He glanced at Ossie who was silent and seemingly miles away.

'What did the Princess look like?' Ossie asked slowly, his voice very low, his eyes staring into the heart of the fire.

'Close your eyes,' Grandpa said.

Ossie obeyed.

'Do you see a beautiful woman?'

Every face turned to look at Ossie. The firelight played on the boy's face. He eyes were shut tight and his face wore a mystical expression as though he partook of the secrets of Tir na n-Og.

'Yesss . . .' he breathed.

'Well, that's her,' Grandpa said softly. 'That's the beautiful Princess.'

There was a beatific smile on Ossie's face. His eyes were still closed and he swayed a little on the horse's back, as though the warmth of the fire and the story had enchanted him.

Grandpa smiled. It was time the children went home. He looked at Tito and winked. Tito stared up at his little brother for a moment and then shook the child's leg. 'We have to go, Ossie.'

Ossie opened his eyes, looked down at his brother. '*No*. I'm not getting down!'

'Your father will be worried about you,' Grandpa said.

'Papa never comes back until late when he's at the drink,' he said stubbornly.

Grandpa went to Ossie, raised his arms to take him down. 'Your father used to be a great man, you know,' he whispered to the child. 'He used to be the King of the Travellers.' He paused. 'The youngest ever,' he added proudly.

'Was he really?' Ossie asked, his eyes now wide awake.

'He was.'

'When?' Ossie demanded.

Grandpa sighed. 'When your mother was alive, your father was afraid of nobody.' He put his hand on the child's arm. 'Come on now, time to go home.'

Ossie pulled back reluctantly, clung to the horse's neck. His head was still full of Oisin turning to dust on the sand. 'I don't want to get old!' he whispered.

'You won't get old,' Grandpa said. He smiled and added, 'At least, not yet!' Then he lifted Ossie down. The child clung to Tir na n-Og, his small hands digging into the horse's coat. Ossie looked up and the white horse lowered his head to look at him and as he did so their eyes met. Ossie became very calm.

'Goodbye, Tir na n-Og,' he said. 'We have to go home now.'

He walked away with Tito towards the towers, great dark monoliths against the night sky, the windows lit with hundreds of lights. Behind the two children the bonfire had settled into hot ash, with one or two spurts of flame from additional bits of fuel thrown by the remaining people who were too tired and comfortable to find their caravans. Grandpa looked at the white horse. Should he try to tether it now? Would it let him? But Tir na n-Og stared after the departing children and then began to follow them. Grandpa turned and ran after him, pulled him by the reins, but the horse moved on as though his mouth was made of iron and the old man could not stop him.

Ossie looked back, stopped and stretched his hand out with delight.

'Can we keep him, Grandpa?' he demanded eagerly.

Grandpa had had enough of this horse. He was satisfied now that the animal would not harm the children. He ignored the prompting from the bottom of his mind reminding him that he was in the presence of an unresolved mystery. He was tired to death and he wanted to sleep and get back on the road in the dawn. He couldn't take the children with him and he bled for them in their confined straitjacket of a life. If the horse made them happy, let them keep it. In any case, the bloody horse would stay only if it felt so inclined. If it were an Epon of the Sidhe, they might wake in the morning and find it gone.

'Where would you put him?' he demanded. 'Where in the name of God would you put him? I'll be gone back on the road tomorrow and I can't mind him.'

Tito and Ossie looked at each other and at the towers and then at Grandpa and burst out laughing together as enlightenment struck.

Birdie stood at the caravan door and looked after the Rileys as they disappeared in the direction of the towers. She knew that her family would soon be moving there themselves and she imagined the interior of their new flat; she fantasised about her own room – would she have her very own room, where she could shut the door?

Her parents were having an argument, but there was nothing new in that. Her father said he'd do what he liked with his money; didn't the welfare people give it to him? The man was the head of the family and the proper person to get it. Mrs Murphy disagreed. She was the one who had to rear the kids; he was only interested in the one thing, that and the drink.

'You didn't exactly take the pledge yourself, you silly old bag,' her husband told her. 'And you never reared a child in your life. Our brats are as wild as the Rileys, and you know it!'

Birdie left the caravan and approached the dying fire. In a moment her mother would take a swipe at her father and then he would take a swipe at her and then she would start crying and then he would say, 'For God's sake, woman, will you give over that racket.' And then he would say in a soft voice, 'Ah now, Bridgie, will you stop that.' And then they would make it up and go out drinking. And guess who would have to mind the kids? She'd lost count of the times she'd had to mind the baby as it screamed and bawled half the night as though someone were taking pot shots at it, while the other two complained that they couldn't get a wink of sleep. She went on her knees and prayed to God to shut it up tonight.

She wondered idly about the Rileys. Would she be living near them or in a different block altogether? Would they be friends with her?

The heat of the fire was warm on her legs. She thought it might be nice to stay out all night, sleep near the embers, look up at the stars in the darkness, be alone. Behind her, the sounds of her mother's furious crying and the whining of the baby spilled out from the caravan. The remaining travellers round the fire looked at Birdie, but made no comment. Birdie waited for the call, which came on cue about five minutes later.

'Birdie, Birdieee. Where are you? Come in here this minute and mind the child.'

The twelve-year-old ground her teeth. 'I hate babies,' she whispered to herself. 'I'd blow them all up if I could!'

On the fourteenth floor of the tower a woman waited with her dog for the lift. She had been waiting for some time and could not understand why the lift was so slow, seeing that the man had been here only two days before to repair it.

'Bloody lift, broken again!' she muttered. Her mind scanned the consequences: if it was broken, she would have to climb down fourteen flights of stairs; she had bunions. She needed to get out so her dog could do its business, but she was not taking her bunions down fourteen flights. She banged on the elevator door.

'Will you come up outta that!' she shouted. Then her face cleared; she heard the unmistakable sound of the approaching lift. There was a strangely heavy clank as the lift stopped. The door opened and a horse stepped out, a child on its back, another behind them. The woman stood as though someone had nailed her to the spot.

Ossie looked down at her from Tir na n-Og's back. 'Out of the way, missus. He doesn't like being trapped!'

The woman, known as Ma Whelan, had occupied number 14F for nigh on twenty years, and was not entirely unaccustomed to surprises, but she started as though someone had jabbed a hypodermic in a sensitive place. 'Holy Mother of Divine God!' she said in awed tones. She watched as the two boys conducted the horse to the door of number 14G and let themselves in.

Chapter Four

The Rileys' flat consisted of two bedrooms, a bathroom, kitchen and sitting room. The interior was bleak; it had not been painted for years and various ancient daubs still adorned the walls. A tough nylon carpet in browns and greens kept the cold of the concrete floor from the feet.

There was a balcony with a view southwards across the city to the mountains so beloved by Grandpa. Sometimes Papa would stand there too, gazing in front of him for what seemed like hours, listening to the sound the wind made and watching the changing light patterns on the far-off hills. He had an old ship's telescope made of brass, which he had won years before in a wrestling match, and he would stare through it on summer evenings when he was at home, showing the boys what was to be seen. Sometimes he trained it on the moon and they saw that it was full of craters. But the children liked most of all to study the traffic and the people far below their concrete eyrie.

If you looked straight down to the ground from this height you saw the concrete paving below, the prams being wheeled out, the children playing and fighting, the unemployed men talking together in the afternoons. Faces would come sharply into focus, would seem so near that you expected them to look up and tell you to stop eavesdropping.

Papa kept the telescope in a box in his bedroom and had told them he would skin them if they ever touched it in his absence. They observed this rule, the only rule. They had no desire to face an irate Papa.

There was a minimum of furniture in the flat; a table and chairs, a battered couch of brown tweed, a television set and a video recorder. Both these latter items had been picked up secondhand and they provided the only entertainment the children had. There was a bunk bed in the boys' room and in Papa's bedroom there was a single divan, with a broken leg. Papa would straighten the leg from time to time, muttering that one of these days he would have to do a proper job on it. But he never did and more often than not the bed sagged on one side with a forty-five-degree slope. Beside his bed was a chair which boasted an overflowing saucer of cigarette butts. Under the chair was a collection of bottles, some with labels and some without. The room smelt of cigarette smoke and spirits. The kitchen contained a gateleg table from which the white melamine veneer was peeling, a few stools, a number of aluminium utensils with burnt bottoms, some Delf crockery, and cutlery. In the window there was a dead geranium in a brown plastic pot.

The flat was hardly big enough to share with a horse, but Tir na n-Og had been installed in the sitting room and seemed content enough. He stood watching television with the two boys perched on his back. The film was a Western and the cowboys were shooting it out with the bad guys in a gun battle. The noise from the television got louder and louder as the battle raged fiercer. The audience were unaware that young Conor Murphy had joined them. With a child's fearless curiosity he had followed them into the tower and up to the fourteenth floor. He had found the door of the flat unlatched and was now regarding the television from under the horse's legs.

Tito and Ossie loved Westerns. In the long-ago days the travellers rode horses in the Wild West and fought the bad guys and the Indians. Tito was trying to interest Ossie in this as a pedigree for his people. He had come to the point now where he was sure it was the truth. It answered all his cravings for a past with purpose and dignity.

'But where did us travellers live then?' Ossie demanded.

'In the West,' Tito answered. He was sucking a Smiley with slurpy noises; he dug in his pocket and offered another one to Ossie. Ossie accepted the proffered confection.

'Are you sure we were the cowboys?' Ossie continued, chewing, a little chocolate dribble escaping from the edge of his mouth.

'Yeah. We had wagons and horses and hats.'

Ossie thought about this. Wagons and horses, yes. But he wasn't so sure about the hats. 'Maybe we were the Indians.'

Tito sighed. There was a lull in the gun battle and during this brief respite Conor announced from between the horse's legs that he was hungry.

The two boys looked down from Tir na n-Og's back and saw their small uninvited guest watching them gravely. His face was streaked with dirt and he was sucking his thumb. Tito took the remote control from his trouser pocket and lowered the volume on the television.

'Did your dad not leave you any money?' he asked.

Conor shook his head. 'No.'

Tito shrugged and held out the remains of his Smiley. Conor reached up to take it, stuck it in his mouth and walked out of the door.

Tito looked after him for a moment. Ossie raised the volume on the television to pre-intrusion levels.

'Ossie,' Tito said, raising his voice to be heard above the din. 'What are we going to feed Tir na n-Og?'

'Hay!' Ossie said, with the air of one stating the obvious, shaking his head with annoyance. Tito was interrupting his viewing.

'But where are we going to get the hay? And he might like oats! We have to do something to make money so that we can buy him food. He must be hungry.'

Ossie turned to look at his brother. 'I'm hungry too!' he said, his face falling, the corners of his mouth turning down. Tito looked at him, turned off the television and slid off the horse. He reached up and pulled his brother by the leg.

'Come on. We're going out. It's time you did your singing act again.'

In the neighbourhood shopping mall, Ossie sang for all he was worth. He gave the evening shoppers the benefit of 'The Rose of Tralee', 'Let Erin Remember' and other notable ditties, but to little avail. The cardboard box he had placed in front of him on the pavement remained empty, except for a five pence piece someone had flung into it in passing, and his audience consisted of just the Murphy children, who had accompanied the boys to the mall, and Tir na n-Og. Earlier someone had dropped in a fifty pence piece and Tito had bought chips with it, which the Murphy children were guzzling.

'We're not getting any money, Ossie!' Tito announced.

Ossie looked into the cardboard box, picked up the solitary five pence and handed it to his brother. 'Why is that? Why am I not getting any money?'

'Because you have to do the bad breathing. Why is your breathing not bad?'

Ossie turned and looked at Tir na n-Og. 'I don't know. It's just okay.'

'Well, you'll just have to pretend,' Tito said desperately.

Ossie took a deep breath and resumed singing 'Danny Boy' with a throbbing asthmatic voice, as though he might not survive long enough to finish the song. His voice wheezed and whined with bronchial misery, which only added pathos to its yearning tone. The adult passers-by looked at him with pity and consternation. 'Poor little kid,' their glances said. 'He shouldn't be here on the cold pavement. Not long for this world by the sound of him!' Coins began to hop into the cardboard box, pinging with various, extremely attractive, high-pitched notes.

Ossie finished the song and surveyed the box with pride. 'Is that okay?'

Tito emptied most of the box so as not to have the punters think that this kid was doing well enough already.

'Make it worse,' he whispered into his brother's ear. 'Much worse.' He glanced at the Murphys. They had finished the chips and looked as though they might eat the paper bag as well.

Ossie took another deep breath, a breath so deep that to his surprise he could feel it all the way down to his tummy. Unaccustomed to the use of his full lung capacity, he loved every delicious second of it, and renewed his efforts with vigour.

When Tito had emptied the box for the umpteenth time and was relatively wealthy, he decided it was time to call a halt. He bought fish and chips, which they and the Murphys ate ravenously, and applied himself to the problem of where he was going to get some food for Tir na n-Og. But the horse seemed in no hurry, apparently happy just to be with the children. He accepted some chips, ones without vinegar, but declined the fish.

'What's your favourite grub, Tir na n-Og?' Birdie asked the white horse, but he ignored her, only blinking at her with his long-lashed eyes.

'Give him some more chips,' Ossie called and Tito bought another portion and fed them to the horse outside the chipper. Then they went off to find someone to sell them hay. On the way they met a group of well-dressed boys who called them knackers. Tito launched a well-aimed kick and there was a temporary fracas. Ossie and Conor joined in and Birdie belted the posh boys with both fists. The poshies were outnumbered and ran away. Tito looked at Birdie with admiration.

'I didn't think girls could fight,' he said.

Birdie looked at him with scorn. 'Girls can do anything!'

Angela made no comment. She had hung back and hoped no one had noticed.

'You were a fat lot of use!' Birdie said to her.

Angela retreated into femininity. 'Real girls don't like fighting,' she said with a simper.

This upset Birdie. She knew she couldn't be a boy, her preferred option, but if she wasn't a real girl, and sometimes she suspected this to be the case, what was she? Some kind of freak?

'Shut your head,' she hissed at her younger sister, making a move towards her, but Angela was practised in evasive action.

'Keep the shit,' Mossy White said. Mossy was the owner of a pony and dray and negotiated the sale of a bale of hay and a bag of oats and bran to Tito. 'Keep the horse shit and put it in plastic bags. You can sell it for garden manure. It's grand stuff for the roses. All the ould ones with gardens go mad for it.'

Tito looked at Tir na n-Og with admiration. You'll make our fortune, he thought. It was all perfectly logical. The more they fed Tir na n-Og, the more shit there would be, and the more shit, the more money. Could anything be simpler?

On the way home from Mossy's the children discussed the history of the travellers.

'They used to be tinkers,' Tito said, remembering what Grandpa had told him. 'That meant that they worked with tin; they made saucepans and stuff. They were craftsmen. They used to go to people's houses and work in the kitchen, mending th'ould pots.'

Birdie listened attentively. 'That's right,' she said. 'They were important. Sure no one would know what was going on if they didn't come calling.'

'Why do people call us knackers?' Angela asked. 'I hate being called a knacker!'

'We're not knackers,' Birdie said hotly. 'Knackers are people who kill horses.'

The children stopped in the playing field to share a box of Smarties. Conor had his hand out all the time and got more than his due. He licked the red Smarties and wiped the colour on his hand, pretending it was blood.

Ossie, who had dismounted, looked up at Tir na n-Og. He thought how terrible it must be to kill horses. Bad guys on telly and posh kids, okay, you could kill them. But not horses!

'We used to be travellers once, Tir na n-Og,' he informed the horse. 'We used to make things outta tin. That's why they called us tinkers. We were like gypsies. We used to tell fortunes and do magic.'

Tito gave a derisive snort. 'Don't listen to him, Tir na n-Og. He was never a real traveller like me!'

'Why was I never a real traveller?' Ossie demanded, furious at being shown up in front of Tir na n-Og.

'Because you were never on the road.'

'Why was I never on the road?'

Tito hesitated. His tone changed. He said in a low voice, 'Because Mammy died and Papa didn't want to be on the road without her.'

'Why did Mammy die?'

Ossie had often asked this question. But the replies were never satisfactory. She had got sick; she had been very tired and her heart had stopped; God had called her. But the more answers he got, the more he posed the question. He wanted her. She was the one thing in all the world that he really wanted. He went to sleep imagining that she came in to kiss him goodnight, to tuck him in, to tell him a story. If he had her, nothing could touch him. He tried to see her face, but it was not in his head and so he made it up, different faces, sometimes with brown eyes and sometimes with blue. He thought about her hair; was it straight or curly? What was she like? Would she smile when she saw him and put out her arms? He knew from Tito, from sensing the tenor of Tito's memory, that she had been wonderful. She had been young. So why had her heart stopped? Or could it be – and the thought was terrible – that she had gone away because she hadn't loved them?

'Well, why did she die?' he demanded again.

Tito looked away. His face crumpled a little. He

had memories, albeit shadowy, to hold on to; the memories were precious, he maintained them in a special place behind a wall of self-discipline, as he did his terrible secret, but the mention of her name was enough to fracture the control.

'I don't know,' he answered abruptly. 'Talk to the horse!'

It was late when Tito and Ossie got home. Birdie carried in the bale of hay and left it, as instructed, in the bathroom. Then she and the rest of the Murphys went back to the encampment.

The two boys went into the kitchen, found the largest saucepan, scraped out the remains of last week's tinned spaghetti, and filled it with oats. That done, they put some water in the bath and tried to undo the twine round the bale of hay. Ossie ran for a kitchen knife and the cord was severed, but the hay, no longer contained, expanded all over the bathroom floor. Tir na n-Og was then invited into the bathroom for his supper. The horse first drank from the bath and then put his nose into hay, worked his mouth in a rhythmic sideways motion as he munched. Tito and Ossie watched in delight.

The door of their father's room was ajar; the boys left Tir na n-Og to his meal and peeped in to see if Papa had come home. If Papa were sleeping it off, that was exactly what he should be left to do. They could tell him all about their adventures tomorrow – if he was in a listening mood.

Papa lay dead to the world. He had a heavy night's

drinking behind him. He snored a little, a low-pitched sonorous sound that came down his nose and was gently ejected. He had half covered himself with his overcoat, but underneath he was fully dressed, still wearing his black polo-neck and trousers, although he had taken off his cracked shoes which lay one on top of the other in the corner. He had a foam rubber pillow under his head, a little stained, and the rest of the bedclothes seemed to have congregated at the bottom of the bed.

The children stood and gazed down at him and were joined by the horse. Tir na n-Og filled the small bedroom. There were flecks of oat bran on his lips and he stared at the sleeping man intently. He whinnied, a horse song of interrogation and reproach. Papa muttered in his sleep, opened his eyes, looked up into the eyes above him. He did not move or register the least surprise that the face directly above his belonged to a horse, but he made a noise of denial, pulled the coat over his head and went back to sleep.

Tito and Ossie looked at each other and shrugged, Ossie with resignation, Tito with sudden anger. Papa was always like this after a night on the batter. Tito could just remember a time when things were different, a time when, holding his laughing father by the hand, he came back to the warmth of his mother's arms. It was like a dream, but he remembered it clearly enough never to forget it and it fuelled a growing, bitter resentment.

The two children left Tir na n-Og staring down at their father and went into the kitchen. They had brought back a litre of milk and they opened it and began to drink it.

'Leave some for Papa's tea. You know the thirst that's always on him when he wakes up after being on the drink,' Ossie said and Tito slammed the milk carton on to the draining board, went into the sitting room and turned on the television. The news was on. This was boring, so he changed channels. There was a funny programme where a fellow was telling jokes and the audience were screaming with laughter. Tito turned the sound up full.

Ossie ran in from the kitchen.

'Turn it down. It'll wake Da up!'

'Good!' Tito said bitterly. 'He needs to wake up!'

The flat reverberated with the noise. Ossie put his hands over his ears.

The door of Papa's room clattered open as he staggered out, past Tir na n-Og who had relocated himself in the hall and was about to return to his stable in the bathroom. Papa blinked at the horse but seemed more concerned with the racket coming from the sitting room. His red eyes glared at his sons. 'Who turned that television on?'

The boys were silent.

Papa lurched towards the television. 'I said, who turned that effing television on?'

'I did!' Tito said defiantly.

Papa turned to look at his eldest son, saw the tears about to spill, the defiant stance, fists clenched as though he were a man. A would-be man confronting a has-been man, Papa thought. He looked at Ossie beside his brother, a baby still, lost in a world where even his father was at sea. Touched and ashamed, he turned the sound down, jabbed an admonishing finger at his children.

'You learn to read. There's too much of this television. You learn to read! Don't be like your father!' He straightened and walked back into his room, brushing against Tir na n-Og's hindquarters which were sticking out of the bathroom. For a moment he felt that the horse had turned away from him in disgust and this impression was intensified as Tir na n-Og farted and filled the air with his personal perfume. This was followed by a putt-putt-putting sound as the horse performed his natural functions and deposited a rope of manure on the floor. Papa looked back at the children.

'Quick,' Tito shouted to Ossie, 'Get the shovel! Tir na n-Og has just done a whopper.'

In his drunken state, Papa didn't mind the smell; on the contrary, it brought back better days, but he felt sudden unwelcome shame pervade him. 'You learn to read, or the horse goes!' he shouted, and went back to bed. He tried to get back to sleep, but part of him was very wide awake. He remembered his youth, the way he could run and ride and climb trees with Kathleen Lee, the wild girl he had grown up beside. He thought of his prowess with a catapult. He remembered killing a rabbit with a single shot and bringing it back for supper. He couldn't read or write, but he didn't need to in those days. Agreements were made verbally and were honoured. Life and stimulus were all around him in the countryside; the evenings would be full of stories around the camp fires, laughter, music.

Then Mary had come and the world seemed fuller than he could have imagined. He thought he had won everything it had to offer: he had a wife he adored; he had a child; he had his own tribe around him; they had even made him the King of the Travellers.

So what was he doing here? In Dublin? In the Towers? Things were not working out the way he had planned. It wasn't his fault. Or was it?

'I wish things had been different, Mary,' he muttered, while tears of self-pity trickled down the side of his nose and on to the pillow. 'Jesus Christ, woman, I didn't ever dream that it would end like that! I wish you were here, with me, with the children. I'd dig your bones up if it would make you come back! I'd do anything, Mary, if I could have you back.' He wiped the tears angrily. 'But you're gone and you cannot even hear me!'

Chapter Five

It didn't take Ma Whelan long to alert the Residents'
Committee to the fact that a horse was living in
apartment 14G. The Residents' Committee, however,
did not entirely believe her. While they were
accustomed to various complaints, this was the first
time someone had alleged that the place was being
used as a stables.

'I saw it myself getting out of the lift, so I did. It
scared poor Fu-Fu out of his wits. It was a huge big
lump of a horse,' and Mrs Whelan gesticulated with
her arms to indicate the length and breadth of the
animal. 'And the child sitting on top of him! Get out
of the way, missus, says he, and out they step as cool
as you please and go into the flat like it was the Royal
Dublin Society.' Ma Whelan expelled a noisy breath
and pulled her lips together with the air of someone
who'd said what she had to say and who wasn't going
to utter another word until something was done.

Mick Cafferty sighed. He drove a bus for a living
and he knew people better than any psychiatrist. He
had to put up with them all day.

'No one in their right mind would try to keep a
horse in an apartment fourteen floors up, ma'am.' He

consulted his notes. 'There's a family living in that flat, people by the name of Riley,' he muttered half to himself. 'Sure there'd be no room. What about feed? What about . . .?' he wrinkled his nose.

'That's precisely what I'm worried about!' Ma Whelan said. 'I don't want to have *that* next door.'

Mick Cafferty looked at the woman, at her fluffy white poodle, at her compressed, outraged mouth, at her varicosed legs. She doesn't look as if she's on the bottle, he thought; she looks as sane as any of us. Oh, Christ, I'll have to dig up Francie Dunphy and go investigating.

Ossie and Tito were in the bathroom washing Tir na n-Og when a reconnoitring party from the Residents' Committee knocked on the door a few days later. The children had cleared out the oats and hay into the kitchen and the bathroom was now full of steam and the sound of water hissing from the shower attachment.

'Give me more shampoo,' Ossie said. He was standing on a chair, busily engaged in making sure Tir na n-Og's head and mane were properly washed. Nobody was going to accuse them of having a dirty horse. Tito was standing in the bath, performing a similar function with respect to the horse's flanks. Ossie worked in the shampoo, grabbed the shower attachment and hosed the horse's head.

'Mind his eyes,' Tito said. 'I hate it when the soap gets in my eyes.'

'Me too.' After a few moments Ossie added,

'Grandpa won't know him when he comes back. When will he be coming back?'

'I dunno,' Tito said. 'Grandpa is only happy on the road.'

'Did you hear the door?' Ossie asked.

Papa heard the door. The furious knocking dragged him out of the thick, heavy sleep into which he had retreated and in which he was happy. He cursed and got out of bed. 'Where in the name of God are those bloody kids?' he demanded aloud. 'A man has no peace in his own home!'

He heard the shower hissing in the bathroom, saw the horse's hindquarters sticking out through the door. An expletive escaped him as he slid to the front door on the wet hallway, opened it in a fury and confronted the self-righteous trio outside: Mick Cafferty, his sidekick Francie Dunphy and Mrs Whelan from 14F. Mick Cafferty introduced himself.

'Mick Cafferty, chairman of the Residents' Committee,' he announced. He spoke stiffly as became the importance of his office and then he turned to the small man beside him, 'This is Mr Dunphy.'

Papa stared at him. What in the name of God did the man want?

'We have reason to believe that you are harbouring a pony. Is that true?'

Papa tried to shake the clinging tendrils of a drunken sleep out of his brains. He looked from Cafferty to Dunphy to Ma Whelan.

'It's a horse,' Francie Dunphy said.

Mrs Whelan pointed at the rear end sticking out of

the bathroom door and her voice rose shrilly on the afternoon air. 'I can see it. There it is!'

Cafferty stared at Papa, saw the bleary eyes, the puffy alcoholic face, looked past him to where Ma Whelan was pointing and saw the hindquarters of a horse.

'My advice to you,' he said after a moment, in which he gave the matter fair consideration, 'is to get rid of it before tonight.' He glared at Papa who wasn't paying too much attention. 'Or else!'

Papa had been leaning wearily against the wall. But he heard the threat and he straightened. 'Or else what?'

'Action will be taken!' said Mr Cafferty.

Papa froze. He took a deep, furious breath.

'We've had enough trouble with you travellers,' Mr Dunphy said and Mrs Whelan's jowls rippled a little in peeved agreement.

'We have to maintain certain standards,' Cafferty added ponderously. 'Keep things civilised.'

Papa had heard enough. He was being threatened by a pipsqueak. He was in his own flat minding his own business and these nosy parkers came banging on his door to hand out insults and threats. He knew how to deal with threats. He reached out and grabbed the pipsqueak by the throat.

'I'll civilise you!' Papa roared.

Cafferty was wearing a suit. He had a tie on and felt that he was about to choke. He had the sensation of being lifted in the air and propelled down the hallway towards the balcony windows. He flailed his arms.

'Help me,' he croaked.

Papa felt only the hot blood surging in his veins and elbowed off the attempt of Francie Dunphy to stop his progress. He kicked open the windows and dangled Cafferty over the balcony. Behind him the small man pulled at his shirt. 'For the love of God, man, don't kill him!'

'Stop, stop,' Cafferty croaked again. He could see the towers from an entirely new perspective upside down. The ground was a long way below him. He could see the shopping mall and the traffic heading towards the airport.

'If you ever come to my door with threats again I'll make a hamburger of you on the pavement below,' Papa roared through clenched teeth. He lifted Cafferty back on to the balcony and propelled him back down the hallway to the door, followed by Dunphy.

The children stood silently in the bathroom waiting for the front door to slam, which it duly did. Tir na n-Og munched hay.

'Did you hear that?' Tito whispered tremulously.

Ossie gazed at him with awestruck eyes. 'Wasn't Papa great? Those people wanted him to get rid of Tir na n-Og!' He raised his voice to a piping child's cry of triumph. 'But he showed them. The King of the Travellers showed them!' His eyes shone. 'Wasn't he great, Tir na n-Og?' he demanded, but the horse did not seem unduly impressed.

Tito began to plait the horse's mane. His mind was full of unease and he worked silently.

'What's wrong with you?' Ossie demanded. 'Why have you gone all quiet?'

'Don't be such a little eejit!' Tito said. 'Do you think Papa can hang someone over the balcony like an old pair of pants and nobody do anything? That's not the end of it. They'll be back, but this time they'll have reinforcements!'

Ossie's eyes darkened. 'Papa'll fight them!' he said. 'Papa is the King.'

Tito looked at his little brother and sighed.

When the police arrived Papa was awake. He had not been able to get back to sleep after he had hung Cafferty from the balcony. He was sitting on the edge of his bed, his head in his hands, when the commotion started. First was the sound of banging on the door of number 14H, which was now occupied by the Murphys. Their 'fifteen' children had obviously made a deep impression on the man from the welfare, judging by the speed of their relocation to the tower. Papa heard Murphy answer the door, shout that it was the next flat they wanted.

Good man, Murphy, Papa thought. One good turn deserves a kick in the arse!

Papa went to the door and opened it. Two policeman and a man in a white coat pushed their way into the flat.

'We're from the department,' the man in the white coat said.

'What are you doing in my house?' Papa demanded angrily, but the men proceeded into the sitting room where Tito and Ossie and Tir na n-Og were watching television. The latter was now looking very chic with a neatly plaited mane and tail.

68

'We've come for the horse,' the man in white said and, as he spoke, opened a small black case from which he extracted a hypodermic syringe. He approached Tir na n-Og who rolled his eyes wildly and backed away.

'Easy, boy, easy,' the man said. 'It's only a little sedative.'

Ossie began to scream. 'Papa! Help! They're taking our horse. Don't let them take our horse!' He ran out of the room and into his father's bedroom, but Papa Riley was lying with his face to the wall. Ossie pulled at him, the tears streaming down his face.

'Please, Papa, I'll promise I'll learn to read. I don't care if you drink. Just stop them taking Tir na n-Og!' But Papa didn't answer or turn his head.

Fourteen floors below, Inspector Bolger sat in the police car and watched the gathering crowd. There was a second police car beside him and a horsebox had been backed up to the entrance to the tower. The fourth vehicle was a police van, a black maria with tinted windows. It contained two policemen in riot gear, their hunting rifles within reach in case the brute gave any serious trouble.

Bolger was wondering how they were going to get the tinker's nag out of the flat and back on terra firma. The thought of it being ferried down in the lift, or coaxed down fourteen flights of stone steps, filled him with a hilarity he seldom experienced on duty. He shared the joke with the garda beside him and they both tittered, trying to keep their faces straight for the benefit of the waiting crowd who peered in at them.

Through the half-open window he heard the comments, 'Jaysus, the pigs are here in force. Where's the action?' And the rejoinder, 'The travellers have a horse in one of the flats!' There was laughter and ribald comment and a woman with a cigarette hanging out of her mouth leaned conversationally towards Bolger's window and said, 'Arresting a horse makes a bit of a change, eh?' but Bolger declined this as a topic of conversation. The gathering was good-natured, prepared to share the joke, waiting anxiously for the moment when the horse would appear and prove that the rumour was true.

Inspector Bolger was a tall, well-built man of six feet who looked, and felt, extremely good in uniform. He had been in the force for twelve years and had moved up rapidly through the ranks. His was a driving ambition, a black sense of humour, a mercenary mind, and a basic lack of principle that stood him in good stead when it came to wielding the executive power with which he was invested. It was the streak of ruthlessness in him which had fuelled his rise to the position of inspector. Ruthlessness, discreetly applied, got results.

Bolger liked the power of being an officer of the law; but he did not like the pay. The drive in him demanded success and the wealth to go with it, and he considered ceaselessly how he would make a killing, become rich, join the ranks of the fat cats whose persons and property he had protected for so many years. He had a new girl friend, Cathy, a pretty socialite who was costing him a fortune and whom he hoped to marry. But he was sure that she would only marry money; sentiment, as such, would never blind her. Bolger came from the country, the son of a small farmer; he had the pragmatic approach to life of one whose forebears had spent generations struggling against the odds. Cathy did not come from a small farm, but her approach to life was not dissimilar. The main difference was that Bolger was head over heels in love, whereas Cathy, while amused and stimulated by her bog man, hadn't the slightest intention of doing anything she might live to regret.

Cathy's presence in the inspector's life was a watershed; she had come as a revelation, an experience, Bolger thought in his passion, like St Paul's on the road to Damascus. He saw his life in terms of before Cathy and since Cathy. In the days before Cathy, women had worshipped him; he thought this was natural. Women were good at worshipping and should be left to get on with it. But now he was the worshipper and he oscillated between euphoria and an uncertainty bordering on despair. Sometimes he was afraid that she was trifling with him. There were few sexual favours; she was seductive one minute and coy the next, but he knew that she liked the uniform and he tried to make sure she saw him in full regalia as often as possible. He dreamed of striking it rich; he dreamed of lotto winnings of two million, of being able to say nonchalantly, 'I'm thinking of buying that little pad in Foxrock, a snip, only half a million.' That would make a difference, all the difference. Whoever married Cathy would automatically belong to the brahmins of Irish society. There was no point in codding himself that love and a crust in a garret featured on her agenda. So as well as the lotto, he had taken to backing the horses and had amassed a rather heavy debt with the bookies. Now he was at his wits' end as to how he would pay it off.

He turned to the garda in the driver's seat. 'What the hell are they doing?' He picked up the radio and spoke to the policemen in the flat.

Upstairs in 14G the man in the white coat was still trying to interest Tir na n-Og in his hypodermic syringe and still getting nowhere. The horse was going crazy, lashing with his hooves and striking the dividing wall. Plasterboard shattered; a large hole appeared in the dividing wall and the blue light from the Murphys' television shone in on the proceedings. Tir na n-Og went for the man in the white coat, his head out, ears flattened, lips drawn back, and the man, who had early in his career fallen foul of a full set of horse teeth, turned and fled down the hall. The two gardai backed away into a corner and one spoke rapidly into his radio.

On the ground, Bolger listened. Then he turned to Kevin O'Dea beside him and said with a certain amount of relish, 'I'm sending up the heavy gang!'

Bolger spoke quickly to the inmates of the black maria. The two men in full riot gear, helmets, combat fatigues and hefting hunting rifles, immediately jumped out of the police van behind the squad car and ran into the tower. Two more squad cars arrived and police fanned out round the tower. Guards ran up the concrete stairs, their pounding boots echoing up the stairwell.

A distraught young woman in a headscarf came

forward. 'I want to go up to my flat!'

'Sorry, ma'am. There's a dangerous horse up there.'

'Holy Jesus!' said the woman, starting to scream. 'There's me baby up there. I only went out for some fags!'

The Murphys had been covertly following the goings-on in 14G. They knew about the horse and were happy enough to have it for a neighbour. It wasn't bothering them. They heard the horse plunging, and listened with interest while they had their tea of frankfurters and beans. The television was on and Mrs Murphy turned up the sound; there was a programme she wanted to watch, but for once the children were not interested in the TV. Birdie strained her ears, but the noise from the telly drowned out the sounds from next door. Maybe she should put a glass against the wall.

When Tir na n-Og's hoof came through into the room, the Murphy children were delighted and took turns watching the rest of the drama through the newly made hole.

'Get back,' their father told them. 'That fellow'll have the wall in!'

The riot squad got the flat number wrong, just as the vet had, and broke the hall door in their anxiety to present themselves as quickly as possible.

'Wrong house! Next door!' Murphy shouted and his wife watched through the hole in the wall, her eyes agog as the riot police charged into the Rileys' sitting room.

'Why have you brought guns to my house?' Papa

roared when he saw the hunting rifles. Ossie went pale. He continued stroking Tir na n-Og who was quivering and sweating, rolling his eyes and flattening his ears.

'Our job is to get him out of here – one way or the other!' was the reply.

Ossie stared at the men and the rifles with disbelief. 'I'll take him down, I'll take him down,' he cried, wheezing, tears starting. 'Don't hurt him!' He scrabbled around for the bridle, found it, climbed on a chair and slipped it on. Then he led Tir na n-Og through the hallway and towards the lift.

All the tenants of the other flats on the fourteenth floor were standing at their doors, including Ma Whelan who was holding Fu-Fu. The poodle started to bark and Ossie put a calming hand on the horse. The vet reappeared and Tito shouted at him in warning, 'Get out of here!' Tir na n-Og reared and the vet took Tito's advice, diving into a doorway with amazing speed.

Ossie thought he had never seen so many people. They stood there, crowds of them, as he emerged from the building. There were big lights trained on the doorway and Ossie blinked, dazzled. There were several police cars and a big horsebox.

The crowd cheered. The cheering got louder and louder, with whistles and cat-calls. Ossie began to feel very important, like he sometimes did in his dreams. He saw the police lower a ramp into the horsebox. It clunked on the ground and Ossie realised what this meant. He turned to his white horse.

'Run, Tir na n-Og. Run! Go!'

Tir na n-Og moved so quickly that no one had time to react. The police closest were knocked sideways. Others gave chase, trying to corner the horse between the squad cars and the black maria.

Inspector Bolger watched, furious at the way the thing was turning out. These knackers and their white brute were not going to make a hare of him. 'Stop it!' he roared. 'Shoot the bloody thing!'

The report of a rifle answered him almost immediately and there was instant silence. But Tir na n-Og kept going, and with a great leap cleared the squad car in front of him. There was a deep intake of breath by two hundred people and then the silence deepened. Ossie smiled. Tito's jaw dropped and he stared after the white horse with wonder. 'How did you do that, Tir na n-Og?' he whispered. Papa, who had followed them down and was standing in the doorway, drew his breath in sharply. 'You found a right one here, Grandpa,' he muttered.

Bolger, too, was stunned. He came from the land and he knew a bit about horses and he knew an incredible feat when he saw one; it was almost a standing jump – the horse had cleared the squad car after three short strides. He looked calculatingly at the horse's finer points, the beautiful small head, the straight back and the spring in the quivering body, the pure creamy whiteness of its coat. This was no tinker's skewball. This animal was a thoroughbred, maybe even another Dundrum.

He smiled, drawing his lips back over his teeth. His mind was already honing in on the main chance. This animal could not have been honestly come by, he reasoned, not by knackers, and what harm done if its disappearance was a little lacking in probity? The knackers wouldn't know the difference.

Ossie looked around at the riot police with the guns. They were reloading. A terrible sinking feeling seared through his insides. They wouldn't miss this time. This time they would shoot to kill like in the movies. The sudden void of a world without his horse, his friend, opened before him. Better lose him than let him die.

'*Tir na n-Og!*' he cried, his shrill little voice cutting the silence. The horse turned in his headlong career.

'Put down the rifles,' Bolger commanded. He watched as the horse trotted towards Ossie. 'Let the boy go to him.'

Ossie, his face tight, led Tir na n-Og into the horsebox. Tir na n-Og wasn't going to die. He rested his small cheek against the horse's leg.

'Let you be good now, Tir na n-Og,' he whispered. 'Let you be good so they don't hurt you. We'll get you back when we can.'

The horse stood impassively as Ossie, his face streaming with tears, walked out of the horsebox. Papa went to him and put a hand on his shoulder, but Ossie glanced at him contemptuously and shrugged it off. The police shut the horsebox. The bolts slid home with a thud and it seemed to Ossie that the ringing of the bolts going home were hammer blows on his heart. All his old loneliness and fear returned.

The horsebox moved off. Ossie and Tito watched it until it turned the corner and was lost to view.

Bolger turned to Papa. 'Who is going to pay for the damage, traveller?' he sneered. 'You are. Not the taxpayer, not Dublin Corporation, but you!' He got back into the squad car. The engine revved and he was driven away. The other garda cars followed.

Papa moved to take his sons' hands. Ossie jumped back from him. Papa picked him up and carried him back into the tower. Ossie hit him again and again, his small fists flailing and banging on his father's shoulders.

'You let them take him away! You let them take him away!' he cried.

Papa said nothing. His face was tired and he looked old.

Ossie hit him again before dissolving in bitter tears. 'It's your fault!'

Papa did not reply. He put his son down and walked slowly away. Tito dragged Ossie into the lift.

When they were back in the flat they surveyed the damage. The door was in a bad way; the hole in the wall had been plugged by a cushion. This was removed and Birdie's face appeared.

'I watched from the balcony,' she whispered sympathetically. 'What are you going to do? Will you be able to get him back?'

Tito was silent, but Ossie spluttered through his tears, 'We'll get him back; he's our horse and we'll get him back!'

'Where are you going to keep him?'

Tito shook his head.

'We'll go and live with him in Tir na n-Og!' Ossie said aggressively.

Birdie shrugged and raised her eyebrows.

'That's a country,' Ossie said in explanation, in case she hadn't been listening to Grandpa's story.

There were raised voices from Birdie's side of the wall, the sound of the baby wailing and Mrs Murphy's voice shouting, 'Birdie, would you shut that fella up!'

Birdie's face darkened and she replaced the cushion.

Chapter Six

'At least I do one effin' thing right!' Papa muttered as he beat the dents out of the car. He worked furiously, trying to forget that his children were in mourning for the loss of Tir na n-Og. He had been told by Inspector Bolger that the horse would be auctioned to pay for the damage done to the flat – unless, that was, he could come up with £155.00 immediately. The inspector had come round personally to tell him this and Papa's hackles still rose when he thought of the smirk on the man's face.

'I can't get my hands on that kind of money!' he told him and Bolger's smirk got wider.

'When will the auction be?' Papa asked, wondering where he might come by the necessary sum and wondering also, even if he did, where he would keep the animal. He was sorry that he had drunk his last few pounds in a wild binge on the night the horse was taken.

'Soon, soon,' was the reply and then the policeman had got back into his car and driven off. Papa looked after him, wondering in a vague kind of way why he was on his own, and why he had come at all; an important class of a guard like him surely had better things to be doing.

The metal groaned and rang under Papa's hands, the bodywork resuming its smooth curves. He fantasised about its gratitude, imagining himself a plastic surgeon with a once beautiful body under his creative fingers. Beside him loomed the tower; the place he called home. It was late evening, edging towards dusk. Papa was wearing his black leather coat, belted round the middle. The blows from his wooden mallet rang out in the still air. He thought of the dog's dinner he had made of his life. His mind went back again to the beginning, something he found himself doing more and more of late. In his memory was the sound of the caravans on the open road. His parents had belonged to the old school; his father was a craftsman, never happier than when working with metal or wood; he made good implements and lovely toys and would sit back and view his handiwork with the pride of the true artisan.

As he worked, Papa remembered the smell of the fires in the evening and the way the smoke would curl in blue eddies over the caravans. They had been almost all barrel-topped in those days, painted in bright blues and reds. Everyone was very poor; many begged, some preyed off the Rozzers, the name they had for the settled people, but the proud lived off what nature gave them, the rabbits, berries, fish, fruit and nuts that were plentiful if you knew where to look for them. He remembered the clear sight being on the road gave you, the 'feel' of different localities, the unobtrusive signs left by other travellers to indicate local friendship or hostility, such as a stick between two stones placed by the roadside. He knew men who would put boot polish on a greying horse or stick nettles up its behind to knock a few years off it. He knew old men and women who spoke Shinti, the travellers' language known only to them. He remembered the sensation that life was an adventure, ever changing, ever challenging, and not just a steady decline into uselessness and monotony.

He thought of the girls he had known and for a moment a smile played on his mouth. Traditionally the girls were married almost as soon as they reached puberty. Life for the women was hard; continual pregnancies wore them out, some died in childbirth. The pretty girl of thirteen or fourteen became the weathered matron of twenty with several children already hanging on to her skirts. But some young women of his generation had resisted and among these was Kathleen.

Papa had known Kathleen Lee all his life. She was his second cousin. She had been a fearless rider, and she and her brother were the only surviving members of a family that had been ravaged by TB. Without parents, Kathleen was under the guardianship of her maternal aunt who could not handle a girl of her spirit and who soon stopped trying.

As teenagers it was expected that he and Kathleen would marry. He used to tease her about it. All she would do was smile, a mocking kind of smile, and say she would marry when she pleased. The young men eyed her, but she seemed indifferent. Papa had ignored any suggestions from his elders that he should look elsewhere, that the girl was wild and would make a bad wife.

'I want to see a bit of the world before I marry,' she had told him. 'Where's the hurry, John Riley?' They were in the woods together, her long red-gold hair held back with a black ribbon, her brown eyes sparkling the way they did when she laughed.

Papa had pushed her back against a tree, kissed her feverishly on the mouth. Her lips were soft and full and the contact surged through him, boiled in his blood.

Kathleen did not seem to react to his kiss. She became very still and then pulled away from him, but he saw that she trembled. She was careful after that not to go into the woods with him. But she smiled and gave him arch sideways looks, driving him mad, making him angry; he decided that she was playing with him, that she had no intention of getting serious. And so the months had passed and a tacit stand-off had arisen between them. Kathleen had the upper hand and seemed to be enjoying it.

By the time Mary Ward had come into his life, Papa was furious with Kathleen, vulnerable to romance and keen for marry, to start his own small tribe.

Mary had arrived with her father one fine summer Sunday, riding on the caravan in a print dress, her bare brown legs swinging over the edge. She was fine-boned, petite and shy, with a doe-like quality of imminent movement about her, as though any sudden change would precipitate her flight. She was everything that Kathleen was not. He could not take his eyes off her. He had the sensation of something happening outside of his control.

After an hour spent in her company, or rather her father's company while she sat on the fringes of the conversation, he no longer felt clumsy and gauche; he felt like a king. By the end of a week he wanted to protect her and be with her and never have another day without her. Her femininity was so delicate, so fresh, that she was a source of continual wonder to him. Their marriage had taken place within months.

Kathleen had disappeared by the time the nuptials were due for celebration. She had gone to England with Jacko, a traveller she had met at a horse fair and precipitously married. Papa had not paused, except very briefly, to ponder how his marriage to someone else might have affected her. Initially, the subdued sense of having turned the tables on Kathleen had been sweet; and he was genuinely in love with his bride, his mind and heart full. Not until a year had passed did he allow himself to wonder if he had hurt Kathleen. He found that he missed her, missed her presence, missed the unrestrained laugh he would hear in the evenings while she joked with the other girls; above all, he missed the challenge she offered him, which forced him into constantly changing his perspectives. He worshipped Mary because she made him a king; he missed Kathleen because she unlocked the doors to his self.

By the time Kathleen came back to the tribe, Tito had been born. She returned without her husband. She was quite open about it; she said that she had left him. This made her position in the tribe ambiguous, a woman who was married and unmarried at the same time. But she quickly re-established herself with her brother Tracker and settled down to her work as a midwife, a skill she had learnt during her time in England where she had travelled with the Romanies. She commanded respect.

Papa noticed that she was changed, that the gaiety had left her. Her demeanour to him assumed the distance of careful cousinly friendship. She did not seem to harbour either resentment or regret and he assumed, with a mixture of relief and involuntary pique, that she had never cared for him in any other way. She made a friend of Mary and would chatter to her about her husband's childhood, something Mary—

'Papa! Papa!'

Papa's reverie terminated abruptly and he was immediately conscious of the huge buildings beside him and the wrecked car dump enveloping him in an atmosphere of immobility and despondency. Tito was running towards him with a frightened face.

'Ossie can't breathe!'

Papa seemed to sag. He put down his mallet. 'How bad is it?' he demanded, keeping his eyes on his work.

'Bad enough!'

'What can I do about it?'

Tito's face registered despair. 'If we had Tir na n-Og back, Papa, he would be all right again. He never had the funny breathing with Tir na n-Og.'

'I know that!' Papa said testily. 'But they want one hundred and fifty-five pound before I can have him back. One hundred and fifty-five pound! That's a lot

of money for a horse we can't keep.' He looked at
Tito's face. 'Well, where do you think we can keep
him? You saw what happened when you tried to keep
him in the flat. Which was a bloody stupid thing to do,
let me tell you. And he's nothing but trouble, what
with that ould Whelan faggot and the Cafferty fellow
banging on the door.' He remembered with a certain
unease that he had hung Cafferty upside down from
the balcony.

Tito was silent, nursing the furious sense of futility
which threatened to overcome the control he had
learnt painstakingly over the years. You did not
confront Papa head on. He loved Papa, but he feared
his anger, feared the sudden flash in his eye and
towering rage which shook him; and he feared for
Papa too, that he would hurt himself, like the time he
had put his fist through the window in a wild surge of
frustration. In a way Tito was nursemaid to two
children and he loved both of them passionately. He
understood Papa's anger in an unformed way; he
knew it in his soul, the fury of a great heart bruised
and fettered. And because of this he forgave Papa
everything.

Papa finished his work and went to the shops. He
bought three portions of fish and chips, two cartons of
milk, some chocolate and a jar of Vick. Then he went
home. The children were in the kitchen; Ossie was
bending over a bowl of hot water which Tito had
prepared and his head was covered with a towel. Papa
opened the jar of Vick, put his hand under the towel
and without saying a word anointed Ossie's upper lip;

Tito looked at the bags of fish and chips on the table and got out some forks.

'Come on now, son,' Papa said to Ossie. 'Eat your supper.'

'I'm not hungry,' Ossie said from under the towel.

'Is the breathing any better?'

Ossie didn't answer.

'The steam always helps him,' Tito answered.

Papa took a bottle of Guinness out of a cupboard. He was trying to go easy on the drink after the last debacle. 'No more spirits,' he had promised himself. 'No more spirits,' he had told Mary in his sleep one night and had woken to terrible desolation.

He opened the bottle and poured it into a glass, watching the head froth creamily at the top. He put the fish and chips on a plate and tucked in. Tito had washed up the day's dishes and Papa was reminded that every single touch that made the place a home came from Tito; not from him, but from Tito who was twelve years old and as tough as any twelve-year-old boots might be.

Papa turned to Ossie. 'Come out from under that thing and eat your food!'

Ossie lifted a corner of the towel and peered out at his father. 'I said I'm not hungry!' He spoke with an asthmatic rasp, in which the authority of his seven years fulminated, and then he retreated under his 'tent'.

Papa pushed a bar of chocolate across the table. 'Maybe that'll whet your appetite.'

Ossie forgot for a second that he wasn't hungry and

that he wasn't talking to Papa any more. The towel lifted a fraction. 'Chocolate!' he yelped with a croak and the bar disappeared underneath the towel.

Tito ate his fish and chips and then he made tea. He put a cup out for his father, but Papa reached for a second bottle of Guinness, leaning back in his chair dejectedly.

'Even if I could lay my hands on that sort of money,' he said to Tito in a low voice, referring to their earlier conversation, 'wouldn't it be better to spend it on doctors?'

Tito met his father's eyes. 'They can't do any more for him. The doctor in the clinic gave him that respirator yoke, but he hates it. He hasn't been as bad as this for a long time.' He set his face. 'He was all right when we had Tir na n-Og.'

Papa bowed his head. 'I know,' he said. To himself he added, I'm a great father! A great class of a father sure enough.

He went into his bedroom and took his priceless brass telescope from its box. It would fetch a tidy sum. He brought it to the balcony for a last look through it at the twilit hills.

Sergeant Brophy had not been at the eviction of the horse from the tower, but he had been told the whole story. He knew Papa by sight; he had booked him once over a brawl. Someone had called him a knacker and had got a punch for his pains which fractured his jaw. Brophy had given him a warning, secretly thinking while he did so that he wasn't one bit sorry for the fellow nursing his jaw. The provocation had been his and the result of it was his due. That, in Brophy's book, was fair enough.

So when Papa walked into the station he needed no introduction, but came forward immediately to the counter.

Papa put a wad of money on the counter. 'That's to pay for the damage. I don't want the horse to go to auction.'

Sergeant Brophy looked at him in perplexity. 'But the horse is already sold!'

Papa gaped at the sergeant. He did not understand. How could you just sell someone's horse? his muddled mind demanded. There must be a law; they had laws about everything. Maybe they made them up as they went along. A solicitor could tell him, but he couldn't afford a solicitor.

'Sold?'

Brophy looked at him with pity, sorry for the hurt in him and the bewilderment. 'Yes.'

'To whom?'

Brophy sighed. 'To a very important businessman in County Meath.'

Papa remembered the lush lands of County Meath, the rich farms, the healthy children. There had been one or two grand halting places with plenty of grass in the 'long acre'. His voice rose in consternation. 'But that horse was supposed to go to auction! That's what I was told.'

Sergeant Brophy saw the desperation in Papa's eyes. 'Surely you knew?'

Papa shook his head. 'No. I didn't know! Nobody told me!'

'Take it easy,' Brophy said. 'Getting upset is no good.'

'What's going on here?' demanded a voice behind Brophy's right shoulder, making him jump. It belonged to Inspector Bolger. He had left his office when he heard the raised voice at the public counter and thought he recognised it. When he realised that it was indeed Riley he had moved quickly.

Drawing himself to his full height, Bolger stared at Papa who was slumped against the counter like a broken man.

'I'll pay the damage money. I want my horse!'

Bolger gave a short, harsh laugh. Beside Papa in his present state he looked magnificent, proud, handsome, informed, scion of the system, his uniform fitted like a glove on his muscular body.

'What are you on about, man? Get the hell out of here before we put you in the cell!' He took out his baton and brought it down on the counter with a resounding wallop.

Sergeant Brophy frowned. He didn't like Bolger whom he knew had blocked his promotion, and he didn't like Bolger's tactics; but he knew which side his bread was buttered. Something shady was involved here; he didn't know what but he was going to get to the bottom of it.

Papa looked at the baton and then up at the inspector. His lips curled in a sneer. 'You're a brave man,' he said, nodding his head sarcastically and fixing his eyes back on the baton. 'I'll not argue with a brave man like you!'

Bolger reddened with anger and Papa walked slowly out of the door.

When Papa was gone, Bolger turned to the sergeant. 'The impertinence of these bloody knackers. He knew the horse was sold. Coming in here pretending that he came down in the last shower.' He looked at Brophy for affirmation, but the sergeant only nodded and turned away. He suspected Bolger's game. If it was the game he thought it was, he'd have a handle on the inspector, but he had to be sure. It would be interesting to check out the precise circumstances surrounding the sale of the horse.

Tito and Ossie went to the top of the tower a couple of weeks later and looked down on the city. They could see for miles, from the mountains to the bay, from the twin pigeon-house chimneys to the airport and beyond. They saw the traffic heading for the capital with its thousands and thousands of houses and offices and streets.

'He's down there somewhere,' Ossie said with a sibilant wheeze.

'How do you know?'

Ossie looked up at his brother. 'I just know.'

'But we've been looking for ages! Come on, let's go in. We can't stay up here for ever.'

Ossie grabbed his brother's arm and pointed towards the countryside. 'Tir na n-Og is down there somewhere,' he repeated, moving forward like someone in a trance. 'Didn't Papa say they'd sold him to an important businessman in County Meath?' He leaned forward, pointing. 'That's County Meath over there. That's where we should go!'

'Stay back, Ossie,' Tito cried in sudden alarm as his brother moved dangerously close to the edge.

Ossie stood still as though he were listening to something. 'He's not happy,' he whispered. 'He's not a bit happy!'

Noel Harnett wanted to own the world. He owned a fair bit of it already, a house in Dublin, a stud in Meath, a flat in Mayfair, a villa in the south of France. The son of a car salesman, he had left school at sixteen, started a building business with a legacy from a great-aunt and made a fortune in the property boom of the seventies when, using inside information for which he had handed out considerable sums in bribes, he bought land about to be re-zoned for a fraction of its true value. Sometimes the land he bought had travellers camping on it and he would move in his bully boys and clear them off. On this land he had built housing estates, charging high prices for poorly built houses. The price of housing was at an all-time high; the children of the post-war years were getting married, settling down. The economy was relatively buoyant. The money flooded in. He couldn't put a foot wrong.

And when the housing boom declined he was ready for it. He knew the cyclical nature of fortune and had already diversified. He sold tracts of undeveloped land at a huge profit at the end of the seventies when the values peaked and then he turned his attention to the food industry, in which he made another fortune. Now he was angling with all his might for the one thing that eluded him: social stature. If he could make it in Ireland's classiest industry, stud-farming thoroughbreds, the long desired status would follow.

Harnett was now in the prime of life, balding, cleanshaven, with a certain formidable hauteur about him which was grounded in privilege and presumption. He was very rich. The money he had made in wheeling and dealing in the seventies had turned him into a multi-millionaire. He was a prudent investor, an adroit manipulator of his fellow man and was possessed of a total disregard for everything except money and power. In this respect he was cut of the same cloth as Inspector Bolger, except that Bolger had not dared to essay the kind of scams that were second nature to Harnett, who stared at millions without blinking. Bolger had never had a million to stare at, a state of affairs he intended some day to change. To hasten this happy future, he had sold Harnett the tinker's horse. The deal was provisional; sums within certain very large parameters had been mentioned, but no money had as yet changed hands.

Bolger had met Harnett through his friendship with Cathy Prendergast and he was the first person he thought of approaching when he decided to appropriate the knacker's horse. Harnett, he knew, would be both interested and not ask too many awkward questions. When he saw what the horse could do, he would pay any price for it; he would recognise it at once as the horse which would put him on the equestrian map.

Harnett had indeed been interested. 'If this animal is as good as you would have me believe, Bolger, you won't find me niggardly,' he said pompously. 'I've been looking for an outstanding showjumper for a long time.' It rankled with Harnett that he had been stung on a few occasions; he had bought horses which seemed to promise great things, but which had failed to star in the end. He knew that a fine horse could come from surprising sources and so he was willing to give Bolger's animal a trial.

Bolger was standing with his prospective purchaser by a paddock at Harnett's stud farm in County Meath. All around him were rolling fields, rich countryside, and in the midst of all this glorious nature was Harnett's beautiful white house, which dominated the grounds around it. The inspector was wearing a raincoat over his uniform and had buttoned it up. His manner was slightly furtive; he did not want to advertise his presence here and he would prefer it if Harnett's staff did not realise he was a policeman.

Tir na n-Og was trotted out of the stable yard to the paddock where a number of red and white pole jumps and a white wooden 'wall' were erected. It was a fine day; the white horse looked elegant and moved beautifully, a different animal already, Bolger thought, to the frightened brute they had taken away from the tower. The movements were fluid, there was coiled strength in the body and the canter was measured and contained. A momentary fear assailed him that its extraordinary feat at the Towers was an exceptional performance, brought on by an exceptional rush of adrenaline. He glanced at Harnett, knew that he would be scathing if the animal did not live up to expectations. Harnett studied the white horse carefully; he liked the look of the animal, but that didn't mean he was capable of the sort of performance of which Bolger had boasted.

'Put him over those jumps,' Harnett said, raising his voice just a fraction and watching the white horse carefully. The rider nodded.

Tir na n-Og flew round the arena, cleared the jumps easily. Harnett's watching face was impassive, although his eyes flickered with a sudden interest.

'Raise the fences,' he called.

Someone rushed forward to raise the fences. Tir na n-Og jumped again, and again he cleared everything with a contemptuous flick of his tail.

'Raise them again!'

Bolger looked at the height of the jumps and shifted his feet.

Again the white horse performed impeccably.

'Build up the wall,' Harnett called. Two men ran forward and the wall went higher, block by block until Bolger could bear it no longer.

'I don't think any animal can go over that,' he said uneasily. 'He's a good horse, but only the devil could fly over a wall that high. He's too valuable to hurt, Mr Harnett.' Jesus Christ, Bolger thought, if Harnett didn't want him there was plenty who would. But he'd injure him if he expected him to levitate like a witch on a broomstick.

Harnett favoured Bolger with a brief, caustic glance. 'You've got to have faith, Inspector!'

Tir na n-Og came forward again, met the impossible wall with a surge of furious energy and cleared it as though it had been a nursery jump set up for a child's pony. Harnett's eyes began to glow as though hot coals from his soul had come to inhabit them. He turned to Bolger.

'Well, well, Inspector,' he said with the air of a man trying to appear nonchalant, although his excitement was perfectly evident, 'it looks as though we will be doing business.' He gestured to his secretary, Morrissey, who was waiting discreetly in the background. The man came forward with a supercilious, sidling gait which annoyed Bolger intensely; he was holding a black briefcase which he opened. The case was full of money.

Bolger felt his heart race. Morrissey, obeying the nod from his boss, extracted several bundles of notes and handed them to Harnett, who gave them to Bolger.

'That's just for starters. But I want a signature. Get the tinker to sign. I want it done properly.'

Bolger glanced around him furtively. Then he took the money and thrust it into his breast pocket.

'You'll have it,' he said. 'You'll have your signature.'

When Bolger had left, an old stable hand who had been watching from the archway to the stable yard approached Harnett, pulled at his peaked cap and asked quietly, 'Can I have a word with you, sir?'

Harnett signalled to Morrissey to rid him of this pest.

'It's about the horse, sir,' the man insisted.

'What about the horse?'

The old man indicated Tir na n-Og who was being brought back to the stable yard. 'That's no ordinary horse, sir.'

'I know that!' Harnett said irritably, moving away.

'Be careful, Mr Harnett,' the man continued softly, raising his voice just a fraction, while his rheumy eyes regarded his employer.

'Why should I be careful?'

The stable hand regarded Harnett with dislike. He was sorry he had bothered, but he didn't want to work in a place where the Little Folk had an innings. Once they had an innings you could expect anything.

'That animal has the sign of the Sidhe on him,' he said in a flat voice. He paused, looking into Harnett's bemused eyes to see if he understood the full import of what he was being told. 'You should send him back to wherever he came from.'

Morrissey turned down the corners of his mouth in pained disparagement; his general demeanour suggested that the old blighter be lifted up with a pair of tongs and deposited in the nearest manure heap. But Harnett only laughed.

'I don't care if he has the sign of the devil on him,' he said. 'Be off about your work and don't be bothering me with such nonsense.'

The old man looked after the departing figures of Harnett and Morrissey. They hadn't seen the horse's shoes – shoes that hadn't been nailed on. 'You've been warned, Mr Harnett,' he muttered angrily. 'You might not care now, but care you surely will!'

About a hundred miles from County Meath, Grandpa leaned back against the half-door of the caravan and thought again of the night before, of what he had seen in the fire. Nothing concrete, just certain shadows in the orange heart of the blaze that always presaged crisis. 'I shouldn't have left them,' he muttered. 'I shouldn't have left the children. I'd better go back.'

He had travelled with unease after he had left the white horse behind him, following his old route south-west; he had intended going to Kerry, rolling out to Dingle, over the Connor Pass, down to the great strand. He saw it in his mind's eye, hungered for it like a lover. But all the time the thought of the children kept intruding. What had they done with the horse? Had Papa sold it and drunk the proceeds? And, most importantly, were they safe?

He stopped at any encampments he passed en route and told stories. The children gathered round him and he whispered to them the story of Cormac Mac Art, son of Conn of the Hundred Battles, and the sad tale of the friends Cuchulainn and Ferdia, and the story of the Sons of Usna. But his heart was not in the recounting as it usually was. He accepted food and drink in exchange for the entertainment and when he left the last encampment someone gave him a bottle of whiskey to take the cold out of his bones. Grandpa loved the odd drop of whiskey, but this time he wasn't tempted to sample it. Instead he left it unopened in the small cupboard in the caravan and turned and headed back to the Towers.

While Grandpa was taking the road which would bring him back to the Towers, Tito and Ossie were out on the Navan Road thumbing a lift. A car stopped. A young man who felt sorry for the two skinny kids opened the passenger door and asked where they were going.

'County Meath, mister. We're going to County Meath,' Tito said, prepared to hop in.

'What part?'

Tito looked at Ossie. 'We want to see an important businessman there.'

'What's his name?' the driver said, already aware that he needed his head examined.

Tito looked uncertainly at Ossie again. 'We don't know . . .' he admitted, his voice trailing off apologetically.

'Go home outta that,' the driver said crossly. 'Go home before you get yourselves in trouble.' He reached for the passenger door and slammed it shut. The car disappeared into the traffic.

The boys decided that if they didn't know where they were going, they had little chance of getting there and so they went home. The flat was empty. There was no food except some bread and one slice of processed cheese which they divided and devoured. Then Ossie found big cardboard box in Papa's room and they cut out a piece big enough for a sign. Then Tito, in his best writing, wrote with a thick felt-tipped pen: 'WITE HORSE LOST – REWARD' and drew a horse, of sorts, in the rest of the available space.

'What's the reward?' Ossie demanded.

Tito shrugged. 'I dunno,' he admitted. 'We'll have to think of something.'

They went out and stuck the sign to a lamppost outside the Towers.

Then they went to bed. They were miserable and hardly talked. There was nothing left to talk about.

Chapter Seven

A week later, Papa had nearly finished work on the car. He bolted the new door to the body, closed it and stood back to survey his handiwork. All she needed now was a good spraying and you'd never know she'd been banjaxed. He visualised his customer's face, anticipated the compliments.

He heard footsteps approaching, looked up, saw a man in an overcoat coming towards him across the muddy grass, knew from his clothes and his briefcase and his face that he was an outsider. He was instantly reminded of the welfare man who had come to see the Murphys. The Murphys had settled in well, but the hole in the wall, which Mrs Murphy had stuffed with a cushion, admitted the noise of every argument and quarrel between the parents as well as the children's fights. 'I must fix that bloody wall,' he said, but Tito seemed unenthusiastic. He conducted conversations with Birdie through the hole. All they had to do was remove the cushion and they could conspire with ease. Birdie was growing breasts and Tito thought this was very interesting and glanced at them at every opportunity. They were very small little apples, but

Birdie was desperate, wondering what she could do to get rid of them.

The man coming towards him was not the welfare man, although he had the same kind of 'I'm a concerned public servant' expression which Papa found irritating. So he looked at him with unsmiling, taciturn inquiry.

'Are you John Riley?'

'Why do you ask?'

'Do you have two sons in St Enda's School?'

Papa drew himself up. What had the bloody kids been up to now? 'I do. Why?'

'Do you know where they are?' the man asked wearily.

'They're at school!' Papa said.

The man regarded him for a moment. 'They're not, you know. They haven't been to school for a couple of months.'

Papa leaned against the car. The dirty little brats, he thought. They trotted off every morning like butter wouldn't melt. ''Bye, Papa,' Tito would say and he would surface from his hangover long enough to say ''Bye, Tito, 'bye, Ossie.' Sometimes Ossie forgot that he still wasn't speaking to Papa and would call, 'See you later, Papa!'

As Papa leaned against the car, something in him, something very unparentlike, wanted to laugh. But he did not convey this to the man with the concerned face because in a moment his immediate response had changed to annoyance and then to anger. What would become of them if they didn't go to school? Why couldn't he turn his back without them having horses in the flat or pulling the wool over his eyes?

'Are they at home now, do you think?' the man asked.

'Come up and we'll see,' said Papa through grinding teeth.

The flat was empty. The breakfast dishes were still on the kitchen table, but there was no sign of the boys.

'They'll probably be back in a minute,' Papa said, trying to give the man the impression that his children were not wild types. They always came home about this time, the normal school homecoming time. He wondered where they were. What the hell did they do with the day if they were not at school? It was different when he was a kid. He had the woods and the streams to explore and the road to follow, but his children had only the towers like bloody Siberian settlements, the encampment, and faceless, sprawling suburbia.

The door opened and Tito and Ossie walked in, jumped when they saw they had a reception committee, dropped their arms by their sides and looked sheepish.

'How long is it since you boys were at school?' Papa demanded sternly.

Tito shifted uneasily. 'A while.'

'About two months!' Papa said. 'Is that right?'

Tito thought furiously. 'Not that long!'

The man from the Department of Education opened his briefcase, removed a folder and consulted it.

'You haven't been at school for precisely two

103

months and four days,' he said drily.

Tito was silent. He glanced at Ossie who was standing with his head lowered, stubbornly jutting out his lower lip.

'Is that right?' Papa demanded.

Tito looked at Papa. 'I suppose so,' he said in a small voice.

Papa surveyed his sons in silence and then turned to the man. 'They'll be in school tomorrow.'

The man looked at the frowning parental face, gave a half nod in acknowledgement, an official kind of nod which inferred that they'd better watch out if they weren't, restored the folder to his briefcase and stood up. Papa went with him to the door.

When he came back into the room he put a hand on each of his sons' shoulders. 'Do you know what they'll do if you don't go to school? They'll take you away for good! That's what they'll do. Is that what you want?' He turned to the television. 'You're always watching that thing. It's going. You've got three months catching up to do before you can watch telly again!' He disconnected it and carried it into his own room. 'It's staying here until further orders – is that clear?'

Before he left to go back to his work, he warned the children, 'Get out your schoolbooks and start working. When I get back I'll hear your lessons.' The children knew that this was an idle threat because Papa could not read.

'Yes, Papa.'

As soon as he was gone, Ossie lifted up a corner of the cushion which plugged the hole in the wall. He saw Mrs Murphy getting ready to go out. She stood in front of the round mirror in her living room and ran a comb through her hair. Birdie had just come home. Her school bag had been dumped against the opposite wall and she was sitting on the couch watching a video, Angela and Conor beside her.

'I'm going out to look for your father,' Mrs Murphy said. 'Stay here until I come back. And mind that baby . . .'

The children grunted. They were immersed in the video. Mrs Murphy put on her coat and left. Ossie could hear her shutting the front door. He turned to Tito.

'Mrs Murphy's gone out. Birdie and everyone's watching telly.' He glanced at his own television-less sitting room. 'It's not fair.'

Tito took the cushion out of the wall, stared in through the hole at the Murphy children.

'Hey, Birdie,' he said. 'Turn the telly round so we can see it.'

Birdie started and then laughed. She complied and moved the couch. Angela used a four-letter word to protest at the interruption of her viewing, but then she too laughed. Having your neighbours watch your telly through the wall was a great bit of crack. Conor giggled.

'Thanks.'

Tito leant against the wall and watched the programme through the hole, one ear cocked for the sound of Papa's return. Chances were that he wouldn't be back for a long time, so he allowed himself to get caught up in the doings of Butch Cassidy and the Sundance Kid.

When Mrs Murphy returned about an hour later, without her husband, she handed her children bags of crisps. 'You've moved the couch,' she said without much interest, unaware that she had interposed her person between Tito's line of vision and the TV set. She didn't know he was there and she stood and watched the television for a moment.

'That's an old movie,' she said.

'Get out of the way, Mrs Murphy,' Tito said, desperate that he was missing the shoot-out.

Mrs Murphy jumped, turned to the wall and saw the face staring in through the hole. She grabbed the cushion and plugged it immediately, making various suggestions as to what Tito might do with himself. But, as she turned, Tito had had just enough time to see that the big guy was lying dead on the ground.

'Didn't even see him get his gun out of the holster,' he sighed, staring at the olive-green cushion which had so abruptly terminated his viewing. He wanted to tear it out of the hole, but felt that crossing Mrs Murphy, whom he had heard in full verbal spate on more than one occasion, would be unwise.

Ossie was sitting with his back to the wall. He had shown no interest in watching the video through the hole, which was not like him; he loved Westerns.

Tito bent down beside him. 'Are you all right, Ossie?' he asked quietly.

Ossie did not reply for a moment; then he said, 'I'm lonely.' He said it in a small, lost voice. Tito realised then that his little brother was crying and that his breathing was bad.

'Tir na n-Og will come back,' Tito whispered,

suddenly feeling his position as family prop to be an insupportable burden.

'When?'

Tito sighed. 'He'll come back when he can. Or we'll find him.'

'When are we going to find him?' Ossie said listlessly.

'Soon. When the time is right.'

Ossie gulped. 'I'm lonely,' he mumbled again.

When Ossie reflected on life he felt that it was a great amorphous place without boundaries, so big that he could drown in it. Papa was seldom at home; he and Tito could do what they liked. No one told them to stay in like Mrs Murphy told her kids. They had to be sensible all by themselves. Once or twice they had gone out late and been chased by big boys. It was frightening outside at night; there was only the darkness and the cold street lights and the lights from the windows where families were together. Once a man had offered them sweets and told them to come with him; there was something funny about him, something that made them feel queer, as though there was a danger near them they could smell but couldn't see, and they had run away.

In the evenings they would hear children being called in for their tea, or told to come in to go to bed. Ossie wished someone would come looking for him to tell him his tea was ready or to bring him home to bed. The other kids said he and Tito were lucky, no one to boss them around, but Ossie knew this was not true. He needed someone to impose rules on his life, to keep him close; he needed it so badly that he was ill with longing for it. He felt sometimes that he didn't exist; that he was invisible and unimportant like a small fly on the wall of one of the great towers. Only once in his life had he lost the feeling that he was drifting and alone and that was when he had called for his mother from the balcony. That was funny, because suddenly he had had a feeling that someone was listening, that someone knew him and was listening. And then, after that, when Tir na n-Og came, he felt he had a real friend. But Tir na n-Og was gone and everything was going back to the way it used to be and he felt that he was fading away. Sometimes the breathing was so bad that he seemed to spend for ever between breaths, clutching at the next mouthful of air and trying to drag it down to where it would work for him.

That night Tito prayed to his mother. 'Mammy, help me. Help me learn how to read so we can get the telly back.' He paused, listening to the sound of Ossie's shallow breathing. 'And you'll have to do something about Tir na n-Og. Ossie's gone all quiet, and his breathing's funny again.'

He angled the bedside light so that it shone on his reader and he prodded at the words with his index finger, trying to break them down into syllables. Eventually the book slipped from the bunk and on to the floor. Tito drifted into sleep, a sleep where an old dream came for him: he was on a beach and she was there and he woke up in horror because of what he had done. He hated this dream and what it meant.

Papa came home relatively sober; he had cele-
brated his successful repair job on the car with a
solitary pint. He looked in on the boys before he went
to bed. He saw Tito's face turned sideways on his
pillow, and the book on the floor beside him. Ossie
was asleep in the upper bunk, his small face pressed
against his hand. Papa turned off the light and sat on
the end of Tito's mattress in the darkness.

'Mary,' he whispered, 'they are fine, good kids,
your sons. You would be proud of them. But Ossie
isn't well. We've had queer shenanigans recently with
a white horse your father brought back, and now,
because of me, we've lost the bloody animal. Ossie
spends all his time thinking about him. If we can get
him back – will you try and get him back, for Ossie's
sake? He's not the same. Something queer is going
on . . . And poor Tito is bearing the brunt of it.' He
paused, leaned his head on his hands. 'Jesus, girl, I
miss you! I cannot bear to think of you in a grave. It
makes me feel so sick inside I want to die!'

He wiped his eyes and went to his room. When he
was gone, Tito turned in the bed and wept. He saw his
mother's face, but when he tried to remember it in
detail, it eluded him. He remembered the feel of her
arms; he remembered sitting on her knee; he
remembered the morning when he was taken away to
Grandpa's caravan and they wouldn't let him back.
'Mammy, Mammy,' he had wept and when he had
heard her moaning he had begun to scream, so that
Grandpa had driven away with him down the road
where he could not hear her any more. He had tried
to run away from Grandpa, to find his mother in the

caravan, to tell her that he was sorry for what he had done. But Grandpa had stopped him, given him sweets, had tried to play with him. 'She'll be all right, she'll be all right.' But the old man's mind was elsewhere; even Tito could see that he was forcing himself to do tricks with cards and marbles. And when they had come back, the night had fallen and Mammy was dead.

They wouldn't let him see her. But he had escaped and sneaked into the caravan. He ran to her, but it wasn't the same Mammy. She lay there, hard and cold, with a thin little smile on the edge of her mouth and her eyes closed. Papa had been so silent and had looked at him with such unseeing eyes that Tito had felt he no longer existed. He had lost Papa too. In one single day everything in his life had been taken from him. Except Grandpa; but Grandpa wouldn't live with them and he never knew when he would even turn up again.

Tito slept and dreamed he was in a big ship crossing the ocean and that Papa and Mammy and Ossie and Grandpa were there with him, and that they saw Tir na n-Og flying up on great white wings out of the waves.

A week later Tito presented his father with the reader.

'I can read . . . well, kind of,' he announced.

Papa looked at the little schoolbook, with its pictures of Dora and Dick and Mum and Dad in their suburban house. He handed it back to Tito. 'You read it then!'

He sat and listened while Tito concentrated, articulating the words syllable by syllable, about how Dick was helping Dad to mow the lawn and Dora was helping Mum to set the table.

'We have to go to bed early, says Mum, be—because tomorrow we go on a . . . trip . . .'

Jesus, Papa thought in wonder. Is that what's in the book? Is that what they have to learn? I never heard such rubbish. Poor kids! No wonder they don't want to go to school!

Tito smiled triumphantly at his father. Papa tousled his hair, left the room and returned with the television set.

Tito looked at Ossie who perked up. 'Can we get a video, Papa? A cowboy film?'

Papa glanced at his younger son, pulled three pounds out of his pocket and handed it over.

'Get yourselves a bar or something as well,' he said.

The two boys got the lift down. It was a fine afternoon. Tito bought two Mars Bars and walked with his brother to the video shop in the shopping mall. The sun was warm on their backs, people were sitting out sunning themselves, even the towers looked better in the sunlight. Ossie wondered where Grandpa was and when he would next come to see them and how nice it must be out on the open road, now that the weather was great, and what were they going to tell him when he did return and found that Tir na n-Og was gone. How were they going to explain that? Would Grandpa be mad with them?

The video shop was almost empty of customers. A

woman searched for a cartoon film for a children's party and a man sat behind the counter watching the Horse Show on television. Tito made a beeline for the cowboy section.

'We've seen all these,' he said after a moment. 'There must be some new ones.' He glanced round for Ossie and saw he had moved away and was riveted to the television programme. Tito paid little heed. But when he heard Ossie begin to breathe as though he were about to expire he whirled round, ran towards him, put a hand on his arm.

'Are you okay, Ossie?'

Ossie did not reply. He just pointed to the television screen where a white horse was jumping in the showjumping enclosure of the Royal Dublin Society. One glance and Tito recognised Tir na n-Og.

'Turn up the sound, mister,' Tito said hoarsely to the man behind the counter.

The man shrugged, turned up the volume and the children listened to the commentator who was now in shot and addressing a middle-aged man with a smug expression.

'This horse has been the sensation of the competition so far. Mr Harnett, you own him; can you give us a little of the horse's history and your hopes for him?'

Noel Harnett inclined his head in polite condescension and smiled at the interviewer. 'National Security is a miracle horse that we hope is going to bring great glory to Ireland.'

'Where did you find him?'

'I bred him myself in Moyglade Stud,' Harnett said smoothly. 'He didn't take to jumping initially, but now we have great hopes that he'll bring back the World Cup to Ireland.'

Ossie stared at Tito, his eyes wide and huge in his pale face. 'That man has him,' he said breathlessly. 'Tir na n-Og is there in that showjumping place in the city!'

Tito looked back into his brother's eyes and began to smile. He had two pounds in his pocket, enough for the bus fare. 'Let's go!' he said.

The children raced from the shop, ran breathlessly to the bus stop. Their luck was in, they got a bus almost immediately. They sat upstairs and watched the city.

'Faster, faster,' Ossie urged, rocking forwards and backwards, as though he could generate enough private momentum to give the bus an extra edge.

When they got into town they began to be afraid they would be too late. They ran to O'Connell Bridge, raced for the terminus of the number 8 and in no time were being swept into the southside, through Merrions Square, Northumberland Road, past Jury's Hotel.

Tito dashed downstairs, Ossie after him.

'Where's the Horse Show, mister?' he asked the bus driver.

The man indicated the building with an inclination of his head. 'There it is. Are yez going to look or to buy?' and he laughed at his joke.

'Our horse is there!' Ossie shouted, jumping up and down, while the passengers looked at each other with raised eyebrows and smiles. The driver let them off outside the Horse Show House and they ran across

Merrion Road to the entrance doors of the Royal
Dublin Society, dashed through and disappeared into
the crowd before the irate ticket clerks could even
react.

Chapter Eight

Papa's nightmare started that evening. He hadn't meant to get so drunk again, but after he had given Tito the money for the video he knew that the kids would be occupied for a few hours and that he could go back to his work. He had another car to unbend. The owner had seen his craftsmanship on the last one, not the filler, but the panel beating, and had been impressed.

It was Saturday and a warm, clammy Saturday at that, no day for the hard work of panel beating. But he worked for a while and then, sweating, his face reddening in the sun, he looked at the dinges in front of him and thought yearningly of a long cool pint; he thought of the creamy froth at the brim and the way it would slip down. Maybe he would have one pint and then he would get some fish and chips for the kids and go home. They'd be watching the video for a while anyway.

When he got to O'Dwyer's he found that it was dim and relaxing there, and that the pint was everything he had anticipated, so he had another one and a chaser to go with it to take the harm out of it, and by the time he staggered home it was already dusk and the flat was empty.

He registered that the place was empty, but his mind was too fuddled to deal with it, and he sank down on his bed, kicked off his shoes and stretched. Sleep took him away almost immediately. He was like the dead when the police came.

They came crashing into the flat. There had been no response to their knocking and so they had broken down the door. The wood had splintered with a crack and then the sound of boots had rung out in the hall. The first Papa knew of all this was when he was being dragged out of bed. He heard a voice shout, 'Here, in here!' and then his arms were being twisted behind his back and he was being bundled out of the room. It all happened very quickly.

The pain of his twisted arms sent excruciating twinges into his armpits. The sound of loud voices seemed deafening, cacophonous, meaningless. He didn't know what was going on, and felt like a child who has unwittingly transgressed some canon of behaviour the existence of which he had not suspected and did not understand. But like a child he accepted for a moment that he must have done something, maybe while he was drunk. Had he hung anyone else out of the balcony? Had he been in a fight? He tried to get his mind to work for him, to remember the last eight hours, to see it in sequence so that he could understand what was going on. But his thoughts were scrambled and his memory would not serve him. So he went quietly, like the shorn Samson with the Philistines.

In the police car he heard the radio play, pop music

fading in and out, and then a news flash came over, a clear male voice.

'Here at the showgrounds people are stunned at the theft of National Security, the brilliant showjumper that has just qualified for the World Cup final in five days' time. The motive is not yet clear, but the police have come under pressure because of the apparent lack of security at the showgrounds . . .'

Papa heard this. It meant nothing to him. He wondered why the police in the car were staring at him. When the car arrived at the station and he was being dragged out, he wondered why cameras were popping. There were men with notepads; journalists. One of them asked him: 'Are you a member of an illegal organisation?' Another shouted: 'Is this horse being held for ransom?' And a third rushed up to Papa and cried: 'What ages are your children?'

Papa thought he must be in the horrors. Nothing made any sense.

The interrogation room was bleak, walls dirty white, windows high up in the wall like a cell, vinyl floor covering faded and worn in places. The lighting was dim, just one lamp on a table. There was a television set in the corner with a video recorder underneath it.

Papa was thrust into a chair, where he slumped like a burst bag of potatoes. In front of him was a table and sitting on the table was Inspector Bolger. Bolger did not look pleased. He clenched and unclenched his fists and the muscles of his hard body rippled under his uniform as he moved.

'Where are your children?' he demanded.

'I don't know,' Papa said.

'You think you can make us look like complete fools, don't you? Where are they?'

'I told you I don't know!' By this time Papa had begun to realise that his children must be the cause of this excessive police attention. He felt alarm rise in him, and self-reproach that he had not been home earlier, and awful dread that something had happened to the two people who constituted his whole world, which had, or could, hurt them for ever.

Bolger, who had been watching his face, suddenly kicked out with his boot, hitting Papa squarely on the knee. The pain shot up Papa's thigh and he jumped to attack his tormentor, but was held back by two policemen.

'What kind of a father are you?' Bolger enquired. 'I ask you, what kind of a father are you? Letting your children do your dirty work for you – like Fagin! But then of course you wouldn't know who he was, would you?'

'I'll burst your head,' Papa said and jerked forward, struggling, but was again restrained. 'I don't know what you're talking about,' he shouted. 'If I knew what you were bloody well talking about, I'd have some idea of how to answer you! Wouldn't I?'

He got another kick for his pains which made him double up.

'Roll that video,' Bolger ordered.

There was a click, and a whirr and then the TV screen brightened with film. The scene was the Horse Show, the showgrounds of the Royal Dublin Society at Ballsbridge. Papa saw a white horse jumping, realised in a moment that it was Tir na n-Og. Then he saw two children, his children, running alongside the enclosure and the next moment the white horse had shied, thrown his rider, and Tito and Ossie were on his back and clearing every obstacle in their race for the exit. Then they were gone; they had got away on Tir na n-Og. Papa thought his eyes were about to pop out of their sockets and a curious kind of pride suffused him. Jesus Christ, but didn't he have the best bloody kids ever made. To carry off something like that! Weren't they the great pair of youngsters?

Superintendent O'Mara arrived at the station. He had been told that the children's father was being questioned and he wanted to supervise this matter himself. The horse was extremely valuable; Mr Harnett was an important man and the minister himself, who was Harnett's personal friend, had already indicated that he wanted the matter dealt with, and solved, without any further embarrassing delay. O'Mara had listened to the ministerial fulminations on the phone. 'Find the bloody little blighters; it can't be that difficult to find two children on a million-pound horse!'

O'Mara looked at the crowd of reporters with a sigh, stepped out of the car and moved towards the entrance. The press clustered round.

'Are the children in danger?'

O'Mara stopped. 'Yes. National Security is a spirited, high-bred horse,' he said.

'Is it true there's a reward offered?'

O'Mara's lips thinned. He thought of two young

children with a price on their heads. 'I sincerely hope
not. This department is appealing for calm. We are
committed to an expeditious and conclusive investigation.'

The reporter looked down at his notes. Before he
could ask his next question, another journalist spoke
up.

'If it's not a political crime, you can't hold Mr Riley
for more than twelve hours.'

O'Mara sought the man's face in the crowd. He was
young, with a northern twang to his voice.

'I am quite aware of that,' O'Mara said drily. He
moved towards the station entrance, indicating with a
wave of his hand that the interview was at an end.

Bolger had seen the smile at the corner of Papa's
mouth as he watched the video and was about to teach
the knacker to respect his betters, when Superintendent O'Mara walked into the interrogation room.
Although he had his back to the door he knew
immediately that the super had arrived because the
two gardai, who did have a view of the door, eased
their grip on Papa's arms and assumed constipated
expressions. So he checked the blow he had been on
the point of delivering and turned with a suitably
concerned mien to meet his superior.

O'Mara approached Papa, looked down at him. He
saw the way he sat, he saw the astonishment in his
face, he smelt the drink. O'Mara was a man who had,
over many years, seen people in all manner of
conditions; watched them cry and fight and lie;
watched them die sometimes, after a fatal stabbing,

or a drug overdose or a horrendous accident. In his young days he had even watched over their corpses to protect vital evidence. The man he saw before him now was in the prime of life and bore all the hallmarks of energy and despair at war with each other. But he did not look like a liar or a knave.

'Will you answer me honestly?' O'Mara asked. 'Do you know where your boys are?'

Papa looked into his face and met his eyes without wavering. 'I do not.'

The superintendent turned, flipped a switch and flooded the room with light. Papa blinked.

'Don't worry,' O'Mara said. 'A white horse is easily spotted.'

He turned to Bolger, looked at him levelly. Bolger failed to meet his eyes. 'Take a statement,' Superintendent O'Mara said coldly, 'and let the man go.'

When O'Mara had gone, Bolger slapped a type-written sheet on the table in front of Papa. 'Sign!'

'I can't write,' Papa said angrily, ashamed that this was the case and angry that Bolger had to know it.

'An X will do,' Bolger said.

Papa looked at the paper, saw the typewriting. 'I'm putting no mark on that paper,' he said in a low voice.

'Sign,' Bolger said through clenched teeth.

'What does it say?' Papa demanded.

Bolger exhaled, narrowed his eyes. 'It's just a consent to sell the horse.'

Papa smiled thinly. 'I'll sign nothing which would make thieves of my boys.'

'They are thieves, bloody thieves – isn't it in their blood?'

Papa sneered. 'That would suit you down to the ground, wouldn't it?'

With two policemen holding Papa back, Bolger shoved a biro into his hand, closed his fingers forcibly round it and slammed it on to the paper, forcing him to make an X.

'That's your mark, not mine,' Papa said darkly when Bolger let him go.

Bolger put the paper in a drawer. 'Get out of here.'

The two gardai escorted Papa off the premises. He was glad that no one was there to witness this sign of contempt. It had taken a whole squad of them to arrest him and everyone had seen that!

Papa went home. He half expected the boys to be there before him, complete with Tir na n-Og. But the flat was empty. He looked out the window. He could see a long way. It was dark; lights twinkled from the other towers, from the city, from the houses stretching out in the countryside. Far below he saw car headlights; a plane went by overhead, dipping slowly towards the airport as though God held it on an invisible string. He saw its wing and tail lights. His children were out there somewhere. They would be back soon and he could get the whole story from them.

He sat in the darkness, head bowed. His body ached where Bolger had hit him. His mind was still heavy from the fumes of the drink. He thought of Tito, only twelve, and Ossie, just seven. He saw their faces clearly. He thought of Mary. He saw their wedding day, her funny little smile crinkling up the corners of her eyes, her dark brown hair. He remembered her in his arms on their wedding night, out under the stars. He saw her face when he went in to see her after she had given birth to Tito in their own bed, the pallor of exhaustion, the triumph. He remembered the celebrations. But the midwife had whispered to him to be careful, that she was small and not able for childbearing. So when she became pregnant again he had suggested she have the baby in hospital. But she had laughed and then refused point blank. 'Our child will be born in our caravan, as is our way. Do you think I'm a weakling entirely?'

Through the wall he heard Birdie Murphy shouting at her siblings. They were watching telly and the younger ones were wailing. 'I'm hungry.' It was Conor's voice. The Murphy parents were obviously out again and Birdie was again babysitting.

Papa needed a drink. He left the flat and found his way to O'Dwyer's, sat up at the bar. The television was blaring. The barman glanced at the screen and looked at Papa. The bar fell silent. There was a news report on the television.

'Police are still looking tonight for the two children who today stole a world-class showjumper from the Royal Dublin Society showgrounds. The theft took place in front of two thousand spectators and a nationwide TV audience . . .'

Papa stared at the screen. 'Give me a bottle of whiskey,' he said to the barman.

The barman did not move. He saw Papa's face. 'Round to the back,' he said.

Papa gripped the counter, raised his voice. 'Give

me a drink before I wreck the place!'

Francie Dunphy, member of the Residents' Committee, was in the pub and recognised the big man at the bar. He was not likely to forget him. The evening that Papa had hung Cafferty from the balcony was still fresh in his head.

'Give him the drink,' he called. 'Look, he's on the television!'

Everyone cheered. Papa turned to look at the TV and, with a start, recognised himself as he was being brought into the station for questioning. Then there was the clip of the boys escaping from the RDS on the back of the white horse, which Papa had seen earlier. The crowd in the pub cheered again. They moved towards the bar and began to buy drinks for Papa.

The television report went on, 'The owner of the horse, Mr Noel Harnett of Moyglade Stud, has appealed for calm.'

Papa drank the whiskies, knocking them back down his throat. He listened then as Mr Harnett was interviewed and heard him voice his concern for the safety of the two children and that to further this he was offering a reward of £5,000.

'This is not just my horse,' Harnett said. 'This horse belongs to all the people of Ireland. We all want to see it win the World Cup. What we want to see is National Security alive and well at the showgrounds in four days' time. I assure you, National Security will be found. There isn't going to be another Shergar fiasco – not in my stud!'

Papa's head was spinning. He stood up and lumbered to the door, tracing his unsteady way back to the Towers. In the shopping mall he saw Murphy and his wife drinking. They were sitting on a bench and were lowering bottles of stout, holding them by the neck.

'Them's two wild lads you have, Papa,' Mr Murphy called.

Papa turned on Murphy, grabbed him by the scruff of the neck. Mrs Murphy backed away.

'Go easy, Papa, go easy,' she muttered in a placatory voice. 'Sure he doesn't mean anything derogatory.' She watched as Papa dragged Murphy into the fish and chip shop nearby and hauled him up against the counter.

'Put your money on the counter,' he commanded. Murphy fumbled in his pocket and brought out a fistful of coins.

'What's wrong, what's wrong?' he demanded, his voice shaking, his eyes darting from Papa to the fish and chip man and back.

'Give this man a feed of fish and chips,' Papa said, addressing the fish and chip man. He stared at Murphy. 'He's taking it upstairs to his children.'

The man looked doubtfully at the money and then at Murphy, but he took the money and proceeded to dish out the fish and chips.

'Now,' Papa said, giving Murphy a shake. 'If I hear that those children of yours didn't get these fish and chips, I'll come through your wall. Do you understand?'

'Right, Papa,' Murphy said. 'Right. Take it easy!'

Mrs Murphy came into the shop behind them. 'What are we doing here, Papa? What are we doing here? Sure he didn't mean anything derogatory!'

Papa went home. But although he had had several whiskies he could not sleep. He anticipated the morning, the thirst, the dreadful head there would be on him and he got up to drink several mugs of water. He'd have to be half way right in the morning.

His mind burned and raced. He thought of the reward of £5,000 offered by Harnett. Lie low and stay out of danger, he told his children silently. There's a lot of people would do terrible things for money like that. Lie low. Use all the tricks that ould codger Grandpa taught you. If you're not back tomorrow morning, Papa will go find you.

Next door Birdie thought of Tito and Ossie. She had seen the television news; she was gasping with delight and admiration. I wish I could be with you, she thought, instead of stuck here minding the bloody kids. She wondered where Tito and Ossie would go; would they go far away on the white horse? She visualised their freedom and the wind and the mountains and the wonderful, delicious danger. They would be sure to send a posse after them. I wish I was a boy, she thought, feeling the breasts under her pyjamas. Jesus, what am I going to do to get rid of these? Is there anything at all that would shrink them?

Her mind churned. She needed to get away; she needed to escape. They would expect her to get married soon and then she would have a clutch of her own children and the whole business would start all over again, the same trap would be sprung. She would

be minding children for the rest of her life. She would
end up like her mother, drinking, or like the other
women around the place who were high on those pills
they gave them to keep them quiet – Valium and
Mogadon. She needed money to escape all that. How
was she going to make some money?

As she drifted towards sleep, it suddenly struck her
– an easy means of amassing a fortune.

When Papa got up in the morning, Birdie's face was
staring into his living room through the hole in the
wall. It was early, much earlier than Papa was used to.
He had slept badly, half of his brain alert and refusing
sleep, waiting for the sound of the children's steps in
the hall.

'Hey, Mister Riley,' Birdie said. 'If you're going to
look for Tito and Ossie, can I come with you?'

Papa jumped. For a moment he thought the wall
was talking to him. Then he saw the face framed in the
hole and groaned privately.

'What are you doing up so early, Birdie?' Papa said
irritably. 'Go back to bed!'

'Can I not come with you, Mister Riley?' Papa
turned to look at the eager young face, the beseeching
expression, the tousled hair, the sleepy eyes. 'Please.'

Papa sighed. 'No, Birdie, you can't come with me.'

He put on his coat, went to the kitchen for a long
draught of water and then he left the flat. Birdie
heard the door shut behind him. She went to the
window and looked down, trying to see Papa when he
left the building, but she glimpsed him only for a
moment before he was out of sight. She turned and

moved back to her bed, tripping on the cat, a half-grown kitten which Angela had found the day before and which had come mincing out of its box to look for breakfast.

'I suppose I'll have to look after you as well,' she said to it. The cat sat down and attended to its toilet, royally impervious.

Birdie got back into bed. Her brain was seething. She began to make plans.

Chapter Nine

Looking back on it afterwards, it seemed to the children that it had been surprisingly easy to reclaim Tir na n-Og. They had sneaked into the RDS without any trouble. The place was full of posh people in nice clothes, women with hats, spoilt kids, and voices booming over loudspeakers. The air was full of the smell of horses. They were everywhere, huge horses and little horses, in paddocks, in stables, in loose-boxes with barred windows, being led on bridles, being ridden; their manes and tails were plaited; some had rosettes pinned to their necks. There were people with Irish accents and English accents and people speaking queer foreign languages. The whole bloody world of the settled people seemed to be there.

They had found the jumping enclosure, crept up beside the very edge of the arena and waited.

They had seen Tir na n-Og as soon as he entered. He moved forward, clearing all the jumps, and Ossie waited until he was within earshot, and was tackling a water jump just on the other side of the fence.

Ossie had called him: 'Tir na n-Og, Tir na n-Og – it's me, Ossie!'

Tir a n-Og skidded to a halt, pricked up his ears and reared, shedding his rider into the water. Tito and Ossie had jumped across the fence and were on his back in a minute.

In retrospect it seemed like a miracle; the speed with which everything had happened was unbelievable. They had fled, hardly knowing where they were going. Tir na n-Og had jumped a gate, raced out on the road, dodged into a side street, galloped down by the canal and eventually on to the railway, his hooves thundering between the wooden sleepers. Behind them somewhere they heard the sound of police sirens.

'Are they looking for us, Tito?' Ossie quavered and Tito said to use his head; what else could they be looking for?

It had been great, just like something from the Wild West. Ossie's blood thrilled to remember it.

They had found a stationary goods train at a siding near the station and an empty wagon near the end, the sliding door ajar, as though it was there waiting for them. It was the work of only a minute to open it, get Tir na n-Og in and bundle themselves in after him. Then they had shut the door and lain back exhausted and laughing, adrenaline still pumping, while Tir na n-Og regarded them sardonically from the corner as though he joined in the joke himself. A thin sliver of light came into the wagon under the door. The boys made plans. 'We can go back to Papa,' Ossie said, and Tito said not to be stupid. The first person they would look for when they couldn't find them would be Papa.

If they went back to Papa, Tir na n-Og would be taken away from them all over again, and this time they might never get him back.

'Are they really looking for us?' Ossie demanded, widening his eyes, and Tito said of course they were looking for them. Ossie shivered with excitement, told Tir na n-Og they were outlaws. Tir na n-Og took the news calmly, snorting softly as though this was a matter of little moment.

Tito had in his pocket the Mars Bars he had bought earlier on the way to the video store and he gave one to Ossie. They munched while they got their breath back.

'What do we do now?' Ossie asked eagerly, stroking the white horse's leg and chewing the bar. Tir na n-Og assumed a thoughtful expression, but was otherwise uninformative.

'We have to run away,' Tito said. 'Until the fuss dies down anyway.'

'Where will we go?'

Tito furrowed his brow. How many options did they have? There was the city and the country and the towns. He looked up at Tir na n-Og. Only in the wildest countryside would they be free, countryside like the Wild West. Of course! They could go to the wild west, the Irish wild west. They'd be just like the cowboys.

'I know where we'll go,' he told Ossie excitedly. 'We'll go where they can't find us. We'll be cowboys! We'll go into the west!'

Ossie whooped in delight, got up and jumped

around with excitement. 'The wild west? Did you hear that Tir na n-Og? We're going to be cowboys!'

The white horse whinnied, and rubbed his nose against Ossie's back.

Tito thought he heard a sound nearby and hissed, 'Shut up, Ossie. Do you want us to be caught?' and Ossie turned to Tir na n-Og, put a finger on his lips and subsided in silence on to the floor.

After a while, when everything was silent again, Tito whispered, 'Ossie, do you have any money?'

Ossie turned out his pockets. A penny fell out on to the floor. Tito stared at it, felt in his own pockets and brought out the contents. He had ten pence, a length of string, a cigarette lighter he had found the day before and a bit of chewing gum which he had chewed and put back in its wrapper for further orders.

He sighed. 'We won't get far on this!' How were they going to survive without money?

'We can fish,' Ossie suggested helpfully. 'We can ask the farmers for some milk. We can eat fruit.' His tummy was full from the Mars Bar, so he wasn't too concerned. He knew that Tito would manage everything.

'Shut up, Ossie. I'm thinking.'

Tito realised that the only thing they had about them of value was the saddle on the back of Tir na n-Og. So there was no two ways about it, the saddle had to go. Anyway, they weren't used to a saddle and would much prefer to ride without it. He jumped up and pulled up a saddle flap to examine the girth.

'What are you doing, Tito?'

Tito put up the stirrup irons, unbuckled the girth and pulled the saddle down on to the floor. It was much heavier than he thought and fell with a clang.

'I'm going to sell this thing.' He looked round at his brother, patted Tir na n-Og. 'You stay here.' He heaved the saddle on to his shoulder and was gone before Ossie could remonstrate.

Tito knew there was a travellers' encampment not far from the station, where there was a rich traveller who sold carpets and stuff. He had seen his caravan many times in his wanderings around the city.

The man was a successful entrepreneur, dealing in scrap, broken pieces of antique furniture, hardware and carpets. He owned a chrome-covered caravan which boasted every modern convenience, including a telephone, music system and television. His BMW was parked nearby. He had contacts throughout the country.

He examined the saddle lovingly. First-class craftsmanship, fine leather, almost new; a prize indeed.

'It's a good saddle,' Tito said, watching the man's face, wondering what it was like to be so big and fat. He saw himself reflected in a mirror and he looked like a stick compared with his prospective customer, a small stick, something the wind might pick up and blow away.

The man stared at Tito and narrowed his eyes as if to say, 'How did you come by this?' He knew it was a good saddle; he knew he would make a handsome profit. He knew the child had stolen it.

'I'll give you twenty pounds,' he said.

Tito's face was aghast. 'It's worth hundreds!' he said.

The man gave a short laugh. 'I'll give you twenty pounds or I'll give you a kick in the arse!'

Tito knew he had no option. He took the money, put it in his pocket and took his leave. He had been cheated, he knew, and he tried to think what he could do to even the score a bit. As he passed the man's clothesline on his way out, he saw the perfect solution. There in front of him was a blanket drying in the breeze and a couple of jumpers. Just what he and Ossie needed. He unpegged them, pulled them off the line and rolled them into a ball. His customer did not look out of the window until it was too late. Tito raised two fingers in a V at the irate figure rapping on the caravan window and ran away as fast as his legs could carry him. He looked back and saw the fat man leave his caravan with surprising speed and head for his car. The engine started, but Tito was already off the road and out of sight.

Tito ran until he was tired, dodging down side streets and doubling back to make sure he had given the man the slip. He hid in the garden of a deserted house. When he judged that the coast was clear he went back to the road and into a shop where he bought a packet of chocolate biscuits. When he came out of the shop he saw the police cars and realised that a road block was being set up. He hurried, tripped on a loose paving stone and was helped back to his feet by a garda.

'Where are you off to, son?' the garda asked. Tito's brain went into overdrive; he bent down, picked up the bundle of clothes from the pavement and ran after the packet of biscuits which was rolling into the gutter.

'Ah, nowhere, mister. I'm just doing a job for me mammy.'

The garda looked at him suspiciously. 'You didn't see two young travellers with a white horse?' Tito thought he would die. He felt his chest constrict, but he looked up at the uniform and shook his head. He couldn't trust himself to speak; he knew his voice would wobble. Suddenly the garda's walkie-talkie began to chatter and the policeman turned his attention to it. Tito moved away as quickly as he could without running.

Ossie and Tir na n-Og were waiting in the goods wagon where he had left them and he flung his illgotten gains in ahead of him and leapt in, closing the door behind him with a sigh of relief.

Ossie gave the chocolate biscuits to Tir na n-Og who chewed them with relish. They were all gone in a minute, much to Tito's chagrin; he had been looking forward to a few.

'Poor Tir na n-Og,' Ossie said when the horse had finished the biscuits and was mopping up the crumbs from the palm of his small hand. 'He's still hungry.' The tone in Ossie's voice indicated that Tito should pay another visit to the shop.

'He'll have to wait,' Tito said. 'He'll just have to wait. I'm not going out there again. He's had a packet of biscuits so he's not so badly off.'

'He wants hay,' Ossie said stubbornly.

Tito was still trembling inwardly from his narrow

escape from the garda. He wanted to rest. He didn't want to run the risk of going out again and maybe being caught. He wanted hay himself. He wanted to lie down on it and go to sleep. He glanced at the horse standing all smug with a whole packet of chocolate biscuits in his stomach.

'It's a pity about him,' Tito said.

Ossie did not pursue the matter. He whispered to Tir na n-Og about there being plenty of food soon. 'When we go to the west, Tir na n-Og, there'll be plenty of hay.'

The two children were both very tired. As it was dim and safe in the wagon they put the brown blanket Tito had pinched and the jumpers on the floor, closed their eyes and slept, waking when the train lurched and moved forward. Then they slept again. For the moment it didn't really matter where they were going as long as they were safe and with Tir na n-Og.

Tito woke some time later, heard his brother's shallow breathing and afraid that he might be cold, took off his jacket and put it over him. Ossie stirred, opened his eyes.

'What's that?'

'It's only me. We've stopped again.'

Ossie felt his brother's jacket with his fingers. 'Are you not cold?'

'I'm not too bad.'

'Is Tir na n-Og not asleep?'

Tito tried to make out the bulk of the white horse in the darkness. He could hear him breathing, smell the musky horse smell of him. They had taken off the bridle and he ground his teeth a little.

'He can sleep standing up.'

'I wish I could do that.' Ossie said.

There was silence for a moment. No sound came from the world outside. Tir na n-Og shifted his feet and his hooves clanged on the wooden floor.

'Tito?' Ossie whispered suddenly in a sleepy voice soft with yearning.

'Yeah?'

'What did Mammy look like?'

Tito felt the catch in his throat and suppressed it. Ossie had asked this so often that he reckoned he should be used to it, but it always took him the same way.

'She looked like you.'

'Was her breathing okay?'

'Except when she laughed,' Tito said after a moment.

'What happened then?'

Tito forced back the tears. He remembered it well, the sudden catch in her voice from laughter.

'When she laughed she couldn't breathe.'

'What colour was her hair?'

Tito swallowed. 'Same as yours,' he whispered.

'Was she big or small?'

'Big. Big. I don't want to answer any more questions. Okay? Go to sleep.'

After a moment Ossie whispered, 'Tito!'

His brother wiped away the silent tears and said crossly, 'What?'

'Thanks for the coat.'

Next morning the roadblocks were dismantled.

Overnight the police had caught plenty of drunk drivers, or half-drunk drivers, and people who hadn't paid their road tax, or were driving uninsured vehicles, but no one answering the given description had been sighted. They had caught Wacko Kelly, the fence Tito had sold the saddle to. Wacko was, in the vernacular of the gardai, 'known to them', and his arrest would, in more normal times, have been a cause of minor celebration.

Wacko said he didn't know where the children were headed; one of them had stolen some clothes and a blanket and if they caught him they should put him behind bars, he told 'the member in charge'. He said this earnestly, to show that he was a concerned citizen.

'You may not know where the children are headed, Wacko, but we know where you're headed,' said the member in charge with heavy humour.

Wacko's reply was not entered into the day book.

Wherever the children were, it was evident that they had given the city the slip. The police had instructions to go home. The search was being moved to the country.

In the goods wagon the boys were unaware of the consternation they had caused and woke up feeling cold and hungry. It was still dark, and the train was not moving.

'This is the longest night I ever saw,' Ossie declared.

'It just seems long,' Tito answered. But he too thought it a bit strange. He tried to work out what time it had been when they had found the train, how

138

many hours they had spent in it. Why didn't the daylight come back into the wagon underneath the door? There was a faint light, like the dawn. But it was a dawn that had gone on too long and didn't get any brighter.

Ossie got up, patted the white horse standing there patiently in the gloom and found the steps to the trapdoor in the roof. He began to climb. He pushed up the door and shoved his head through, and immediately hit it on something hard.

'Ouch!' Ossie cried, on the verge of tears from pain and shock.

'What's wrong?' Tito asked from below.

'We're in a tunnel!' Ossie wept.

Tito thought quickly. He went to the door and slid it open.

'I'll be back in a minute,' he said, jumping down on to the track.

Ossie ran to the door and stuck his head out after him. 'Tito, Tito, don't leave me. Come back!'

Tito hesitated, looked back at Ossie's white face. 'I'll be back in a minute,' he repeated.

Tito climbed up the embankment, into someone's rear garden, and then out on to the bridge. A woman was walking along the pavement, pushing a baby buggy. Tito approached her. He didn't like having to ask questions, but he needed some vital information.

'How far are we from Dublin, missus?'

The woman looked at him as though he were mad. 'What?'

'How many miles is it to Dublin, missus?' Tito repeated.

'This is Dublin!' the woman said.

Tito drew a deep breath, opened his mouth. 'Oh, is it?' he said.

The woman stood and watched him.

As he turned back to the railway, Tito heard the clanking and banging that heralded the emergence of the goods train from the tunnel. His eyes nearly fell out of his head. Ossie and Tir na n-Og were leaving without him. Slipping and sliding down the embankment, Tito ran as fast as he could, but the train was faster. When he tried to put up a last burst of speed he tripped on the gravel and fell. The full horror of the situation paralysed him. He sat on the edge of the track, his head in his hands, while the train disappeared down the line. He had lost Ossie and Tir na n-Og. He had no idea at all what he could do to find them. He wondered where the train was going, Where would Ossie and Tir na n-Og end up? What would he say to Papa?

In the midst of his despair he heard a horse whinny and he turned to see Tir na n-Og with Ossie on his back approaching behind him.

'Tir na n-Og didn't want to wait in the wagon,' Ossie explained.

Tito embraced his little brother, his relief immeasurable. 'I won't leave you again. I promise, Ossie. I'll never leave you again.'

The woman who had informed Tito that he was in Dublin was watching from the bridge with her mouth open and, as Tito jumped up on the back of the white horse, she shouted after them in shrill tones, 'I know who you are! I know who you are!' but her voice became thin and distant as the horse and riders vanished down the line.

Grandpa found his way back to the Towers the day after the children's flight with the horse. He had not seen a television; he could not read the paper; he did not know that his family were embroiled in a scandal of sorts, that his grandchildren were regarded nationally as some kind of heroes. The day before, he had gone into a shop to buy bread and heard a customer discussing some kids who had stolen a horse. 'Kids who could do the like of that!' the man said. 'Jesus, but they have great spunk.'

'Sure an animal like that would eat you,' said another, shaking his head.

'What about the owner?' the shopkeeper asked. 'It's hard on him.'

'Noel Harnett?' said the first man. 'That's one man that's not short of a few bob.'

Grandpa had taken little notice, being pressed by a sense of urgency to keep moving. But when he was on the road again he found that the name Noel Harnett reverberated in his head. What was it about that name? He puzzled over it, and then put it out of his head. He was in the middle of his supper of bread and cheese when he remembered. He remembered a man who had bought land where the travellers had a camp, who had cleared them out with dogs; he had done so even though a young pregnant woman was about to give birth. Harnett wanted the land for building. Yes, he remembered that story all right. He also remembered the aftermath.

The following morning, a fine morning with a nip in the air, Grandpa saw the Towers again. He saw them with a sense of foreboding, the old feeling of claustrophobia giving way to a different kind of anxiety. He flicked the reins on old Dan's rump to hurry him along.

When he entered the travellers' encampment he looked around, expecting to see the strange white horse, but there was no sign of it. He went to the car dump, expecting to find Papa, but he was not there. So he tethered Dan and walked to the tower.

He got the lift up. It was like being in a tomb, he thought, to be trapped in this thing. What if it got stuck? But the lift deposited him at the fourteenth floor and he went straight to number 14G and knocked. There was no answer. He knocked again. Again no answer – puzzled, he left.

Birdie heard the knock. She was at home minding the children. It was Saturday. Her parents were asleep and Birdie had had to get up early to feed and change the baby. Then she had made porridge for Angela and Conor. She told Angela that she was going out and to mind the other two until she got back.

'Where are you going?' Angela demanded. 'I want to come too.'

'Well, you can't,' Birdie had hissed, 'and if you start whingeing I'll break your head!'

Birdie went to the bedroom she shared with Angela, shut the door in her sister's face and scrabbled for her savings which she had hidden in a special hole she had made in the bottom of the wardrobe. This money was intended to facilitate her running away from home when the time came. But it grew so slowly that she had begun to despair. She counted it out – five pounds and twenty-two pence. She put it in her pocket. Only then did she let Angela into the room.

'What were you doing?' Angela asked suspiciously.

'Mind your own business,' Birdie said.

She went out and spent the money on Smarties. When she got home she produced the sweets. Her siblings began to clamour for them, but she told them to shut up and listen. She explained carefully what they had to do. She told them she would give them a reward if they did it right. If they didn't, she'd beat them up.

When Birdie heard the second knock on the Rileys' door she went to investigate. She recognised Grandpa at once, although she didn't know his name.

'They've gone, mister.'

Grandpa stared at her. 'Gone? Do you mean they've left? Where did they go?'

Birdie considered the bewilderment in his face. Was it possible that he didn't know what had happened?

'The boys ran away with that horse that was here, and their da's gone looking for them. Didn't you know?'

Grandpa looked as though he would have a heart attack. 'I shouldn't have gone away,' he said. 'I shouldn't have left them with that horse.'

'Come in mister,' Birdie said, 'and sit down. I'll tell you about it.'

Grandpa went into the Murphy residence and found two other children there, sitting at a table, eating sweets. At least he thought that was what they were doing. They had two bowls in front of them. One was filled with multi-coloured Smarties. They were sucking the colour off the Smarties and putting the little sweets, now white, into the second bowl.

'I've every one of them counted,' Birdie hissed to them as she invited Grandpa to be seated. 'If you eat any I'll kill you!'

Grandpa looked at Birdie. He remembered her. This was the girl who had tried to jump the fire.

Birdie told him the whole story. Then the old man took his leave, visibly shaken.

'I'll look for them in the city encampments first,' Grandpa muttered to himself as he took the lift back to the ground. Then he went to his caravan and filled an old basin with water, shut the door and looked into the water in the half-light. He sat for a long time, staring into the basin, his eyes glazing in trance. Then he opened the door, climbed up on to the caravan seat and flicked the reins. It was only when he got to the camp at Ringsend that he made a fire and put down a kettle. His head was beginning to lift for want of a cup of tea.

Papa checked with all the sites around the city, just in case they had news of the children. When he came to Ringsend he saw that Grandpa's caravan was there before him, his fire burning outside with a kettle over it. He pulled his car into the nearest parking spot with a screech and jumped out.

'Where are they with that bloody horse?' he shouted at his father-in-law. 'I presume you know what's after happening to my boys?'

Grandpa was standing by the door of his caravan and he looked at Papa without moving.

'They're okay. The kids are okay,' he said softly.

'What stupid stories did you fill their heads with?' Papa demanded. In his mind the source of his woes was his father-in-law. It was he who disapproved of his life, who taught his children to hanker for the old ways, who told them stories fit to turn their heads.

'Calm down, Papa,' Grandpa said equably.

'If you weren't an old man,' Papa said, breathing deeply, 'I'd crack your head open!'

Grandpa was not perturbed by this intelligence. He surveyed the man before him, saw the bleary eyes, smelt the telltale, stale scent of last night's whiskey.

'You would try, Papa,' he said softly.

'Stupid bloody superstitious stories,' Papa went on. 'That's what killed your daughter!' He paused and added bitterly, 'That's what killed Mary!'

Grandpa recognised guilt when he saw it, but it did not prevent him feeling hurt and suddenly desolate. 'Don't blame me for Mary's death,' he said in a low voice.

'I had her in my arms, begging her to go to hospital,' Papa went on, 'but she wouldn't go. Why do you think that was? Why?' He paused and glared at Grandpa. 'And now she's rotting in the earth because of bloody superstition!'

Grandpa stared back at his son-in-law. 'She's not rotting in the earth, Papa.'

Papa snarled. 'Where is she then?' he demanded, looking around him, gesticulating wildly. 'She's not here! She's not getting up in the morning whistling to herself!' He thrust his head forward and stared aggressively into his father-in-law's eyes. 'She's not turning my heart upside down with her little smiles!'

Grandpa turned his head away. 'You never grieved for her, not properly, not in the old way,' he said bitterly.

There was the sound of a car pulling up, but Papa didn't notice. It was the police and they watched the altercation between the two men without interfering.

'Never grieved?' Papa shouted. 'I've spent seven years in hell without her. Seven years blaming myself for letting her die.' He clenched his fists, his lips curled back over his teeth. 'Seven years crying when no one was looking!'

Grandpa saw the blind anguish in Papa's eyes and felt the grief storm him. So much pain! The world was full of pain and John Riley had had his share.

'You can't be afraid to let people see you cry, Papa,' he said. 'You can't hide death.'

Papa looked at him contemptuously, jumped on a rock beside him. 'You want me to make a big act of it, like a Traveller King? Hah? Is that what you want?' He jumped down, turned to Grandpa's fire, bent down and shovelled his hands into the warm ashes at the edge of the fire, withdrew them full of gritty white ash.

'Ashes,' he shouted, pouring them down on his head and face. 'Is that what you want?' The ashes stuck to the tears wetting his face and he rubbed the

146

rest of them down on his shirt. 'Is this good enough
for you?' He raised his face and looked round at the
other travellers who were watching in silence and
then at the occupants of the police car who were
watching with amusement.

Papa stared at them for a moment like something
from a Greek tragedy. Then he approached the car.

'What are you laughing at?'

The driver revved the engine and drove slowly
away. Papa followed, shouting, 'Do you want to fight
me? Hah? If anything happens to my boys I'll set fire
to that station of yours!'

Later that day Birdie began to sell the produce of the
morning. She had spent a large part of the afternoon
scouring dustbins for Mogadon bottles, Valium
bottles, any bottles with a tranquilliser prescription,
and had filled them with the bleached Smarties. She
approached all the likely women, the young ones
trying to cope with progeny ten floors up, the older
ones who had developed dependency. They bought;
they were desperate. They had prescriptions but not
ones that met their requirements any longer. They
needed much more than their doctors would pre-
scribe. So they bought from Birdie without any
investigation. Birdie began to find that enterprise
paid off, that all you had to do to achieve anything in
life was to have enough neck and not be backward in
putting yourself forward.

Chapter Ten

Ossie held on to Tito's back and surveyed the
countryside, saw the light playing on the land and the
shadows from passing clouds scudding across one
field and then another. They were in the hills already
and could see the city behind them, stretching out in
all directions round the bay. They stopped, traced
with their eyes the urban sprawl below them, saw the
twin red and white Pigeon House chimneys, looked
further to the left and saw the Towers, rising out of
the northern end of the city like some strange
prehistoric stones. 'They're over there,' Tito said,
pointing. 'I hope Papa isn't too worried about us.'

'We'll send him a card from the west,' Ossie said.
'You can write it, Tito.'

Tito was silent. 'Don't be an eejit, Ossie,' he said
after a moment. 'If we send a card then the postman
would know where we'd gone and he might tell the
police and then they'd know where to look.'

'How would the postman know where we'd gone?'
Ossie asked.

'Because they put a mark on letters and cards with
the name of the place where they were posted. That's
how!'

They traversed high ground, keeping to open country for the most part, away from the road. The gorse was still in bloom, bright yellow, and it stirred Tito, to whom the countryside and the pungent smell of gorse brought back early childhood memories, almost to tears. Ossie was awed. He had seen countryside like this on the telly, but had never been there before. Some instinct, part of the unconscious memory of his race, stirred in him, too.

'Is this the Wild West, Tito?'

'Not yet.'

The horse and riders made their way through a wooded area. As they came out of it they saw more fields ahead, and beyond them the mountains. They stopped and stared.

'It's the Rockies!' Tito shouted. 'Let's go!' Tir na n-Og needed no further encouragement. He whinnied. 'Heigh-ho, Silver! Away!' Tito roared and they galloped off across the fields.

The boys had never had such fun. They sang while Tir na n-Og trotted and they were bumped up and down on his back. They laughed when he cantered. When he walked, they planned what they would do in the wild west.

At one point Tir na n-Og stopped, neighed and refused to go on.

'What's wrong with him?' Ossie demanded.

'Maybe he doesn't like singing,' Tito said. He kicked with his thin legs, but Tir na n-Og seemed impervious to his urging.

Then, as they stood there, they heard the hunting

horn. Tir na n-Og began to edge off the track and made for some woodland.

Looking back, Tito and Ossie saw the riders in scarlet appear over a distant skyline. The local hunt was out cubbing, breaking in the young hounds.

'What's that?' Ossie asked breathlessly.

'It's the cavalry,' Tito answered. He didn't know what it was, but he gave the answer best suited to Ossie's expectations.

They saw the riders start down the hill. From somewhere nearby they heard another horn. Tir na n-Og turned and galloped into the wood, and the two boys ducked to avoid the low-hanging branches. Their mount slowed and stopped in the lee of a big fallen tree. They listened, but there was silence except for the wind soughing through the foliage. And then suddenly Tir na n-Og leapt from their hiding place and dashed for the open country. The hounds came ululating, streaking across the fields like low-flying magpies. The boys looked back in horror. Tito's eyes widened in fear and Ossie closed his, preferring to concentrate on the sensation of rapid movement, the power of the horse beneath him, buoyed up by his immovable, childish faith.

There was a ruin on the hill. Tir na n-Og reached it and brought his riders inside. But the fox had seen it too and it raced into the ivy and up into the old rafters. Tir na n-Og and the boys hid in the joist pit of the collapsed floor which was now overgrown with ivy and brambles. The horse stood perfectly still and the boys did not move a muscle as the hounds tore up the hill. They were young, inexperienced hounds pursuing a young, not so inexperienced fox, but their gusto lacked for nothing. In a moment the whipper-in caught up with the pack and was followed by the whole field who circled the building. The field master blew his horn and the whipper-in dismounted, awkward from age and his hours in the saddle, and stumped towards the ruin, shouting and kicking at the hounds.

They were year-old hounds that the hunt had fostered as puppies to its members and friends, but were now in the kennels where the discipline and maize porridge were not to their liking. Two of the hounds found Tir na n-Og's hiding place. They jumped at the children, fawning, tongues lolloping. Ossie, who had only a passing acquaintance with dogs, did not recognise canine worship. All he saw were the jaws, the cruel teeth, the dripping saliva, and opened his mouth to scream, but his brother quickly clamped his hand over it.

'It's okay, it's okay,' Tito said urgently into his ear, breaking the impetus of the mounting panic. He turned his head to look for a way out and as he did so he saw the fox in the rafters and looked for a moment into its wild, calculating eyes.

Suddenly the baying was deafening; the whole pack was on them. The fox, a young vixen, surveyed the confusion both of scent and purpose she had created by hiding in the derelict building. She gave a sharp bark of derision before leaping out of Tito's sight on to the rotting wall plate and away across the countryside, her sloping red brush almost skimming the ground.

'Tally-ho!' roared the whipper-in and the master blew his horn – to no avail. The hounds in the ruin were trapped there by those still struggling to get in. The field master and the whipper-in were trying to restrain the few old hounds from deserting the trainees and taking off after the insolent fox. If that happened there would be no more cubbing for the rest of the week; the time would be taken up trying to find the cub hounds who were lost, strayed, or had decided upon desertion.

Order was eventually restored and the pack streamed off across the fields in pursuit of their original, and now safe, quarry, and the hunt followed them, leaving Tito, Ossie and the white horse in a sudden, wonderful silence. Tito turned and looked at Ossie.

'Phew!' he said shakily.

Ossie was silent, quivering. He felt Tir na n-Og's warm back shudder beneath his legs and saw his brother's drawn face before him. Adventures were somehow not the same when you tried them for real. He wished Papa were here to take him down and carry him in his arms. And then he remembered that Papa might be drinking and would only want to sleep.

When the hunt had disappeared, Tir na n-Og and his riders set out from the woodland, turning their faces to the higher country. The fields gave way to coarse land; the heather bloomed purple around them and Tir na n-Og walked carefully. Sometimes they disturbed nesting larks who flew out almost from under Tir na n-Og's feet, making him start. The larks would fly up and up in sudden soaring motions and the boys watched them with wonder, their ears full of the sweetest, clearest sounds they had ever heard. They were tired but Tito said they would rest later.

'I'm tired now, Tito,' Ossie said petulantly. 'Tir na n-Og keeps bumping me around and my bottom is sore and my legs are all broken.'

'Your legs are not broken, they're just a bit stretched. We'll stop soon.'

About a mile further on, they came to a grotto with a statue of Our Lady. There was a pair of rosary beads dangling from her hands and a piece of cardboard, with a legend inscribed on it, sitting at her feet.

'What does it say?' Ossie asked.

Tito perused the writing. 'It says . . . God bless the . . . travellers!' he announced triumphantly.

Ossie smiled. 'You've got good at the reading, Tito. Is it hard?'

Tito shook his head. 'Not if you break the words down.'

'Can we rest now, Tito?'

Tito groaned. 'Will you stop. How can we go anywhere if all you want is to rest and eat?' But he looked at the grotto and the place beneath it, which was like a small cave, enough room for two boys who wanted to sleep.

'All right so! But only for a while. We don't want the priest catching us.'

They slid to the ground, tethered Tir na n-Og to a

bush and lay down beneath the grotto on the blanket. In no time at all they were asleep.

The annual horse fair in Ballinafest was an event which attracted dealers from all over the country. Short of the thoroughbred, almost every type of horse could be found, from the humblest nag to the sprightliest new possibility for the jumping arena. There were Connemara ponies and Irish draught horses and cobs and children's ponies. The air was redolent of horse manure, hay and the smell of beer and whiskey.

Noel Harnett had been to the Ballinafest Fair only once before, when as a child he had accompanied his uncle, a farmer who was on the look-out for a bargain. He regarded it now with distaste. His nature was a blend of the coarse and the exquisite – coarse in his morals, exquisite in his tastes. But his was not the artist's eye; he could no more discern the true and the authentic underneath poverty and deprivation than he could fly to the moon.

He was busy interrogating a member of the travelling community as to his knowledge of the whereabouts of the horse he referred to as 'National Security'. The man indicated that he had 'been seen all right'.

'Who saw him? When and where?' The traveller to whom he was speaking was obsequious but curiously uninformative.

'He left yesterday.'

'Bloody thief!' Harnett said.

The traveller moved his face a little nearer. 'Who are you calling a thief?'

Harnett gesticulated angrily. 'All of you. Why don't you get off your arses and do a bit of work?'

The travelling man was not accustomed to taking insults without some measure of retaliation. He was on the point of lashing out to hit Harnett, but the omnipresent Morrissey immobilised him before he could do anything.

Harnett looked down at the traveller as he lay on the ground, and carefully stepped over him as if afraid of contaminating his shoes.

It began to dawn on him that he was being sent from one place to another, from one traveller to another; and none of them knew anything. The exercise was calculated to keep him on the move, to stop him from following any one course which might lead to the rediscovery of his miraculous white horse, the horse which would put Moyglade finally on the map as a stud to be reckoned with. What he really needed was a decent tracker; and he needed to mobilise the people who would be able to help him. Someone had told him in awed whispers about a traveller who could follow anyone in any circumstances, a man who had a pet crow which spied for him, a man who was very old and looked young because he dabbled in things human beings should have no truck with. And then someone else had whispered, 'Speak of the devil . . .' and everyone had melted away and Harnett found himself confronting a man whose face he could not bear to look at.

'I'll track the horse for you, sir,' the man said. 'What will you pay me?'

'What do you want?'

'Sure I'll take the reward that's offered and one other thing.'

'What's that?'

The man paused. Harnett avoided his eyes.

'The children,' he said softly. 'I'll take the children.'

Tito and Ossie slept like the dead. Exhaustion and fright had drained them and they slept through the long evening and did not waken until the dawn of the following day when the birds began to twitter. The birds were funny, Tito thought; first one or two gave a few tweets and then the whole bloody choir got going and after that you might as well get up because there was no sleep to be had at all.

The boys got up, shook out the blanket, rolled it up and secured it to Tir na n-Og's back. They realised that they had left the bridle on him all night and, full of contrition, took it off for a while. The horse walked to the stream for a drink and grazed for a bit by the bank. They were hungry, but there was nothing for them to eat.

'I'm hungry, Tito.'

'Well, you'll have to stay hungry,' Tito responded. 'We've no food. We'll get some later.'

They set off again on the back of Tir na n-Og. They were still full of the adventure they had embarked on, but all either of them could think of was where they could get something to eat. Where was the nearest shop? They scanned the countryside and saw no shop, nor any sign of human habitation save one old farmhouse. Tir na n-Og moved in its direction and Tito became alarmed. The last thing he wanted was to put themselves in a position where they would be caught.

'We don't want to go towards that house,' he told the horse and he pulled on the left rein to turn his head. But Tir na n-Og was impervious and brought them swiftly to the shadow of an old orchard wall and they saw above them a branch with fruit, green fruit. The orchard was near the house, but they were on the far side of the orchard wall and could not be seen.

'What's that fruit?' Ossie enquired.

Tito looked up, saw the greengages over his head. 'Whatever it is, it's not ripe,' he announced.

'How do you know it's not ripe?' Ossie asked scornfully. 'It looks all right to me.'

He leant his weight on Tito's shoulders and pulled himself into a standing position on Tir na n-Og's back. Then he stretched up and picked the fruit within reach, handing it down to Tito who looked at it doubtfully, sniffed, felt that it was soft and took a bite.

'It's okay . . . It's good,' he announced, but even as he said this a bloodcurdling growl was heard from the other side of the stone wall, a growl full of menace, and in a moment the silence was shattered by wild barking. Tito stuffed the greengages into his pocket, turned round to help his brother regain his seat behind him.

Ossie was trembling. Tito urged Tir na n-Og away.

He was gone in a moment, leaving the orchard and the old stone farmhouse far behind.

When the barking of the dog could no longer be heard, the boys stopped to examine the fruit. Tito took it out of his pocket, four green fruits. He divided them, two each, and they ate them and both declared them to be very good.

'You should have got more while you were at it,' Tito grumbled.

They travelled for most of the day, resting only for short periods, and soon put a good stretch of country behind them. Towards evening they stopped in the ruins of a Norman castle. The castle was about five hundred years old and was covered with ivy, convolvulus, and blackberry brambles on which tight, ripening fruit grew in abundance. The children looped Tir na n-Og's bridle over a branch and left him to graze while they foraged. They picked whatever ripe berries they could find, stuffed them into their mouths, but the hunger pangs, which had disappeared only temporarily after their breakfast of greengages, continued more or less unabated.

'I can't eat any more of this stuff,' Ossie announced eventually, staring down at the last few berries in his hand. 'It only makes you hungrier!'

'We'll find more berries,' Tito said, remembering that in theory it was supposed to be possible to live off the land. After all, Grandpa did it, no bother. Every cowboy worth his salt did it.

'I'm starving!' came Ossie's petulant little voice again. 'Why can't we go to the shop?'

Tito sighed. 'Cowboys don't go to the shop. That's

giving up.' He said this, but what was really exercising him was caution, fear of discovery, of being made to return to the Towers and an irate Papa, of losing Tir na n-Og. Ossie stared at the fruits of the earth. His tummy rumbled.

'What would you get in a shop that cowboys would eat?' Tito demanded.

Ossie furrowed his brow. 'Beans!' he stated categorically. He could taste them already, fat and soft with plenty of tomato sauce. Tito felt his mouth water.

'Yeah, sure. Okay, I'll go.' He looked at his small brother's suddenly cautious face, knew how much Ossie hated being left, especially after the last time. 'I won't be long, Ossie. Honest!'

Ossie drew him by the arm and said, 'Tito, we're being watched.'

Tito nearly jumped out of his skin. 'Where?' he demanded.

Ossie pointed to the branch of a tree where a crow with a white wing tip was sitting, looking at them. Then he laughed.

'You and your jokes!' Tito said sourly. 'It's only an ould bird. You gave me an awful fright!'

Tito thought of food all the way to the village. He thought of fish fingers and spaghetti and potatoes and hamburgers and fish and chips. It was as though some other person lived inside him, who directed his body, who made demands. The demanding person in his body knew nothing about money, didn't care that you couldn't eat without it. But Tito knew he had little money and that he had to mind it.

Baked beans, he thought, were cheap. And he could get some chocolate too. Lovely, lovely chocolate.

The village shop doubled as a kind of supermarket. Ossie found the shelf full of cans, selected two tins of baked beans, picked up six bars of chocolate, brought them to the counter. Jack Farrelly who owned the shop watched the boy, saw him glance at the *Evening Press* on the counter, saw him take a copy and hold it behind his back. He also noticed the way the boy glanced out of the window at the street where two police cars had stopped and policemen were conferring. He heard some sort of public announcement being made by the police, but couldn't catch it properly.

'How much?' Tito asked the shopkeeper.

Jack Farrelly totted up the bill. 'Two cans of beans, six bars of chocolate . . . Is that a paper?'

Tito started and brought the paper round from behind his back. 'Yeah.'

'Why have you got it behind your back?' Jack said irritably.

'I didn't steal it!' Tito said hotly. He had it behind his back because he had seen the pictures on the front page and didn't want the shopkeeper to see them too. He knew this exercise was futile but he did it anyway.

The shopkeeper sighed. 'Who said you did?' He glanced at the till. 'Three pounds twenty-five.'

Tito paid and left the shop. The shopkeeper took up the evening paper and glanced at it. He saw the photographs immediately, read the headlines, saw the sum offered as reward. He expelled an exasperated breath of understanding and put the paper back.

Tito sneaked back to his hideout at the ruined castle via several side alleys and bent down behind walls and hedges. Ossie was still there, sitting beside Tir na n-Og and carrying on a monologue about the Wild West. The white horse grazed and looked at him occasionally from deep black eyes. This was sufficient response for Ossie. He knew that Tir na n-Og was interested and that was all he required. Tito gave his little brother some chocolate, lit a fire and puzzled over the words in the paper.

'What does the paper say?' Ossie asked.

'It says we stole Tir na n-Og.'

Ossie looked at the white horse. 'Stole him? But he's ours!'

Tito shrugged. 'I know. Anyway, we can't go to jail.'

'Why not?'

'Because we're too young.' He glanced at his brother. 'But we can be sent to a home, though.'

Ossie looked doubtful. 'Don't we have a home, Tito?'

Tito thought. 'I'm talking about a home where they don't let you out,' he said after a moment.

'That's a jail,' Ossie said contemptuously. He glanced at the paper, asked hopefully, 'Is there a reward for us?'

Tito was silent. He had put the tins of beans on the fire. Dusk was falling. He smiled teasingly at his brother.

'Is there?' Ossie demanded.

Tito didn't believe in giving away vital information too readily. He squinted his eyes and laid his head on one side in a considering attitude, as though he was trying to remember what it had said in the paper.

Ossie became incensed. His forehead crinkled and his eyes became furious. 'Tell me, Tito, or . . . or I'll kill you.' He launched himself at his brother, lay on him, pummelled him with his small fists. 'I bet you there's a reward!'

Tito grinned and held up five fingers.

'Five pounds?' said Ossie indignantly, sitting up.

Tito smiled, shook his head.

'Not five hundred?'

Tito shook his head. 'Five thousand pounds,' he said, letting each syllable slip slowly through his lips.

Ossie's eyes brightened. He got up and jumped up and down with joy. 'Brilliant! Wanted dead or alive, Tito and Ossie.'

The boys began to whoop round the ruined castle, forgetting that they were cowboys and behaving like Indians. But the night was falling and they were hungry and they soon returned to the fire which was now blazing merrily. The tins of beans were in there among the glowing embers and Tito pushed at them. How was he supposed to get them out? How was he supposed to open the tins? He wished he had a pair of tongs. Suddenly there was an explosion. In the quiet of the firelit evening it was deafening. The two boys were immediately covered with a sticky, scalding goo. Ossie cried out with pain.

'What was that?' Tito demanded crossly.

His brother tasted the substance stinging his face. 'Beans,' he said philosophically.

The second explosion followed quickly. The boys had moved back from the fire, but they and Tir na n-Og were covered with baked beans and splodges of tomato sauce. Tir na n-Og stretched out and started to lick the beans from Ossie's face. The boys picked off the still hot beans from the back of the white horse and ate them ravenously.

'Why did they explode like that?' Ossie demanded. 'I'd much rather eat them out of the tin.'

'I dunno,' Tito said wearily. A lot of things didn't make sense to Tito. Cowboys never had to put up with this sort of crap.

Later, having cleaned themselves up a bit, the boys lay wrapped in the blanket. They looked up at the stars blazing in the dark sky. The remains of the fire sent up occasional darts of light, illuminating the immediate surroundings for a minute. Tir na n-Og was a reassuring presence in the darkness. They could see his white body easily, and hear the hoarse intake of his breath. Neither of the boys could sleep. They had gorged themselves on the chocolate, drunk water from a stream, picked one baked bean after another from the flanks of Tir na n-Og, but still they were hungry.

I'll catch a rabbit in the morning, Tito thought, and we'll eat it for lunch. We'll have a real lunch tomorrow. He had seen plenty of rabbits in their travels; there were burrows in the nearby field.

He thought Ossie was asleep, but then he heard the whispered question: 'Are you awake?'

Tito didn't want to talk or explain anything. 'Not really,' he said.

'What do you think Papa's doing right now?' Ossie demanded.

Tito didn't need to think. He answered, 'He'll be at the drink.'

Ossie sighed. 'Yeah. Would you say he'll be mad at us?'

Tito thought of his father. What they had done was worse than mitching school. 'He might beat us this time,' he admitted.

Ossie agreed sleepily. 'Yeah, he might.'

Next morning Tito tried to catch a rabbit. He went to the field beside them, which was riddled with burrows, and took up position. They had watched the field for a while, seen the rabbits running in and out of their burrows. He had assured Ossie that he would catch the first rabbit that came out; he would grab him by the ears. He made Ossie wait behind the hedge as he did not trust him to keep quiet. Ossie therefore had an excellent view of what was going on. He watched his brother crouch beside his chosen burrow for a long time. He saw the long-eared, rabbity heads stick themselves out of every single burrow in the place behind his brother's back. Gradually the field behind him seemed to fill with rabbits. They were all looking at Tito and then they looked at each other. Insofar as rabbits could laugh, they laughed.

Ossie didn't like rabbits making a fool of his brother. 'They think you're mental!' he shouted suddenly, bursting from cover. Tito was furious until Ossie told him what the rabbits had been up to.

'When I grow up I'll bomb them!' Tito said in rage. He looked at the field of burrows but all was still.

Later, as though providence had been watching, they found a rabbit caught in a snare. It was alive; its leg was bloodied and broken and it was struggling frantically to escape.

Tito approached it. 'There's lunch for us,' he announced.

Ossie's eyes became very large and sorrowful. He saw the round frightened eyes of the little animal, the fluffy white tail, the blood on its leg, its gentle whiffling nose.

'He's alive,' Ossie cried.

Tito released the rabbit from the snare and held it by its ears, aware of his brother's mounting distress.

'We need to eat, Ossie. This rabbit would give us a meal,' he said defensively.

Ossie began to cry. 'Don't hurt him, don't hurt him!' he screamed.

Tito, whose own heart had quailed at the prospect of wringing the little creature's neck, complied. He loosened his grip on the rabbit's ears and watched while it ran away on three legs, with a lopsided gait like a ship in a storm, dragging the broken leg behind it.

Lunch was gone. Tito turned to his brother with a show of irritation. 'We'll starve to death if you keep going on like this!'

Ossie ignored the comment. 'Will anyone mend his leg?' he asked, his eyes still fixed on the burrow into which their lunch had disappeared, and Tito looked at him in exasperation.

'Oh yes, they'll send at once for the rabbit doctor!'

The sarcasm was lost on Ossie. He smiled.

Back in the Towers, Birdie looked at the wealth she was amassing. It was unbelievable. She had fifty pounds. She had only invested five pounds and twenty-two pence and she had fifty pounds. She still had plenty of 'Mogadon' to sell. There were other 'drugs' too, depending on what pill bottles had been found in the rubbish bins. She and her work force had filled them all with the sucked Smarties. She could not believe the success of her enterprise. Soon she would be a rich girl and she would never have to mind children again.

But what would she do with the money? She had intended to use it to follow Tito and Ossie. But now she wasn't so sure. Making money had become an occupation in itself, one not to be sneezed at. She calculated how much she should spend now on Smarties; how many she would have to give the work force to keep them sucking. So far they had been amenable; they had sucked another three packs and she had given them eight Smarties each as reward. But she had had to rescue some of her stock from her mother who had been on the point of throwing them out. 'What's this? Sucked Smarties? Don't you want to eat them?'

Birdie had had to be quick to save that lot from the bin. They should really only work when the parents were comatose. God, but life was not so boring when you were making money. You could buy things. She had seen some vanishing cream in the shop. That was the name on it. 'Vanishing Cream'. She had made her first purchase from her earnings and had rubbed it into her breasts. With a bit of luck . . . Well, even for a year or two it would be worth it. Jesus, who wanted to have boobs sticking out at twelve? It wasn't fair.

She heard the ring at the door. It was a new door, put up since the riot police had demolished the other one. She heard her mother answer it.

'Birdie,' her mother called anxiously. 'There's gentlemen here from the Drug Squad who want to talk to you.'

Chapter Eleven

Once word of the reward was out, Tito and Ossie and the white horse were seen everywhere. The calls came flooding in, from the thirty-two counties of Ireland, from Britain, even from France.

'Does anyone know bloody French?' someone shouted and Superintendent O'Mara who had just come into the incident room, took the call. The caller was excited; the French was rapid. O'Mara listened carefully, learnt that the quarry was now in the Dordogne.

'*Oui, oui. Je comprends*,' he assured the caller, who was stretching O'Mara's knowledge of French to the limit by the speed of his communication. He took a note of name and address.

'Anything in that, sir?' Inspector Bolger asked, coming in with a file.

'Moonshine,' O'Mara said. 'I knew it would happen if he offered that reward.'

Bolger handed the file to his superior. He did it reluctantly, but he had no option. O'Mara had asked for it the day before.

'What's this?' O'Mara asked.

'It's my file on the matter as requested by you, sir.

It contains the signature authorising the sale of the horse.'

'What signature?'

'The knacker's,' Bolger offered.

O'Mara looked at him coldly. 'You mean Mr Riley?'

Bolger had had enough of the Rileys. He was on the point of losing the only chance he had for sudden preferment in a harsh world. So he made the mistake of losing his temper.

'I mean that drunken, bloody, lay-about, no good, sponging knacker!' There was silence. Brophy tried not to smile. Bolger looked at the faces before him.

'I have the perfect solution to the knacker problem,' he went on. 'Put them all on one of the Blasket Islands with forty barrels of whiskey and one barrel of knives – and come back in a month's time and hang the survivors for murder!'

Bolger noted the perfect silence which greeted his levity and flung angrily out of the room.

O'Mara put down the file. There was another call and for a change this one seemed promising.

Kathleen remembered John Riley well. She had known him for years, been friend to his wife Mary, held her hand while she was dying. To Kathleen, John Riley was friend and cousin and a source of pain. He had gone; he had left them all after Mary had died, taken the kids and gone to live with the Rozzers, the settled people. The tribe was poorer without him and the tribe did not forgive him. And neither did Kathleen.

What did she remember of John Riley? She remembered the skinny boy, shinning up trees, building a tree house and weeping with anger when he had to leave it because the tribe moved on; making catapults and bows and arrows and using them to bring down rabbits. She remembered him growing into manhood and changing towards her, becoming careful of her, not expecting her any longer to climb in the old way, or even ride as she had used to. For her part she had worked to prove him wrong, by climbing higher than he would dare himself, or putting her uncle's piebald pony over higher fences.

She remembered the kiss. Even now, years later, she could remember the taste of it, the thrill of it. It was as though, by pinning her against the tree and pressing his mouth on hers, he had opened the door to an entirely new world, to a different reality. She had denied this reality; she had been too young. By the time she began to realise what John Riley meant to her, it was too late. He had fallen for the winsome Mary Ward and was engaged to her. But then she had always known he would. She had seen it.

Kathleen had married to escape. Her husband Jacko belonged with a different tribe. He was a quiet, thoughtful man, whose basic requirement of life was that it leave him alone; but there was a sweetness to him which had decided Kathleen. Traveller women were not used to sweetness in their men.

The marriage had not been happy. Jacko had retired more and more into his own world, had decided to settle, dreamed of a permanent fireside.

Kathleen felt stifled, and when the sense of suffocation became unbearable she had returned to where she belonged. By this time John Riley was the father of one son and had been made the King of the Travellers. His tribe was the happiest and the most prosperous of all the tribes. His people loved him, relied on his judgement in times of trouble and accepted his decisions. The tribe now called him 'Papa'. He had welcomed Kathleen back with a brotherly embrace and she had taken her place in Tracker's caravan and brazened out her ambiguous status.

Tall, slim, red-haired, and with a quirky proud mouth, Kathleen was possessed of the elusive quality known as 'presence'. You would know if she was nearby, even if you did not see her, because the air would become charged with a sort of excitement; she emanated a subtle kind of danger. Sometimes she looked into the crystal ball with deadly effect, and read the tarot, but only rarely. She was reluctant to tell fortunes, having reason to believe that in her hands neither the tarot nor the crystal ball were jokes. They were instruments which gave her glimpses into the truth about the future and she knew that the future was better left alone.

She knew the past; she knew that she had lost most of her family to TB at the age of four; she knew how she had been befriended by John Riley and that she had grown up beside him, only to lose him in a matter of weeks to a gentle stranger. She knew that her own failed marriage was the direct result. How could she live with Jacko when she had known what life had tasted like with John?

So, knowing the past and the pain of it, and suspecting that pain was hidden in all the turnings of Time, she preferred to be as ignorant of the future as everyone else.

Kathleen saw Papa before he saw her. She knew about the 'theft' of the white horse, knew that the children involved were his. She'd reckoned it was only a matter of time before he came back to his own for help. Where else would he go for it?

She saw his tall frame looking down on the encampment, a big man in a black coat standing outlined against the sky. She saw him before anyone else did and she felt the surge of recognition climb all the way up her spine.

The encampment was a sheltered spot for a camp, a dip in the ground, surrounded by open hilly country. Papa saw the caravans, some new, some old, but only one was barrel-topped. His eyes were drawn to it. There it was, over at the edge of the camp, lonely as an abandoned house. The grass was untrampled around it. There was no fire before it and no pony was hobbled nearby.

Papa felt the sting of unshed tears behind his eyes, but he moved forward down the incline. It was then that he was spotted and a party of teenage boys on horseback came to block his path. He scanned their faces keenly. He knew them; he knew every one of them. Seven years had made a difference. They had been children when he left and now they were angular

173

adolescents, raw with new power, but they were still recognisable.

'Out!' they shouted. 'Keep back there!' From behind the horses a man in an old reefer jacket came forward. He had a closed, shrewd face, in which hardship and bitterness were etched. Tracker Lee, Kathleen's brother. He and Papa looked at one another for a moment and then he spoke.

'You remind me of someone. Do you know that?'

Papa ignored the bitterness in his voice. 'I need help, Tracker.'

Tracker raised his eyebrows. 'Don't you get it from the welfare man?' He paused, while his sarcasm settled over the space between them. 'We got along without you, Papa.'

'I need you to track my boys,' Papa said stubbornly.

Tracker looked behind Papa and saw the police cars encroaching on the skyline. Papa thought that he had given them the slip. He'd known that he was being followed, but he had doubled back several times, gone down one-way streets, thought that he had lost them. Now he realised that they probably knew where he was headed. Where else, after all, would he go for help?

Tracker sneered, gestured towards the police. 'Papa Riley is here. Bad luck is not far behind!'

From the shadow of her caravan Kathleen watched the exchange between Papa and Tracker. She saw the mounted sentries, the police cars, and she strode forward, throwing back the long red hair which streamed down her back. She was not going to stand by while John Riley was driven away from his own.

'Let him through!' she commanded in a voice which carried right around the camp.

Papa turned to stare at her; her eyes met his in challenge. The way she stood with her hands on her hips, leaning back slightly, her face haughty and still, made him think that he had never known her. Something had changed in her. The girl had become a woman and the woman had been touched with cynicism and knew a thing or two about the twists of fate. But as he stared at her, there passed between them something elemental, like lightning, a surge of electricity which both felt but neither acknowledged. Kathleen turned proudly away. The boys on horseback moved aside obediently to make way for Papa and he walked through the camp.

No one spoke to him. He saw faces he knew and he attempted a greeting, but they turned aside from him. The camp felt different; it was a place which no longer responded to him, to his will, to his anger or to his laughter. He felt that he had died and that it was his ghost which traversed the field full of familiar faces which did not see him. He moved, slowly and almost reluctantly, as though drawn by invisible strings, towards the weathered, barrel-topped caravan he had seen from the road. He surveyed it for a moment, his face set, and then he opened the door.

The inside was almost unchanged; it seemed faded and smaller, but it had the scent of another world and another life. Everything was covered in dust and a colony of spiders had moved in. The air in it was different to the air outside, as though it had trapped something of an old vitality and kept it against the attrition of the years. But there was a lonely melancholy where once there had been joy. Papa looked around, opened a small cupboard, recognised in sudden astonishment the old tea caddy in which Mary had kept some odds and ends, prised off the lid and looked inside. There, at the bottom, was a photograph of his dead wife, holding two-year-old Tito in her arms. She was gazing up at him with her sweet, slightly lopsided smile. Papa took up the photograph and devoured it with his eyes. The grief welled up until he felt almost weak. Then he replaced the photograph in the box and closed the lid with a snap.

When he came out of the caravan he moved away unsteadily, like a man in a dream. He didn't hear the shouts of 'Papa Riley! Papa Riley!' until the burly owner of the voice was almost on top of him, crashing towards him down the hill.

'Jesus, is it you?' the man roared. 'Papa Riley, is it yourself?'

Papa stared and recognised the owner of the voice immediately. It was his old friend Barreller Kiely, a man who resembled a bear in size and strength. He flung himself on Papa, hugging him fiercely. Papa felt as though the breath was being squeezed out of him. Then he got a slap on the back which winded him.

'I knew you'd be back!' Barreller thundered.

'Barreller,' Papa said, when he got his breath back. 'What am I going to do? I've lost my boys!' He looked into his old friend's face and saw the sympathy in his

eyes. It was as though no time had passed, as though
he had never gone away.

'First you come away and let me warm you up,'
Barreller said, dropping his voice to a gentle
gruffness. 'Are you still a drinking man?'

He threw an arm round Papa and drew him to his
own caravan, laughing playfully like a child.

Evening fell. Kathleen prepared a meal by the fire
and sat with her brother to eat it. Tracker was as cross
as two sticks, and she knew why. He had a deep, black
soul which remembered everything. He was not a
man who knew how to forgive and he had no peace;
he nursed his old grievances until they put roots into
him and corroded him. Perhaps it was this very
tenacity over minutiae which was the basis of his
famed abilities as a tracker. He was now looking at
Barreller's caravan where Papa's voice could be
heard in animated talk as he ate and drank by the fire.

'Wouldn't you think Barreller would have an ounce
of wit,' he sneered, 'to be letting John Riley sit by his
fire and eat his food.'

Kathleen listened for a while in silence. Tracker
drew a word picture of a traitor, a man who cared
nothing for his own, but who left them for the safety
of a welfare cheque and a small concrete burrow
halfway to heaven, a man who, when severely tested,
was found wanting.

'He might have changed,' she said eventually.

'I don't see it,' Tracker said sourly.

Kathleen listened to Papa's voice coming across to
her in the firelit darkness.

'Mary Riley died in his arms giving birth to his child. Don't you understand? Don't you know what that did to him?'

'He blames us for Mary's death,' Tracker said after a moment.

'He blames himself!' Kathleen whispered.

Tracker stared moodily into the fire. He gave a sideways jerk of his head. 'They're to blame!'

Kathleen looked at her brother. She knew whom he was referring to, but she pretended ignorance.

'Who?'

'Them!' Tracker said bitterly. 'Them! The settled people!'

Kathleen sighed. 'She died because she didn't make it to a hospital. That's all.'

There was silence for a moment and then Tracker said, 'He's one of them now anyway, that's all I'm saying.' He watched Papa across the clearing, saw him get up and go with Barreller to another caravan.

'Are you sure?' Kathleen demanded. 'Are you sure he's one of the settled people?'

Tracker turned to look at his sister. She could see the firelight in his eyes and the weary, bitter curl to his lip. And he saw something in her face, like a current deep down in a still pool, which disquieted him.

'He's a stone,' Tracker said. 'When you throw a stone in a lake it's not happy until it hits the bottom.' He surveyed his sister and then he added, 'Just make sure he doesn't bring us all down with him.'

Kathleen finished her meal and sat back, wrapping her old sheepskin jacket tightly round her. The flames picked out the lights in her hair and the brooding expression of her eyes. She heard the music start up, first some preliminary squeezes on the accordion followed by a few warm-up screeches on the fiddle; then the pipes started and soon the whole camp was filled with the sound of music. The musicians had gathered round a fire lit in an oil drum in the middle of the site and soon the young people got up and began to dance. The music played faster and faster and the dancing got wilder and wilder, until it seemed that the fairies had come to play for them and that the dancers were held by some old enchantment, so furiously and tirelessly did they turn and whirl and stamp to the tempo. Bottles of stout were passed around among the spectators. The night was filled with music; the stars seemed within reach. Barreller clapped the musicians on the back. 'Play up, play up,' he laughed. He clapped Papa on the back: 'You need a bit of that yourself!'

Papa heard the music as if it spoke to him. It was like a spell, but he was wary of its easy seduction.

'Barreller, I must find them quick,' he said. 'With the reward that's offered, anything might happen.' He turned to his old friend. 'Will you come with me?'

Barreller blew into his cheeks. 'All I would be is company.'

'I need that too, Barreller,' Papa said. 'I need that as well as a tracker.'

Barreller wanted to dance. 'Dance,' he roared. 'Go on, dance!' and he pushed Papa towards the dancers. But Papa resisted. He wanted to be off at once, to find his children who were alone somewhere under the stars with a white horse.

179

'You won't find those boys in the dark,' Barreller went on, lowering his voice. 'They're traveller kids. It's the police you have to worry about for now, Papa.'

When Bolger turned up unexpectedly, he found his constables in the squad cars looking anything but bored as they watched the activity in the camp below. There was discreet tapping of police boots against the car floor.

'Shit, here's Bolger!' someone exclaimed. Cigarettes were rapidly extinguished. The guards jumped out of the cars and went to meet their superior.

'What's going on?' Bolger demanded.

'They're dancing.'

Bolger looked down at the scene below. He saw the light from the fires and the caravans, heard the wild music, saw the forms turning and stamping in the firelight.

'I can see that,' he said. 'How long have they been dancing?'

'About an hour.'

Papa did not see Bolger approach. The inspector and his men came out of the night like ghouls. Papa was dancing; his feet and his body remembered the music which spoke to him like his own heart beating. The blood surged through his veins, he stamped his feet in the frenzy of the dance. Barreller passed him a bottle, but he waved it away. What need did he have for bottles now?

When he heard the voice of his old tormentor, he

thought for a moment that he was dreaming.

'Stop it, stop it!' Bolger roared. 'Dancing like an animal and your children on the road without a mother or father to look after them!'

Instantly there was silence. The music stopped. The travellers stared at the police. The only sound was the hissing of the fire. Kathleen watched from her vantage point by her caravan, but she did not move.

'I'll take the kids off your hands once and for all when I catch them,' Bolger went on with sly triumph. 'I'll give them a proper home.'

Kathleen rose and moved forward. She confronted the inspector with cold hauteur. 'This is my home,' she said. 'Nobody asked you to come here!'

Papa drew back and glowered. The inspector sneered. He turned to his guards. 'Call me when the animals leave,' he said and moved away.

Papa sprang towards the inspector. Kathleen and Barreller caught his arms. 'That's just what he wants,' she said.

The travellers did not resume the dance. It was late and the joy had left them. The fires were burning low and they sought their beds. Papa went back to the caravan which had once been his home, sat inside in his old leather coat, leaning against the canvas wall. Silence descended like a shroud, except for the soft half-whinny of a horse, the movement of dogs as they turned in their sleep, one or two voices from nearby caravans.

After a while the silence deepened. He was cold, colder than he should be. The cold seemed to seep into him from the caravan itself. Here, in this space, he had loved and fathered and lost. It was like coming back to live in a tomb. Here Mary had laboured to give Ossie his life. He had begged her to go to hospital when the labour started. No, she said, drawing in her breath sharply with the first pains, she'd be fine. But what did she know? She thought it was unlucky to give birth other than in your own caravan. He should have insisted. He should simply have insisted. There was something wicked about setting dogs on people, about frightening a pregnant woman the way the landowner had. Being moved on like that had hastened a cruel birth.

'It's a boy!' Kathleen had said, holding up the new morsel of humanity. Mary's eyes had followed the infant and Kathleen had wrapped it in a towel and put it, crying, against his mother's face whose glazed eyes registered relief and joy. But the haemorrhage had started and nothing Kathleen, or the other midwife, could do would stop it. Mary had slipped away from him then, slipped away easily, too exhausted to fight, looking into his eyes and smiling a little as she always did in the face of the inevitable.

'Call her,' Kathleen had commanded. 'Call her, John. We're losing her!'

Papa remembered it, remembered calling her until they pulled the sheet over her face.

'Oh Mary, Mary,' he whispered to the listening canvas of his old home. 'Oh Mary, why did you leave me behind you?'

There was no answer, only the night breeze which buffeted the canvas, and crept in through the open door.

Papa went to the cupboard and took out the tea caddy, found her photograph and lit a match to study her face by its light. 'Our boys are gone, Mary. I don't know where they are. I need your help!'

He waited as though he expected a response to come to him somehow out of the night and when it did not, he stood up with a groan and stumbled down into the darkness outside.

Kathleen saw him. She had not gone to bed, but sat in the shadows near her dying fire. Her mind was full of the events of the day and she went over them carefully, weighing in her head the demeanour of the man they still called Papa. From the caravan beside her she could hear Tracker's snores. He had not joined in the dance but had had a lot to drink and now he was deeply asleep. She had allowed her fire to die and she sat very still. Her eyes were smarting; she had looked into the flames for too long and had seen there what she had seen.

She watched to see if Papa was going away and when it became apparent that he was merely sleeping outside, stood up and moved towards him and was seated beside him before he was aware that she was there.

'What's wrong?' she asked softly.

'I can't sleep, Kathleen,' Papa said. 'I can't sleep in that caravan.'

Kathleen nodded in the darkness. She couldn't sleep either, but for entirely different reasons. She had felt the ice cold in her veins, which was the precursor of trance; she had seen the warning in the fire. She knew that for reasons she could not fathom, forces from another dimension were out and searching. She knew that John Riley needed her.

'I can help you,' she said after a moment.

'How?'

'I can track as good as my brother.' She glanced up the hill to where the police cars were still waiting.

'Why won't your brother come?' Papa asked.

'Tracker doesn't trust you, John.'

Papa sighed. He looked back at his caravan. 'He thinks I should bury her like a traveller. Burn the caravan. Let her soul go free,'

Kathleen did not look at him. But she whispered after a moment, 'Maybe you should.'

Papa was silent and after a while Kathleen returned to her caravan.

In the morning Papa washed in the river. Then he went to his car which he had brought down into the encampment the previous evening and listened to the radio news. He heard the voice of Noel Harnett, the businessman who purported to own Tir na n-Og, being interviewed.

'Time is running short,' Harnett said. 'National Security is Ireland's entry in the Jameson World Cup showjumping finals. The event is only two days away. If we don't recover the horse in the next two days, we can say goodbye to Ireland's participation in the World Cup final on Sunday. It's an outrage!'

Kathleen was nearby washing horses and Papa opened the door of his car and turned up the volume.

'. . . What is most galling is the irresponsibility of the travelling community, their lack of care for their children, allowing them to run wild, unsupervised in any way. This sickens all civilised people . . .'

Kathleen looked up at Tracker who came to help her with the horses.

'You stay, Tracker,' she said. 'I'm going.'

Kathleen brought the horses to where Papa and Barreller were preparing packs for the journey. Papa looked up at the horse, a big hefty piebald animal. 'I haven't been on a horse in seven years, Kathleen.'

Barreller looked at the brute Kathleen indicated as his. 'Jesus, Kathleen, I'm not fit enough to get up on that thing!'

Kathleen laughed. 'Well, you'll be fit soon enough!'

The voice of the interviewer came from the car radio. 'What do you feel should happen to the runaway children?' he asked Noel Harnett. The latter did not reply at once. He seemed to consider his response carefully.

'This is very difficult. Obviously it is more dangerous for them to be living alone with this father who does not seem to care, or notice, whether they come or go. They need proper care and there are institutions that can provide that care . . .'

Kathleen saw Papa's mouth tighten in anger. He mounted his horse without a word. Barreller followed suit, with some initial difficulty. Kathleen rode off ahead of them. Behind them the police car radios blazed into life.

'Shit, they're leaving. We can't drive after them. They're going cross-country!'

In the open fields the three riders rode abreast.

'We've no radio now,' Papa said.

Kathleen pulled a small transistor radio out of her pocket, flipped the switch on and then off again.

'Begod, Kathleen,' Papa said, 'but you think of everything!'

Chapter Twelve

When Papa had furiously driven away from the Ringsend encampment, Grandpa had got out the tarot cards and played them, letting them slip through his fingers in a dreamlike fashion. He saw how they fell; no matter how often he played them they gave the same reading.

He was very troubled. He felt that the boys were safe enough for the time being at least, because no human agency could harm them now. He knew that Papa would find the boys and he also knew that he would not find them until the time was right. He wondered what he should do. He had served no purpose in the city; he had come too late to influence events and now he might as well make his way back across the country, be there when it ended. He knew perfectly well where it would end.

He was tired. Old Dan was tired. The sun was warm. Grandpa decided to go back to the encampment by the Towers, give Dan a bale of hay, rest there for a while before setting out again on another journey. But when he got back to the encampment beside the Towers and while he was unharnessing

Dan to give him a rest, he was approached by the curious.

'Is it your grandchildren that stole the horse?'

'They didn't steal it! The horse was mine. I gave it to them.' Grandpa knew that the horse was not his, that it could not be appropriated by anyone, but he wasn't going to get involved in explanations.

'The Rozzers say they stole it!'

Grandpa made a gesture of exasperation, lifted one wry eyebrow and slipped the hobble over Dan's hind leg, tethering him to the caravan. The people drifted away. As he was climbing into the caravan he heard a girl's voice: 'Hey, Mister Ward.'

He turned. It was Angela Murphy, one of the children he had earlier seen in the Murphy residence sucking the colour off the Smarties. Her brother Conor was at her heels.

'Hello,' he said gruffly.

'Is there any news of the two boys?'

'Not yet.' He looked past her, expecting to see her sister who had wanted to join in the search. 'Where's your sister?'

Angela shrugged and said in a smug voice, 'She's helpin' the guards.'

Grandpa stared at her in astonishment. 'What?'

Angela shrugged again. 'Yeah. She got into trouble over the Smarties.'

Grandpa tried to understand. A child in trouble over a few sweets? 'What do you mean, Angela?'

'She was selling them, putting them in bottles and pretending they were drugs.'

Grandpa managed to keep a straight face although for an unguarded moment he wanted to laugh out loud. 'I see,' he said, then added, 'Did she make a lot of money?'

'I dunno.' Angela made a disparaging face. 'She hid it. She didn't give us any, did she, Conor?'

Conor shook his head. 'She gave us sweets. If we sucked the Smarties the way she wanted, she gave us eight for ourselves every day!'

Grandpa nodded. You had to pay the work force. If they weren't unionised, that was their problem.

Conor looked up at the old man. 'Will you tell us a story?'

'Where are your parents?'

'Me Ma's in the flat and me da's at the pub.'

Grandpa sighed to himself in silence. He saw the figure of Birdie approaching; there were tears on her face and she grabbed Conor by the hand and said harshly, 'Where were you?'

'Have the police gone?' Angela asked.

'Yeah.'

'Are they going to arrest you?' Angela asked hopefully.

Birdie gave her a hard look. 'They took away the Smarties. I told them they were only sweets, but they didn't believe me.'

Grandpa pieced the whole story together. His respect for the elder girl grew. Wasn't she the great little character? Again he wanted to laugh, but instead he said, 'I was going to tell them a story, Birdie. Do you want to hear it?'

Birdie, on the verge of fresh tears, nodded and the three children sat in front of Grandpa while he told them the story of the three children of Lir.

Birdie listened, heard how the children had a curse put on them by their wicked stepmother which changed them into swans, doomed to spend hundreds of years on different lakes.

'. . . Three hundred years on this lake, three hundred years on the Sea of Moyle, three hundred years on the Sea of Erris,' Grandpa's voice droned on. 'Then you will hear the sound of a Christian bell and the spell will be broken.'

The story went on to tell how the children came back to their home after nine hundred years had elapsed, but the place was gone, with nothing to show for the happy home they had once known but a wilderness of brambles and a few stones.

When the story was over the Murphy kids looked back at the Towers as though to reassure themselves that they were still there. But Birdie's face remained tearful and pale.

Grandpa beckoned to her. 'Don't worry your head,' he said. 'You sold a few sweets, so what? They'll soon find out they're not drugs.'

'Me Ma says they'll put me in jail.'

Grandpa gave a derisive snort. 'Divil a jail. Did you know that they have no jail for girls?' When he saw that Birdie brightened, he dropped his voice and asked her gently, 'Tell me, Birdie, do you go to school?'

Birdie nodded. 'Sometimes,' she said.

Grandpa regarded her for a minute. 'Do you like school?'

Birdie sighed shakily. 'No.'

'Can you read and write?'

She nodded. 'Yeah, 'course I can.'

Grandpa thought of his own grandchildren, of their schooling. 'You want to get away, don't you?'

Birdie nodded.

'You know, Birdie,' Grandpa said solemnly, 'the best way of getting over a problem is going through it. With those books you have and the brains you have and the school and everything, sure you could do whatever you wanted to if you put your mind to it. The ould lessons would be no bother to you. You could become anything,' he continued, warming to his theme, 'a teacher, a lawyer, a doctor. You could represent the travellers, stake a claim for us all!'

Birdie was silent.

'Would you like to do it, Birdie? Eat up everything in those books, show the lot of them? Will you do it?'

Birdie turned shy blue eyes on him. Her mouth was compressed.

'You'd never have to bother with sucking Smarties for a living again!'

The girl smiled. 'I'll try, Mister,' she said to please him.

Grandpa shook his head. 'It's a terrible mistake to "try", Birdie. That's the way people give up. Just make your mind up and, if you want to do it, then do it! But don't "try"!'

Birdie nodded at him and walked away with Conor

by the hand, Angela trailing behind.

Grandpa leant back in the sunshine against the half-door with his eyes closed. He was not aware that he had more company, a dark traveller, a thin, shifty-looking man with black hair who was standing beside the caravan sizing him up, until the latter spoke.

'Where d'you think those boys, your grandsons, have gone?' he asked softly.

Grandpa started, opened his eyes and felt the instinctive welling of alarm. He looked at the man closely, saw that he did not meet his eyes.

'I don't know,' he said. 'But they'll be back when they're ready.'

'That horse might bring them on a strange class of a journey,' the man went on as though Grandpa hadn't spoken.

Grandpa narrowed his eyes, looked at the spare figure before him, so thin that he seemed to continue in one line from his neck without any noticeable angles.

'Where do you come from?' he demanded sternly. 'Why so interested in that horse?'

The man raised his eyes and Grandpa found himself looking into two black eyes with slits for irises, like a cat's.

'The horse? Who said I'm interested in the horse?' he said softly, and he turned away.

Grandpa heard the words, but by the time their possible import hit him the man had disappeared behind the caravans. Grandpa stood up and looked for him, but the man had gone.

Grandpa sat down again and closed his eyes. He could see the horse in his mind's eye and the children with him. So many entities could be watching for them. When the other world was disturbed, when the normal balance was broken, there was turmoil between the realities of Time and those, both good and evil, ravelled up and hidden in eternity. Grandpa knew that these realities could not all be named or counted, but all of them moved in some strange tandem with the passion and the restless emotions of human beings.

'I have been used,' Grandpa thought. 'There was a Sending and I was used!' He thought of the queer-looking man with the cat's eyes and a shadow fell on the peace of his heart. Where had the stranger come from?

Words from the Book of Revelation, once told him by a priest, came to him: 'And I looked and behold a pale horse and the name of his rider was Death.'

Grandpa went inside his caravan, took out a photograph of his daughter and gazed at it. 'Mind them, Mary!' he whispered.

Inspector Bolger was off duty. Normally he could not bear to be away from the incident room; he wanted to follow up every clue which might lead him to the recovery of the elusive horse. But he had promised Cathy that he would take her out and he dared not renege on this promise. Cathy didn't take kindly to being treated as second best, even if it was only his work which came between them.

'Really, Phil,' she had told him when he had phoned to explain on the last occasion, 'if your work is so important and I'm not, I don't know why you don't just do the work all the time and forget about little undeserving me!'

This had scared Bolger a little. 'Sweetness, you know that you're the only thing that's really important in my—'

Cathy had hung up.

He had seen her briefly since then, taken her for lunch in the Westbury, very aware of the male eyes on her and in particular the eyes of Hubert Greyson, whom they had encountered while leaving the hotel.

'Hello, Hubert darling,' Cathy said and had introduced Bolger to him. Greyson was a tall, distinguished-looking man of forty-five, a widower and friend of Cathy's father. A bit old for her, certainly, but, judging by the age gaps between plenty of people who married, by no means too old. Greyson scared him, scared him so much that he had gone out and bought a ring. He wanted to present it to Cathy tonight. It was a diamond, an impressive stone sitting in solitary splendour on its twenty-two carat ring. It has cost Bolger his shirt, or to be precise all the money he had left from Harnett's down payment. He was in dead trouble now, he knew, if they didn't get the horse. Harnett had made it clear to him that if the horse was lost, not only would he not pay the rest of the proposed price, he would claim back the money already paid. Harnett had clout, political, financial, and commercial clout, and was not a man to mess with. And Phil Bolger could not pay that money back.

He had spent most of it in satisfying some of his more pressing creditors, the bookies with whom he had managed seriously to compromise himself financially. The balance, which should have gone to other bookies to get the last of them off his back, was a round sum of five thousand pounds, and this he had blown on the magnificent ring for Cathy.

He picked Cathy up and drove to the restaurant where he had booked a table for two, a small, discreet place; French, with exquisite nouvelle cuisine, candle light, silver cutlery and a bill that would cross his eyes for a week.

Cathy looked wonderful. She was wearing a cream silk dress with a gold belt. A plain gold band shone at her neck and a gold bracelet at her wrist. Her hair was simply done, straight, with its own natural bounce. She had varnished her nails pink and her lips were painted red and she seemed to Bolger to encompass all the glamour in the world.

He looked at the menu. Christ, all in French. Cathy was more familiar with the language than he was, although even she asked the maitre d'hotel to explain some of the delicacies on offer. Bolger could see how the latter approved of her.

He examined the wine list, with which, being fond of wine, he was more at home. But he ordered champagne.

'Are we celebrating something?' Cathy asked in her slightly breathless voice, leaning towards him across the pink damasked table and fixing him with her dark blue eyes. He could smell her perfume, L'Air du Temps, a young woman's perfume, and

desire for her filled him, suffused all the hidden nooks
and crannies of his body and his soul. Her skin was
creamy, with a slightly golden glow to it, and he
imagined all of her skin, all of her body, with a
desperate longing.

'We are celebrating you,' Bolger said in a moment
of chivalry and then sat back with the glow of having
delivered himself of a good line.

'How's the hunt for this wretched animal progress-
ing?' Cathy asked as she tucked into lobster. 'Haven't
you found it yet?'

Bolger had to admit that they were still searching.

'This is the horse that's going to make your fortune,
Phil, isn't that right?'

He agreed that it was. He felt uncomfortable under
her steady gaze and when she asked him where he had
got the horse in the first place, he said he had bought
it off some tinkers who didn't know a good animal
when they saw it.

Cathy chewed meditatively. 'This is simply delicious.' She held out a morsel on the end of her fork.
'Taste?'

Bolger tasted. He knew it was delicious, but
because he was on tenterhooks with what he intended
for later on, he found it difficult to give it the
adulation that was its due.

'Superb,' he murmured. 'Like yourself, Cathy.'

Cathy smiled, but she did not respond to the
compliment. Her reaction suggested that it had been
a little bit awkward and this put Bolger less at ease
than ever.

'How much did you say you were expecting for the

horse?' she asked lightly as she raised her glass to her lips and glanced around the restaurant as though to ascertain who else was there.

'About a million,' Bolger said laconically, annoyed at her inattention and capable himself of a game or two.

Cathy lost interest in her surroundings. She turned back to him with slightly raised eyebrows. 'Are you serious, Phil darling?'

'I'm perfectly serious.'

'Noel Harnett would part with that for the horse?'

Bolger put down his fork. 'He's paid that before for an animal, I'll bet.'

Cathy nodded. 'Probably, but that would be for a thoroughbred, a racehorse with a pedigree as long as your arm. Whereas this brute . . .'

'He's no brute,' Bolger said shortly. 'You should have seen him.'

She smiled at him then, an arch smile which wooed him a little.

When the meal was over and they had finished coffee and liqueurs, Bolger drove Cathy to Howth and up to the summit. From here they could see the whole of the bay, the lights of the city twinkling all the way from Greystones right round to Sutton. He leant over and kissed her, forcing himself to be slow and very gentle. He took her lips between his and she kissed him back. He looked at her lovingly.

'Cathy,' he said, 'I have something I want to ask you.'

She said nothing and sat quite still. He reached into his pocket and extracted the morocco box containing the ring. He opened it and the light from the street lamp beside them picked up the fire in the stone. He took her hand and said simply, 'Will you marry me?'

Cathy looked at the ring. She gazed into Bolger's eyes.

'Phil,' she said after a moment, 'the ring is beautiful, but I need some time. I think we should give ourselves some time. You are so rushed at the moment. Don't you think we should wait to make such a big decision until you have finished with your present pressurised case, eased the workload, found that horse of yours and so on? I mean, you can't really know your own mind with all that on your plate!'

Bolger sat and looked at her, the open ring box in his hand. Disappointment rose in him like a corrosion. He shut the box and put it back in his pocket.

Cathy leaned forward and kissed him on the mouth. 'I am very fond of you, Phil. It's just that marriage is such a big step. Ask me again . . . in a month or two when I have had time to think.'

Bolger looked at her with a half smile, trying to contain his sense of rejection. She kissed him again and he kissed her back fiercely.

'I won't let you go, you know,' he said into her ear. Privately he swore, I'll get that effing horse if it's the last thing I do.

Grandpa asked around among the travellers if they knew who the man with the black hair and the strange eyes was and one, an old woman, had immediately volunteered: 'I haven't seen that fellow for years. I thought we were well rid of him.' She crossed herself almost surreptitiously.

'Who is he?'

'He used to come round in the old days, when some of the women got involved with – ah, a dangerous class of carry-on with bits of dead animals and stuff like that.'

Grandpa stared at her. He knew that this woman was talking about the black arts. The man who had asked him where his grandchildren were was a black magician.

She looked at him with worried eyes. 'I hope he won't be round here again.'

'You haven't told me who he is.'

She shook her head. 'We never knew his name, just a kind of nickname because of his eyes – Catspaw. He could track anything. They used to say he had sold his soul to the devil. He had a crow, an evil looking yoke with a class of white feather; they said the devil had put his soul into the crow and that it spied for him.'

Grandpa had heard enough. He moved as fast as his legs would carry him, harnessed old Dan once more to the caravan and found the road.

Chapter Thirteen

Tito and Ossie left the shelter of the ruined Norman castle and the company of the rabbits in the nearby field. But first they buried the fire, remembering the rules that Grandpa had preached. That way there would be nothing for the posse to find, no clues. They watched out for signs of rain, but the clouds were fairly high and the breeze was fresh.

The children had slept well, curled up together in the blanket under the fifteenth-century stone archway, and Tir na n-Og was in good form. He had grazed plentifully and drunk his fill from the small river. When the children got on his back he moved forward with great energy and brought them at speed through fields and over hedges. Sometimes it seemed to them that they were flying, but they knew that this was silly. Horses didn't fly. They went through flat countryside, where there were wide open spaces and many horses, but the horses did not seem to notice Tir na n-Og, although he passed within biting distance of some of them. They lifted their heads and stared at the children and then resumed their grazing. At one point Ossie shouted to his brother, 'Hey, Tito. Stop.'

Tito reined in Tir na n-Og. 'What's wrong with you?'

'There's an old saucepan back there in the ditch.'

Tito clicked his tongue in annoyance. 'So what?'

'I'm getting down, Tito,' and he slipped from Tir na n-Og's back, found the saucepan which was battered and had a broken handle, and returned with it triumphantly.

'What do you want that for?' Tito demanded, man-oeuvring Tir na n-Og to a boulder so that Ossie could use it as a mounting block. He bent over to help his brother up behind him.

'For beans,' Ossie answered. 'For the next time we have beans! If we have them in a saucepan, maybe they won't explode on us.'

Tito agreed that this was a possibility and the white horse moved off again.

A little later they heard a plane overhead and, looking up, saw that it was a small aircraft, that it was going slowly as though it were checking the ground for something.

'They're looking for us,' Tito said, his heart turning over with sudden fright.

Tir na n-Og moved in among a flock of sheep, all of whom were as white as himself. He stayed there, moving a few paces with the flock, which ignored him, until the small biplane disappeared.

'Were they looking for us, Tir na n-Og?' Ossie whispered. But the horse only rattled the bit.

The day wore on and Tito thought that he would die of hunger. The episode with the plane had made him reluctant to stop near shops and the rumbling in his belly was reaching an all-time crescendo. As though echoing his thoughts, Ossie exclaimed suddenly, 'Tito, I'm starving!'

Tito half turned his head. 'So am I,' he said, 'but if we go to the shops now, we might be caught. It would be better to wait until the evening and try to wear a disguise.'

'What's a disguise?'

'It's wearing other people's stuff so no one will know you.'

Ossie thought about this. 'There might be a scarecrow somewhere and we could steal its clothes.' He had seen a children's programme where a scarecrow provided most of the action and where the young hero had ended up impersonating it.

Tito raised his eyes to heaven. 'It's our faces, you eejit. It's our faces we have to disguise. They have our picture in the papers, remember!'

Ossie remembered, but he was still hungry. 'I'm still hungry, Tito.'

The flat country had given way to bog and Tir na n-Og picked his way through heather and soft black terrain. The bog was full of cut-away sections, where dark water lay very still, reflecting only the clouds and the occasional shiver of the bracken and the long coarse grass which grew among the heather. The boys dismounted and walked beside Tir na n-Og in silence. It had occurred to Tito that they would be less visible from the air on foot and they felt that Tir na n-Og must be tired.

When they came to a field with several cows and other cattle Ossie had a brainwave. 'Tito, I'd love some milk. Let's take some milk!'

Tito stared at the cows. There was a black and white one and a red one and they were grazing very calmly, although they did raise their heads to look at the children. But how did you get milk out of a cow?

Ossie raised his saucepan triumphantly. 'We can use this,' he announced. 'I'll do it!'

Tito held him back. 'Ossie, you don't know how to milk a cow.'

Ossie sighed irritably. He pointed. 'Look, their things are full of milk. They won't mind. All you have to do is squeeze. I saw it on the telly.'

He dodged away from Tito's hand and ran towards the red cow who raised her big wet muzzle at him. Tito watched while he crouched underneath her and commenced operations. First he put the battered saucepan on the ground beneath her udder and then he squeezed a teat. His hand was small and he clutched the warm rubbery teat near the end and nothing whatever escaped from it. He took another teat and redoubled his efforts. This time he used his thumb and index finger and applied pressure halfway; the cow moved and kicked his saucepan; a small jet of hot milk caught him on the face. He jumped up and down with delight and started to cheer. 'Did you see that, Tito? She squirted milk!'

He picked up the saucepan and followed the cow. Tito ran to hold the cow's head, but as he did so he saw the bulk of a huge animal raise itself up on a ditch at the far edge of the field. It was a great black bull, with hefty shoulders and an enormous head and it let out a bellow which paralysed the children with dread. They turned and stood still, unable to move, as the bull lowered its head and stared straight at them. It had a ring on its nose and its front hooves were pawing the ground.

'Jesus, Ossie, run! It's a bull!'

Ossie didn't know anything about bulls, but he knew peril when it stared him in the face. His body began to shake; he wanted to cry for Tito who had run to the fence at the edge of the field, but when he opened his mouth no sound came out. He wanted to run after him, but his legs wouldn't move. The cow had moved away. He saw the bull gather himself up and come charging at him down the field. Time stood still. He felt the ground shaking as the great animal charged. It came towards him, slowly, so slowly, that afterwards he wondered why he hadn't moved, run, sprinted after Tito. It seemed to Ossie that he had had all the time in the world. But Tito knew differently. He looked back to see Ossie standing frozen, a small fragile figure straight in the path of the bull who was coming at him full tilt down the field. He picked up a stick and ran, waving his arms at the thundering brute who paid no heed to him.

'Tir na n-Og!' Tito screamed. 'Help! Tir na n-Og, help!'

There was a second thunder of hooves. The white horse flashed by Tito and ran between the bull and the small child. Ossie's hypnotic state was broken. He turned and fled back over the fence. The bull, when he saw the white horse, turned sideways and careered to the other side of the field, his muzzle dribbling with foam, his mean eyes red with fury. Tir na n-Og came back to the children who were stretched out panting on the ground on the safe side of the fence. He nuzzled a weeping Ossie.

'I only wanted some milk,' Ossie said, in angry floods of tears. His lips were trembling and he was crying so hard that shudders were going right through his body. 'Why did he have to do that just because I wanted some milk?'

Tito tried to comfort him. 'Bulls are funny. They're very cross. Come on, we have to go.'

As they were about to get up to remount Tir na n-Og, they heard a voice behind them and turned to find an old man leaning on a stick and looking at them. He had white hair, was thin and a bit stooped, and was wearing an old tweed jacket; he had a dog at his heel.

'That ould bastard is pure bad!' he informed them, indicating the bull with a wave of his stick. 'There's many a good man he's had a go at. Ye shouldn't have set foot in that field.'

Ossie stared at him and started to cry again.

'My brother was only looking for a drop of milk, mister,' Tito said defensively.

The old man looked at the children and glanced at the horse. His face was full of the bemused astonishment of a man who had gone out to count his cattle and who had found children materialising out of the grass like leprechauns. But his face was also full of kindness and years of laughter.

'Sure if it's a drop of milk ye want, why didn't ye come to the house?'

Tito looked round. Beyond a small clump of trees, smoke was rising from a chimney.

'Ye can have all the milk ye want and a bit of bread and butter too if ye feel like it,' the man went on. As though the matter were decided, he turned towards the house. The dog came sniffing at the boys, licked their faces, wagging his tail exuberantly.

Tito and Ossie looked at each other and followed the old man in silence to his cottage. Tir na n-Og trotted discreetly behind.

The little house was thatched. There was an open fireplace with a black kettle hanging from a crane over a turf fire. There was a picture of the Sacred Heart with a small red lamp glowing in front of it. The house smelt of turf smoke. The kitchen was dim, the light being admitted through a half-door and a small window. On the table was a tall lamp with a glass chimney. The room contained neither radio nor television.

The man got out a tall brown jug from a cupboard and poured two mugs of milk. Then he took a cake of brown bread from a bin, cut two thick wedges, slapped butter on it and handed them to the children.

He sat down by the hearth and looked at them while they ate. 'Where would ye be from?' he asked.

Tito looked into the shrewd old eyes. 'Dublin.'

'Where are your people?'

Tito mumbled. He was stuffing his face so fast he couldn't talk.

His host cut some more bread and buttered it. 'Pitch in, pitch in,' he said and he reached for a pipe on the mantelshelf, took some plug tobacco and a box of matches from his pocket and commenced to light the pipe. There was silence until the pipe was lit, except for the sounds of the children gulping and the soft putt-putt of the pipe smoker lighting up.

'Are ye going far?'

The children stared at him.

'We're going to the wild west, mister,' Ossie blurted.

Tito gave his brother a dig in the ribs, but the old man nodded as though this did not surprise him. 'Ah, the west,' he said and his eyes assumed a misty, faraway look. 'They had great men in the west.'

Tito and Ossie exchanged glances.

'I was reading something the other day in the paper,' the man went on, 'about two children who stole a horse up above there in Dublin,' and he suddenly stared very hard at his two small guests. 'Ye wouldn't know anything about that, I suppose? A white horse?' he added helpfully.

Tito and Ossie prepared to bolt. But they saw that the man made no move to detain them and that the door was open. Not far from the door Tir na n-Og was grazing.

'We didn't steal it, mister,' Ossie cried. 'He's our horse. Grandpa gave him to us and they tried to take him away from us!'

The man nodded, drew a breath from his pipe and

expelled tobacco smoke into the kitchen. 'Sure in that case what are ye worried about?'

'He came from Tir na n-Og,' Ossie said. 'From the land under the sea. That's where he got his name.'

The man leaned back in his chair, clearly impressed. 'D' ye tell me! That's a long way to come. The Sidhe must have sent him, or maybe 'twas a spirit.' His eyes twinkled. 'Of course there's an easy way to find out,' he added, 'whether he's from Tir na n-Og or not.'

'What way is that?' Tito demanded suspiciously.

The old man lowered his voice and looked from one child to the other. 'It depends on how he's shod.' He stood up with a private laugh and the dog rose from his position by the hearth where he had been staring into the fire and followed his master outside.

Tir na n-Og looked up from his grazing as the man approached and danced away from his outstretched hands. 'It's all right, Tir na n-Og,' Ossie called.

Tito whispered furiously in his brother's ear, 'Why did you have to go and tell that ould fellow everything? I told you there's a reward for us!'

But Ossie was too excited to reply. He ran up to Tir na n-Og who was now permitting the old man to lift his leg and examine his hoof.

'Well, mister?' Tito demanded, standing with his hands on his hips. 'He's wearing shoes the same as every horse. But that doesn't mean he's not from Tir na n-Og!'

The old man appeared shaken. He stared at the hoof for a long time and then dropped the horse's leg as though it might burn him.

'I'll tell you this,' he whispered, trembling visibly, 'that horse was not shod by any blacksmith I ever knew.' He looked at the children with a changed expression. 'I'll give ye a bit of advice. Go off home like good children and let that horse be off about his business.'

Ossie drew close to Tir na n-Og and wrapped his arms round one of his legs. 'He'd only come after us.'

The old man had heard enough. 'Let ye be off with ye so. Off with ye now!'

The boys mounted Tir na n-Og and turned him towards the open fields.

'Don't tell them about us, mister,' Ossie cried as the horse moved away.

The old man raised his stick and turned back to the house. 'There was never an informer among the Touhys,' he muttered under his breath. 'Never! Not in two hundred years.' But he crossed himself as he regained his cottage and carefully bolted the door.

The sun was going down, a great orange ball sinking behind the hills. Ossie was now riding up front, holding the bridle, and when his efforts to pull up the horse proved fruitless he shouted out, 'Tir na n-Og, Tir na n-Og, you're pulling my arms out of their sockets.'

Tir na n-Og slowed. Ossie had been thinking about the Land of Eternal Youth that Grandpa had told them about. How would it work? he wondered – staying young for ever. Would it mean that time didn't pass, that it was just one long day that never ended?

'Maybe the sun doesn't set in Tir na n-Og,' he said. 'Maybe no one gets any older there because there are no nights. I don't want to grow up. I don't want to grow old like Oisin.'

'What?'

'I don't want to turn into dust!'

The sun disappeared behind the hills, leaving a lingering grey light which turned the mist into a shadowy presence. Tir na n-Og stopped.

Tito sighed. 'I'm getting down,' he said, ignoring Ossie's line of conversation. He didn't want to grow up either and the nearer he got to this inevitable state of affairs the less attractive and the more complicated it seemed.

He slid off Tir na n-Og's back, but found as he hit the ground that his legs would not support him; instead of the limbs made of muscle and bone that he was used to, he was now possessed of wobbling appendages which were no use to him whatever. This had never happened to him before. His mind raced to the story Grandpa had told of Oisin. It was happening to him, just like it had happened to Oisin.

'My legs are gone. . .'

'What?'

'My legs are jelly, I can't stand. I'm getting old,' he cried, his voice rising in a wail of genuine distress. 'My bones are going to dust!'

Ossie stared down at him in terror. 'Are you okay, Tito?' he quavered.

Tito tried again to rise and found that his legs would not support him. He fell back on the ground shouting, 'No, I'm getting old!'

Ossie's heart was thudding. He loved Tito. If Tito died, he was lost. He wouldn't know where to go. He wouldn't know what to do. And if Tito died and blew away in a handful of dust, it meant that he couldn't get off the horse either or the same would happen to him. He was doomed.

'No, no, Tito. No! Help! Mammy!' He raised his face and screamed, 'Mammy, Mammy, Mammy, Mammy, Mammy. . .' He screamed for all he was worth and the wind blew the words away.

Tito stared up at him, watching the trancelike way his little brother sat so still while he called for his mother into the wind. Tito scrambled up, finding that life had come back to his legs. It was only temporary paralysis due to non-stop riding. He could not bear what Ossie was doing and yelled at him, 'Ossie, stop it!'

Ossie moved, his voice trailed away and he stared shakily at his brother.

Tito leant against Tir na n-Og. 'I'm okay, Ossie.' After a while he asked in a very low voice, 'Mammy is dead. Why were you calling her?'

Ossie looked bewildered. 'I thought Papa would come, Tito,' he said, with the air of someone who didn't really know the answer.

Tito frowned. 'You thought Papa would come?'

'I miss Papa.'

'So do I,' Tito said.

They moved on in silence. Once or twice the white horse stumbled, but quickly righted himself. It was getting very dark.

'Tito.'

'What?'

'I'm afraid.'

Tito put a hand on his brother, but said nothing. When Ossie wanted to dismount he helped him, reassuring him that it was all right.

Tito and Ossie were now very tired. The hunger had begun to gnaw at them, a kind of ache in their bellies which would not go away. They wanted to lie down in a warm bed; they wanted a hot dinner. They knew that cowboys did not bow to these exigencies, but they wanted their beds and hot grub all the same.

They were walking alongside Tir na n-Og, and Tito was holding him by the bridle. Ossie looked around him at the countryside, so mysterious and dim in the twilight. It was cold. The clouds were low. The air was full of a threatening downpour. There were no warm beds or hot dinners in sight. There was no Papa.

'I don't want to stay out tonight!' Ossie announced suddenly.

Tito pulled the remains of the money out of his pocket. 'We've got four pounds and twenty-six pence. We can either eat or get a hotel. Which do you want?'

'I'm hungry,' Ossie said.

Tito shook his head. 'We can only have one.'

Night was beginning to fall; the rain was starting and an owl hooted suddenly in the woods nearby. Ossie looked nervously around. He couldn't see the owl, but he could make out a crow on a tree straight ahead, black except for one white marking. It was the same crow, head cocked and watching them. Why was it watching them?

'Let's get a hotel,' Ossie said, his voice quaking and trailing away to a whisper.

The nearest town was small, a collection of two thousand souls called Ballyhaney. It boasted four pubs, one small hotel, twelve shops, a cinema and a very large Catholic church built of limestone. It was night and there was little traffic.

Tito and Ossie walked down the street with what they could muster of a cowboy swagger. Tito saw the sign – Midlands Hotel – and approached the place carefully, saw that it had a bar and that it was not unlike the establishments favoured by cowboys. He told Ossie to stay outside and he went in and approached the clerk behind the counter in the lobby. The lobby gave directly on to the bar and the clerk had in fact two occupations, being clerk as occasion demanded and pint-puller the rest of the time. Now he stared at the youngster crossing into the lobby while he delivered himself of the punchline of a joke.

Tito came to the counter, thumped the bell and looked up at him.

'What do you want?'

'How much is it for a room?' Tito demanded.

'For whom?'

'Me and me brother.'

The clerk examined him. Here was the makings of a bit of crack.

'Are you travellers?'

Tito saw the faces of the men at the bar staring at him with amusement. He scowled. 'We're cowboys!' he said, raising his voice.

The clerk laughed. He turned to his customers at

the bar and their laughter filled the room.

'No, we don't take cowboys here,' he gasped, leaning back and howling with laughter at his own extraordinary wit. 'Get out before I plant me boot in your arse!'

Tito backed away. He did not want to let go of the fantasy, so he turned at the door, lifted his right hand, pointed his finger and pretended to shoot the clerk. Then he ran back into the rain.

While they sheltered from the rain in a side exit of the cinema, Tito concocted his master plan. Ossie could buy a ticket for the picture, hide under his seat before the lights came up at the end, and open the side door when everyone had left.

'You get into the pictures and when everyone leaves, open this door for me. Okay?'

Ossie was delighted. 'Have you got any money for popcorn?'

'We have to try and keep our money,' Tito said reluctantly.

'I'm starving,' Ossie piped, screwing up his face as though he was going to cry.

'Okay,' Tito said. 'Okay.'

Tito thought the film would never end. He leant against the wall in the lee of the building, out of sight of the main street, while the rain came down in torrents. The steam rose from Tir na n-Og's neck; the bridle became wet and unpleasantly slippery. Only the fact that they were out of the wind saved them from being completely saturated. Tito was glad of the warmth of the horse under his bottom. But his hands

were so cold they were turning blue. He imagined
Ossie in the warm cinema, watching the film and
munching popcorn and after a while he began to feel
very sorry for himself.

Eventually, when he had begun to feel that he was
beyond human succour, the cinema emptied, the side
door opened and Ossie appeared.

'Where were you?' Tito demanded, glad that he
was still able to speak.

'Come in quick,' Ossie whispered urgently. 'Oh
Tito, you should have seen it, it was great!'

'Is that right?' Tito said. 'Well it wasn't so great out
here!'

Tito brought Tir na n-Og through the door and
then he bolted it securely behind him. Bliss! He was in
a warm place out of the rain. Ossie beckoned the way
to the foyer and Tito and Tir na n-Og followed, the
latter's hooves clopping softly on the carpet. Ossie
touched a switch and the foyer was flooded with light.
Tito's eyes widened. There before him was the
promised land: popcorn, sweets, chocolate, a Coca-
Cola fountain.

He got the popcorn machine open, shovelled out a
heap of the contents for Tir na n-Og, stuffing his own
face at the same time. And then he found a plastic
bucket in a closet and filled it with Coke for the horse.
Tir na n-Og slurped greedily and when he was offered
a bar of chocolate he demolished it at once.

The children were very happy. Tito took off his wet
jacket and put it over a radiator which was still warm.
Then they got into the projection room, threw every
switch they could find until they got the machine

working. Having managed by this process of elimination to discover the secrets of the cinema, they turned the unnecessary lights off again and settled down to watch the film. There was no doubt about it, this was their best night on the road.

They were snug and safe when the police car went by outside, patrolling the town, looking for two children on a white horse.

Papa was silent for the first part of the journey. He tasted the hint of rain in the air and the smell of the earth. He watched the rise and fall of the land, the shifting of the light, the movement of the birds. His horse flung him around at the trot but he sat well down into the canter, letting the rhythm take him. After a while he felt that he had never left the old life. He felt its peace claim him, the sense of belonging to something great and real, something that really mattered.

As he rode the wind whipped round his ears; his nose ran at the gallop and the world around became a blur as the sense of speed subsumed him, a sense he never got from a motor car. And there was also, although he blocked any acknowledgement of it, the magic of seeing from his peripheral vision Kathleen's red hair stream behind her in the breeze.

They lived, as Tito and Ossie did not, off the land. Papa made a catapult from a piece of old tyre tube and a strong cleft stick which he broke from a tree. This enabled him to take down a few rabbits, which they cooked over their evening fires. Barreller tickled trout and brought them back to the camp with much pride. Were it not for the serious nature of their journey, the pleasure in it would have made them linger.

'Do you remember the old days?' Papa asked Kathleen when he came back with two rabbits for supper. 'Do you remember how we used to run wild? Do you remember the time we jumped the river and you fell in?'

Kathleen smiled. She had deliberately refrained from alluding to the past, to their intertwined history, to their childhood, to their adolescent love. Let him bring it up if he wanted to.

'I remember,' she said. 'I remember everything.'

Papa turned carefully to look at her. Into his mind flashed the image of a breathless teenage Kathleen pinned against a tree trunk offering him her soft red mouth.

The trio moved speedily for the first part of the journey. The radio news had given them the lead they needed: a shopkeeper from the village of Rathclery in County Roscommon had informed the police that one of the children had been in his shop. They got there at night and camped a good distance from the road, watching out for the police.

In the morning, which was clear and cold, they found the boys' camp. Kathleen was a good tracker. Papa saw the care with which she watched out for clues, broken twigs, tamped-down grass, a white horse hair on a bush, a trail of horse hooves in a muddy place. The hoof marks seemed to astonish her.

'How was that horse shod?' she asked in a very

careful voice and Papa had to admit that he didn't know.

'Why do you ask?'

She looked up at him, squinting against the morning light. 'Because there's no nails, John Riley. How do you hold a shoe on a horse without nails?'

For the first time Papa felt the hairs on the nape of his neck stir a little, and a shiver went through him as though it had become suddenly cold. 'What do you make of it, Kathleen?'

But Kathleen was not forthcoming and merely shook her head. Barreller, who was patient and cheerful, and who distrusted any suggestion that the escapade on the white horse was anything other than a childish prank, suggested that the fellow who'd taken the horse to make a showjumper of him must have developed some newfangled methods of shoeing a horse.

Kathleen just looked at him. 'They've a blanket with them, anyway,' she said, pointing to the spot in the shelter of the old castle wall where the boys had slept and where it was evident from the flattened grass that someone or something had lain there.

'Sure that could have been anyone, a courting couple – it could have been a cow,' Barreller offered and Kathleen smiled and shook her head. She pointed to the horse manure and Barreller laughed. She pointed to a sward of grass. Barreller looked puzzled until she leaned down and with a stick raised up a sod of earth about a foot square. It had been cut out of the ground and replaced. She put her hand underneath it and withdrew a charred piece of wood, part of the remains of the fire, and a scrap of what might have been a tin can.

'They've gone about six hours,' she said. She turned to Papa. 'Your two boys seem to know the tricks of the traveller.'

'Who taught them?' Barreller asked.

Papa saw the face of his father-in-law in his mind's eye. 'Their ould codger of a grandfather!' he answered angrily. 'He had them all jizzed up with the old ways and the old stories, until he turned their heads! Why do you think they went off on the road?'

Kathleen looked at him strangely. 'Is that why you think they went away?' she asked in a low voice with just a trace of mockery. 'Their grandfather's stories?'

'Whyever else would they go?'

She looked into his eyes. He saw that hers were red-brown, narrowed in private speculation, and that they hardly looked at him at all, but rather through him and beyond him.

'Maybe they were sent for, John Riley.'

He started. 'What do you mean, Kathleen?' but she merely turned and looked back at the tracks in the damp grass.

'They're headed due west!' she murmured. 'If we hurry we may be in luck.'

Later, when the two men were busy with the horses after their midday meal, Kathleen walked away from them and got out the tarot pack, silently dealing out the cards and staring at them in fascinated disbelief. She shuffled them again and again as if she was dreaming.

As they continued on their way, Papa asked her to

explain what she had said. 'What did you mean when you said they may have been sent for? What class of a thing was that to say?'

'If it bothers you, ignore it,' she softly.

Papa held her eyes. 'It bothers me,' he said sternly, 'but I will not ignore it.'

'Haven't you heard of a Sending?' Kathleen asked, her voice very quiet.

Papa's face tightened. He saw the long silken lashes, the way the afternoon sunlight caught the tawny irises. 'Bloody superstition!' he said.

She raised an eyebrow, smiled. 'Maybe. And what is superstition but belief. And don't you know anything about what belief does to the twisting threads of fate?' She paused. 'I read the cards, John Riley, and they do not lie to me!'

Papa cleared his throat with a deprecating sound. 'Superstition,' he said, 'is superstition.'

Kathleen glanced at him and saw the war in him, shrugged and looked away.

'What did you see?' he asked almost angrily.

She stared into his face. It was perfectly serious. 'So much depends on the order of the cards as they fall,' she murmured. 'You know this. But I will tell you that I have seen the Fool and the Fallen Tower together and also Death.'

Papa made a noise deep in his throat and urged his horse to a canter.

When Papa and Kathleen and Barreller came to Ballyhaney, they came in a downpour. It was as though the floodgates of heaven had been opened and every drop dammed up since the beginning of time was being dumped on the world. The men wore wide-brimmed hats and Kathleen wore a rainproof cloak with a hood, and the water streamed off them and down their horses' sides. They passed the Midlands Hotel and the Savoy cinema, unaware that the two boys and their horse were snug inside the cinema, eating popcorn and watching the film. Their horses' hooves clattered on the deserted wet street. It was late and there were few signs of life.

The travellers were hungry and tired and when they saw the sign above the fish and chip shop, they stopped the horses, tethered them to a lamp post and entered the shop. The girl behind the counter looked at them nervously. In a corner were three bored locals who were finishing their chips. Each of them wished he belonged to Dublin or London or Timbuctoo, anywhere away from Ballyhaney and the parish priest and the rain.

The locals stared at the travellers as Papa placed the orders. The fluorescent light made them blink, showed up the hollows of fatigue on their faces.

'Begod lads, it's the cowboys,' one of the locals suddenly commented, staring at the three tired people before the counter.

'You're wrong, Tommo, it's the Indians,' said another.

'It's the last of the Mohicans,' offered the third with a cackle.

Kathleen felt Papa tense beside her, felt Barreller's disquiet. But neither of them moved and they waited quietly for the assistant who had fled to the room behind the shop, emerging with the proprietor.

'Are you going to serve them, Rico?' one of the local louts demanded, and Rico, who had come all the way from Naples a thousand years before when he was eighteen, recognised trouble.

'No trouble here, lads, no trouble,' he said in a beseeching voice.

'There'll be no trouble from us,' Papa murmured. Kathleen, as though oblivious of the flexing of male biceps around her, took off her hood and shook her hair loose. The locals stared at her.

'One of them's a squaw, lads,' came the whisper, a loud whisper.

There was laughter.

'Cross me palm with silver, Tonto,' Tommo said mincingly.

The provocation went on. The travellers did not appear to hear.

'Ah now, lads,' Rico said looking at the three men in the corner. 'Give it a rest. They're doing no harm.'

'Don't you know that these are knackers, Rico?' came the voice of Tommo, a plump, peeved fellow who was old enough to have known better, but who longed for anything at all to break the tedium of Saturday night in a downpour with nothing to look forward to except tomorrow's tedium in what was quite likely to be another downpour. In a way he envied the travellers their lives of movement, their contempt for the strictures which had him trapped. He too would have liked to have taken off into the night on horseback with a lovely slim woman with long red hair.

Kathleen turned on Tommo, saw the unwholesome colour, the soft belly, the disappointed face.

'My people were poets and seers on the roads of Ireland when yours were still in the trees picking the lice out of their fur,' she said. She said it reasonably, as the simple truth, and her voice, which was low and deep, filled the little shop.

There was silence. The squaw had answered back and what was more she had got him in the soft underbelly of his pride.

'Where's your child?' he demanded. 'I never met a tinker woman without a baby.'

'She must be a virgin so,' said another with a snigger.

Barreller held on to Papa's arms.

'She doesn't look like a virgin,' Tommo said knowingly. He glanced at Papa and Barreller, but their profiles gave nothing away and they did not turn to look at their tormentors. Tommo was heartened by this. 'Are the knackers too drunk to look after you?' he asked on a high note of licence.

Kathleen turned, walked towards Tommo who shrank back from her towards the wall. She looked into his eyes and then reached for his hand, turning up the palm. Tommo found himself unable to react. He sat as though he had been frozen while Kathleen studied the palm.

'You've a short life line,' she said slowly, studying the hand before her, 'and no heart at all.' Tommo stared at her, his pupils dilating. Fear, of a short life, of a tinker's curse, of a pointless death, invaded him, terrified him.

'Stay out of here, you tinker's whore,' he shouted, standing up and raising his hand to strike her.

Papa turned. He moved with speed and certainty, grabbed the raised arm and brought it down suddenly so that Tommo cried out in pain. Then he picked him up. Barreller, meanwhile, grabbed the other two youths and held them like children in the grip of his huge arms.

Tommo felt his head being banged off the wall, felt himself being lifted up and dropped like a sack of potatoes, felt the kick to his rib cage, heard the woman shout, 'No, John, no; he's not worth it!' and then the shop door opened and the travellers had gone.

Papa walked out into the rain. He lifted his face to the night sky, to the low black clouds which covered the sky like a pall. And then he smiled. Kathleen pulled her hood back over her head, glanced at him and smiled too.

Later, in their makeshift tent, Papa woke with a start and a shout. He sat up, breathing heavily, his heart racing. Beside him was Barreller and on the other side of Barreller lay Kathleen who could not sleep. Barreller was snoring, light little snores which trembled in the air. Kathleen sometimes gave him a sharp knuckle in the ribs and then the snores would change pitch for a while, or he would say, 'What, what?' from the depths of his sleep. Occasionally he stopped for a few minutes before starting up again. Now she looked over at Papa.

'Take it easy, John,' she said.

Papa drew a deep breath. 'I had a terrible dream. Will they take the children away from me, Kathleen?'

'It was only a dream,' Kathleen said, and paused, measuring the words as they dropped into the silence. 'They need a mother.'

Papa heard the words, acknowledged the truth of them. 'I know,' he said. After a while he added, 'Why did you leave your husband, Kathleen?'

She sighed in the darkness. 'He didn't want to be part of us no more, of the tribe. He wanted his slippers by the fireplace at night.'

'Did you ever see him again?'

'I met him in England one time. He was happy enough, but he couldn't look me in the eye.'

She heard Papa move, as though he turned towards her in the darkness.

'He had the smile of a child when I married him, John.'

Papa could see her face. It was very pale in the darkness.

'What keeps you on the road, Kathleen?'

'What keeps me on the road? Because we're all out together – everyone for each other. Out there,' she gestured with her hand to the world of settled people beyond the tent, 'you're alore, you're part of nothing!'

Papa smiled. There was fire in this woman. He liked to see the fire in her. He remembered it well, but he knew too that once, long ago, he had seen it die.

'Good to see you smile, John,' she said.

At this point Barreller's snores stopped. He gave a kind of whistling sound instead. 'Two chips and three spaghettis please,' he growled.

Kathleen clamped her hand over her mouth to stifle the shriek of laughter and Papa turned, spluttering, and buried his roar of laughter in the crook of his arm. When he had contained himself he raised his head and looked across the sleeping body of his friend. He slowly lifted his right hand and reached across until he touched Kathleen's face. She did not move.

'I don't deserve you, Kathleen,' he said. 'But thank you.'

At home in the Towers, Birdie had just received a walloping. Her father had belted her a few times and had gone off to the pub. The men from the Drug Squad had come back and her da knew everything. They said they had established that the pills were really sweets, that she wasn't selling drugs; the people in the laboratory had tested them. But they warned her not to do it again and told her to give the money back to the people she had deceived.

Birdie was terrified. She was sore from her beating, her ma was mad with her and Angela had a smirk on her face, apparently delighted that her elder sister was in the dog house. Birdie wished she had a room of her own where she could get away from the lot of them. She hadn't the slightest intention of giving the money back to the women who had bought the 'pills' from her. They'd kill her. The police wanted to know where the money was, but she said she'd spent it. This was untrue, because she had put the money into the hole in the wardrobe.

Birdie knew the only thing to do was to run away. She had fifty quid and that was enough to get her to England. She'd be able to get a job there, doing waitressing or something. So when her mother was finished telling her off, Birdie went to her room. Angela was there reading a comic.

'Get out,' Birdie said.

Angela smiled at her archly. The balance of power had shifted and she was going to make the best of it.

'I won't!'

'Get out or I'll kill you!'

Angela eyed her big sister carefully. She looked like she meant it. Her face was streaked with tears and she was pale and tense. Angela stood up and sidled out of the room. When she was gone, Birdie put a chair against the door and went to the hole in the wardrobe. She put her hand in, moved it around in disbelief. The hole was empty; the money was gone.

She ran out after Angela, beckoned her to come into the room.

'Did you take my money?'

Angela's eyes widened. 'What money?'

'The money I had in the wardrobe.'

Angela shook her head, ignorance written all over her. Birdie wondered if she should believe her. And then she thought of her father and the red face of him and the way he had money recently for drink, lots of it.

She drew a deep breath and sat on the edge of her bunk. 'It's Da!' she whispered.

What was she going to do? She was trapped. Ma was pregnant again; there would be another baby to mind. She looked at her school bag and thought about what Grandpa Ward had said to her. She thought of her schoolbooks and how boring they were. Jaysus, but her own life just lately had been more exciting, what with the Drug Squad and Tito and Ossie rescuing Tir na n-Og and being on the telly an' all. Maybe she should write about that, it would be more like a real book than schoolbooks. Maybe she could sell the writing to a magazine and get money that way – or even a proper book, for the library and such. That wouldn't be boring at all. She might get lots of money for that. She dragged her school bag from the corner, pulled out a copybook and a biro and lay down on the bed. She would write it as if it were a letter to Tito . . .

Grandpa felt the weariness in his bones. He had been hours on the road and old Dan was beginning to flag, twitching his ears interrogatively from time to time as much as to say, 'Why can't we have a rest? Where are we off to in such a hurry?' Grandpa had made him trot a good deal and old Dan felt he was getting a bit too old for it. A nice sedate walk, with plenty of stops for a graze and a drink and a bit of a chat, was what he was used to. Not that Dan could talk, but he appreciated Grandpa's company and affection and he liked being talked to.

Grandpa's mind was in turmoil. He desperately needed to think; he needed also to sleep, but he could do neither. The cards had only indicated that no human agency could touch the children. But this dark fellow who was so interested in them, what of him? Why was he so interested in the children? 'Who said I was interested in the horse?' he had whispered in his soft mocking voice. Grandpa tried to marshal the facts: Catspaw was a black magician; he had said he would find them and Grandpa knew he could take this as fact. The question was who would find them first? Papa, who had gone back to the tribe for help, or that creature? Or maybe even the garda. The old man slapped the reins on Dan's rump, but the horse only quickened his pace marginally. His head was drooping and Grandpa could hear that his breathing was laboured.

'I'm an old fool,' he whispered to the horse. 'I'm full of blather and that's all I'm good for!' Dan snorted in disagreement. He plodded on, his movements saying that Grandpa was not an old fool, just a man who expected too much of his horse.

Grandpa looked up at the sky, saw the clouds, saw the evening shadows stretch out lazily over the fields, heard the rattle of the caravan wheels over the road. This is too slow, he thought. But even if I had one of those helicopter yokes, what good could I do? The boys have a horse with them that should be able to protect them. But then another part of his mind whispered, 'But can it protect them from Catspaw?'

He groaned. 'My fault, my fault! All my fault!' He remembered the morning he first saw the animal on the beach; he should not have left it behind with the children in the Towers. 'Were you mad?' he asked himself out loud. 'Didn't you know there was no one to mind those kids, that their father is useless? You should have stayed behind with them!'

He leant against the half-door, felt the wood under his hand. The wheels hit another pothole and the caravan juddered. But Grandpa's self-interrogation continued: 'What could I have done for them if I had stayed?'

He shook his head. He knew the answer. He could have watched over them so that this business with the horse would never have happened. But he had not watched over them. And now there was no way he could trace them himself. He did not know where Papa was. He had no one he could warn of the danger the children were in. He needed help.

He let Dan amble on for another mile or so and then he reined him in where a stretch of the long acre was wide and full of grass, got down, unharnessed him and hobbled him. He knew where he could find help, but it would come at a price.

Old Dan bent his head to graze, wrenched mouthfuls of grass with a tearing sound, lifted his head to munch and regarded his master quizzically. Usually Grandpa whistled, made a fire, put down his old black kettle, and went about preparing himself some supper. But not this evening. Instead, the old man was silent and there was fear in his eyes.

Chapter Fourteen

Tito and Ossie and Tir na n-Og spent a happy night in the cinema. Ossie was asleep by the time the film was over and although it was a Western, Tito too found that he could not keep his eyes open. Even Tir na n-Og lay down for a change and rolled and stretched out on the carpet.

In the morning the children were awakened by the sound of doors opening and closing, the rattle of a bucket and mop and the sound of a Hoover being dragged from its hiding place in the foyer closet and plugged in. Mrs O'Rourke in a wrap-around apron, curlers in her hair, was about to start the morning's cleaning. She leant over into the closet to pick up the polishing rags and as she did so Tir na n-Og padded up behind her, snorting gently. She thought it must be Una, the other cleaner.

'Still got that ould cold?' she enquired, her head still in the closet. Tir na n-Og was hungry. The popcorn was all gone and he thought Mrs O'Rourke might have a lump of sugar or some chocolate in her pocket, so he rubbed her bottom with a quivering lip.

The cleaning lady shot up, turned and looked straight into the horse's eyes.

'Jesus, Mary and Holy Saint Joseph,' she howled. 'Go way outta that!' and she ran for the door and out into the street, while Tir na n-Og gazed after her in puzzled disappointment.

Mrs O'Rourke's howling alerted Tito and Ossie to the fact that hanging around any longer would be the second best plan. They looked down from the balcony where they had slept and saw Tir na n-Og wander back into the parterre.

'Come here, Tir na n-Og,' Ossie hissed and the white horse positioned himself obligingly while the two boys jumped down onto his back from the balcony. The balcony was not very high and the horse stood very still but as, one after the other, they hit the horse's back with a thump, it seemed to both Tito and Ossie that now they had finally graduated in the school of Wild Western proficiency.

Tir na n-Og made for the emergency exit, through which he had entered the place the night before, and in no time horse and riders were clattering down the street, Ossie's euphoric voice shouting, 'Heigh-ho, Silver! Away!'

However, such had been Mrs O'Rourke's success in alerting the authorities that there was something queer, involving a horse, going on in the cinema, that the children's escape was not unimpeded. They met a police car coming to investigate; there was a screech of tyres, the sound of running feet and the children turned to see the boys in blue in hot pursuit. In front of them another squad car materialised. Tir na n-Og swerved round the police and down a side street, and from there to the outskirts of the town.

The children found that shaking off the police was no light task. Inspector Bolger, who had been immediately advised that the white horse had been found, arrived in jig time and soon the children found that they had quite a posse on their tail. In panic Tito steered Tir na n-Og down another side street, which turned out to be a cul-de-sac. Before them, at the end of the short street, was a concrete wall as high as a house. The street itself was lined with terraced houses.

'How did we get into this mess?' Tito demanded and Ossie replied petulantly that it wasn't his fault. Behind them the police cars blocked the entrance to the street. It looked as though the game was up.

Bolger came striding down the street, grinning now as he saw his quarry helpless and cornered. But he reckoned without the prompt action of a girl who lived in one of the houses and had seen everything from her front window. She was aware, like the rest of the country, that a valuable white horse had been stolen by children, and in solidarity with the world of children she ran to open the front door.

'Come in here,' she hissed and Bolger rushed forward as he saw his quarry disappear through the open front door of a house. He reached it too late. The door was firmly shut in his face and all he heard was a small voice telling him to go away. 'Go away or I'll report you!' the child said to him through the letter box.

'I'm the police, open the door,' Bolger said, pounding on it, but to no avail. The child stood stubbornly behind her door eating her knuckle. She didn't give a straw for the police. She knew she was a kid and that they couldn't touch her.

Meanwhile Tir na n-Og surprised the rest of the family who were in the kitchen. The table was set and breakfast was being prepared. The horse clopped through the small room and the astonished owner ran to open the back door at Tito's behest. 'He'll wreck the place if you don't,' Tito informed him. 'Sorry for barging in.' Then he looked at the woman of the house. 'Will you give us some food, missus?' This was attended to with alacrity, cuts of bread and marmalade were thrust into the children's hands and then they surged forward out of the back door, through the garden and up into the fields behind.

Bolger, feeling that he would explode with rage, stood impotently outside the front door of the house while the little girl continued to survey him through the letter box. By the time the child's father came to open the door, the runaways were well gone.

'I'll have you up for obstructing the police!' Bolger roared and the man indicated such genuine bewilderment that the inspector turned aside, muttering something to himself about useless bloody gobdaws and the state of the country.

One of his guards rushed up with a radio. 'It's the super looking for you, sir.'

Bolger ground his teeth. 'Tell him I've gone, that I've signed off,' he said.

Tir na n-Og seemed to have sprouted wings. He sped across country with the children clinging to his back.

'I'm bleedin' freezing!' Ossie announced when he got his breath back.

'So am I,' Tito said.

'Tito?'

'What?'

'Why do you think Oisin came back?'

Tito thought for a moment. 'Maybe he was lonely.'

'Are you lonely?' Ossie demanded.

'No,' Tito lied. 'Are you?'

Ossie sighed. The corners of his small mouth turned down. 'Not much,' he said in a small voice. Then he added, 'Tito?'

'What?'

'What happened to his dust?'

'What dust?'

'Oisin's dust.'

Tito groaned silently. 'I suppose it just blew away to nothing.'

On they went. The clouds were massing in the west, promising more rain. The cold was eating at their hands. After a while Ossie announced suddenly, 'Let's go home, Tito!'

'Why?'

'I miss Papa. I'm hungry. Let's go home for one night. We'll be cowboys tomorrow.'

Tito turned to look at his brother. He tried to maintain a judicial expression, but he had been longing for some time to suggest precisely the same thing. Now he weighed the pros and cons as a big brother should, and said, 'Okay.' He pulled on the right rein to turn Tir na n-Og, but the horse behaved as though he had got his tongue over the bit. 'Turn, Tir na n-Og, turn,' he shouted.

'He'll only go towards where the sun goes down,' came Ossie's small voice behind him. The boys kicked and Tito pulled on the rein, but Tir na n-Og only became more obdurate, rearing up and whinnying. The children screamed.

'Tir na n-Og, stop!' shouted Ossie. 'Turn back, Tir na n-Og. We want to go home!'

But the horse which had always been amenable to their requirements now seemed to have undergone a complete change of attitude. Tir na n-Og gathered himself up and galloped to the west.

Exhaustion began to grip the two boys. It seeped up into their heads and down into their bones and they just held on, aware for the first time in a vague kind of way that this horse had an agenda of his own and that they were simply passengers being carried towards a destiny they no longer had the energy to resist. They trusted the horse but they feared, as only children fear, the forces of law and the status quo closing around them. So they went towards their destiny, wherever it might be, if it would only let them shut down their minds for a while and rest.

The Shannon came as a surprise, a great spreading river, with no end to it as far as the eye could see. It flowed broad and wide, whispering and murmuring and lapping along the edges and among the reeds. The children came to it in the evening of a day which had included not only the escape from the village of Ballyhaney, but also hiding in copses, sprints across open stretches of country and the knowledge that they were utterly lost. They were unaware that this was the longest river in both Britain and Ireland, that it divided the west of Ireland from the rest of the country; but they did realise, as soon as they saw it, that they had a formidable obstacle ahead of them.

They looked at it in dismay; they would have to find a bridge. It was too big a river to try to cross on Tir na n-Og's back; the current could easily sweep either or both of them away and neither of them could swim. They dismounted and watched for a while from the cover of a thicket; there were a few pleasure cruisers far out on the water and a scattering of tiny reed islands; they heard the lonely cry of a moorhen. The sky and the clouds were reflected in the water and on every side the flat land stretched away in varying hues of green to the infinity of the horizon.

The children covered Tir na n-Og's back with the brown blanket and led him along the river bank by the bridle. After a while they saw, some distance ahead of them, a village beside which an old cut stone bridge stretched out over the Shannon. On the other side of the river, watching the approaches to the bridge, was an old fort, its stone walls and emplacement points for cannon still intact. This thrilled the children. They hid in the shadow of some trees while they made up their minds as to what to do. They tethered Tir na n-Og and slid forward on their bellies, hidden by the rushes, in an attempt to ascertain the extent to which the bridge was watched.

'If you open your mouth,' Tito informed his little brother, 'I'll kill you!'

Ossie gave him the look of someone who had been seriously offended; he was quiet for a moment or two until he could contain himself no longer.

'That old fort place is empty,' he whispered. 'There's no soldiers in it!'

'Shut your head,' Tito hissed back. 'It may be empty, but the police cars on this side of the bridge are not!'

Ossie drew his breath in sharply. 'I can't see any. How do you know there are police cars there, Tito?'

Tito was feeling quite proud of himself. The bridge looked innocuous enough from their vantage point, but if you looked under the arch of the bridge you saw the reflection in the water of the blue cars parked by the river on the near side with GARDA written on them, albeit upside down in the water. He pointed this out to Ossie with a minimum of ceremony, clamping his hand over his brother's mouth as he spoke. Ossie bit him.

'Don't do that!' he said peevishly when Tito snatched his hand back. 'You make me think I'm going to suffocate! Anyway, your hands are filthy dirty and taste of horse.'

Tito pursed his mouth and examined the pink teeth marks on his grimy palm. 'Look,' he hissed furiously, 'I'm going home if you won't do what I tell you! I don't care if I have to walk. They'll hear you if you open your little squeaky gob again.'

Ossie stared at him in fury. 'It's not a squeaky gob!'

Tito's response was to clamp his hand over Ossie's face once more. He saw a garda appear on the bridge, look down onto the river and survey the countryside through a pair of binoculars. Tito put a finger to his lips, looked at his brother meaningfully and they both crept away to the shade of the trees where Tir na n-Og was placidly grazing.

'What are we going to do, Tir na n-Og?' Ossie whispered to the horse. 'They're watching the bridge.' He indicated the broad sweep of the river. 'Do you think you could carry us across?'

Tito wanted to scream. 'We can't do that! Just shut up and let me think.'

Ossie looked as if he was going to cry. He sat down, or rather crumpled onto the ground and leaned against Tir na n-Og's grazing head, stroking him and whispering to him.

'I'm tired,' he said. 'I'm so tired I want to go to sleep for ever.' He put his head down on his arm and when Tito looked at him next, his small face was tucked into the crook of his arm and he was sound asleep.

Tito sat and watched the shadows in the river. He thought of the fish who lived there in deep, dark pools, fish who never had to worry. He watched the swallows swooping and soaring above the water; they didn't have any worries either. He thought of the people in the nearby village who hadn't a real bother between them. He wondered why all the worry in the world belonged to Tito. A little voice in his head prompted him to wake Ossie, walk away and leave this white horse behind them. Maybe they could claim the reward themselves! Another, darker, voice prompted him to leave both horse and Ossie. He could disappear, never be seen again, and he could still claim the reward. Papa wouldn't miss him and Ossie didn't deserve him.

He wondered what his mother would think of her children if she could see them. She would probably dote on Ossie, like Grandpa did, and not take any heed of him. 'Do you remember me, Mammy?' he whispered to the air. There was no response. Tears of self-pity gathered in his eyes. 'I bet you don't remember me.'

But Tito knew that, no matter what dark promptings he had, he could not leave Ossie and he knew that Ossie would never leave the horse. He could not make up his mind what was the best plan. He thought they should wait until night and try to cross the river at another bridge. But then he realised that all the bridges would probably be patrolled, just as this one was. How long was this river? he wondered. He had worked out, from the sun, that it was flowing from north to south. Should they try to follow it north and continue westwards above the point where it rose? Where did it rise? He tried to remember geography classes in school. He wished now he'd paid attention to some of them. He hadn't had many.

Anyway, he thought, we'll stick together. He looked at Tir na n-Og and saw that the horse was watching him from inscrutable black eyes. 'We'll stick together, isn't that right?' he repeated aloud, but the horse chewed grass with a grinding sideways motion and did not answer.

It was still daylight when he heard a voice on the boreen, an overgrown former thoroughfare which they had followed for a short while when they first saw the river. He positioned Tir na n-Og so that he could not be readily seen by whoever was passing by. Then he crept to the hedgerow bordering the boreen and saw a traveller's caravan approach, an old barrel-topped caravan, like Grandpa's. But it was not his grandfather who was driving; it was an old woman in a black skirt and shawl, her hair white and shining and flowing down her back. She stopped, got down from the caravan and approached her pony. She ran her hands down the animal's legs, lingered on one leg, examined the hoof.

'Lame!' she exclaimed, putting her hands on her hips and looking the animal in the eye. ' 'Tis yourself has the great sense of timing!'

The pony, a black and white skewbald, moved its ears while she spoke to it and sneered at her with its big rubbery lips.

Tito wanted to laugh. He hadn't had a good laugh in ages and some kind of giggle must have escaped him, for the old woman turned and in a jiffy was gazing at him through the hedgerow.

'Get out of there, young fellow,' she cried, 'and help an old woman instead of sniggering.'

Tito came out sheepishly, picking twigs and bits of brambles from his clothes. He felt the fierce scrutiny of the old sunken eyes, eyes that took him in from top to toe. He looked back at her brazenly.

'Ha,' said the old woman. 'Half starved and bold as brass! But can you cure a lame horse, young fellow?'

Tito shook his head.

'Maybe you have a horse you could lend an old woman?'

Tito immediately had the sensation that things were slipping out of his control. He tried not to move his head, because he did not by word or gesture want to give away the presence of Ossie and Tir na n-Og in the copse behind him by the river bank.

But to no avail. The woman narrowed her eyes and stared beyond him.

'Good boy yourself,' she said. 'You brought me a horse!'

Tito cursed himself silently as he followed the crone to the river bank. This ould one represented trouble, he thought. Ossie was still asleep and Tir na n-Og was still placidly chewing, although the grass was eaten down to the ground all around him.

The woman looked down at Ossie, a strange expression on her face. Ossie's mouth was open, revealing a gap where he had lost a milk tooth. Then, without as much as a by your leave, she began to untie Tir na n-Og from the tree.

Tito rushed forward. 'That's our horse, missus!'

The woman continued what she was doing. 'Did I say it wasn't?'

Tito put his hand on the bridle. 'You can't have our horse!'

Her eyes were on him, and when he met them it felt as though everything had become silent and the energy had left his limbs and he knew he could not prevent her from taking the horse if she wanted to.

'Come along,' she said tersely. 'Bring the little one and follow me.'

Tito stirred Ossie with the toe of his shoe. 'Get up, little one!'

Ossie woke, hissed in instant belligerence, 'What did you call me?' and then he saw that Tir na n-Og was being led away by a stranger. He jumped up and ran after them. 'You can't take Tir na n-Og.'

She laughed, a soft chuckle. 'No one can "take" this horse, child,' she said drily. 'But the two of you kids might be glad of soft blankets this evening and a safe conduct into the west.'

'Who are you, missus?'

She chuckled again. 'I've many names and many faces.'

When they got to the caravan, the woman brought out a bowl and a rag and began to apply blacking from the bowl onto Tir na n-Og.

'She's ruining him,' Ossie wailed as he saw the big black patches appear on Tir na n-Og's coat and down one side of his aristocratic face. 'Stop her, Tito!'

But Tito was silent and was beginning to smile.

The old woman pointed to the skewbald pony in the traces. 'In a minute you won't know them apart. And then we'll be over the bridge and the Rozzers will never know!'

Tito stood still in admiration. 'Why do you want to help us, missus?'

'I need a horse and you need to cross the river. They're watching for ye at all the bridges.'

A short time later a battered barrel-topped caravan driven by an old woman approached the stone bridge. The caravan was drawn by a black and white skewbald and another one, seemingly lame, was tied behind. A garda appeared on the bridge as the caravan approached and put up his hand to stop it.

His comrade watched from the police car.

'Where are you going, ma'am?'

'Wherever the road leads me!'

He stared at her, at the long silver hair and the weathered face and the eyes like gimlets.

'You didn't see two children riding a white horse?'

She gave the matter some thought. 'Which children would that be now?' she enquired. 'There was a child on a white pony beyond in Tullamore and there were other children with ponies in Birr for a class of a gymkhana. But, two children on a horse . . .' She pursed her lips and frowned doubtfully.

The garda was about to signal her to move on, but she raised her left hand in sudden recollection: 'Wait! Unless ye mean that ould white beast I saw back in Roscrea . . .'

The guard's eyes brightened. He took out his notebook. 'Where exactly was that, ma'am?'

''Twould be the far side of Roscrea; but there were three children and a cat up on the back of him.'

The garda sighed and shut his notebook with a snap. His eyes dwelt for a moment on the caravan, rested on the closed half-door.

'What have you got in there?'

She raised her eyebrows. 'Me bed and me table and me chair. Do ye want to come in and I'll read yer palm for ye?'

He met her eyes and then looked quickly away. 'No thanks,' he muttered. He stood back and the caravan rumbled on its way, over the bridge and down the road on the other side of the river, taking the first right turn towards the west.

When they stopped as the evening shadows fell, Ossie pulled at the woman's sleeve and pointed to a crow standing watching them on a tree by the roadside.

'That bird has been following us, missus,' he confided in tones calculated to impress.

Tito turned to see the offending creature and glanced apologetically at the woman. 'Don't be such a little eejit, Ossie,' he said. 'The country is black with crows.'

But the old woman did not seem amused. She turned to look at the bird sitting there above them, its black head and cruel yellow beak turned sideways and its glittering eye fixed on them. Her eyes narrowed and she began to mutter to herself. 'Ah, Catspaw,' she whispered, 'is it your old self that's in it?' and she bent and picked up a stone, lobbed it upwards, but the bird had already taken off in flight. The stone crashed through the foliage and its target sustained only a glancing blow. The creature squawked and continued on its way, but a black feather fell from it to the ground.

'Fetch that feather,' the old woman commanded and Ossie ran to find it. Tito followed him, but they could not locate it.

'Will you stop going on about that bird,' Tito said, plainly embarrassed. 'Your woman will think you're mental!'

'It was the same crow,' Ossie insisted. 'I saw the white mark on him.'

Tito felt uneasy and went back to tell their silver-haired deliverer that they could not find the feather.

She did not seem surprised, but she put a hand on each of their heads as though in benediction. 'Watch out for a man with eyes like a cat,' she murmured in a strange flat voice. 'Remember what I'm telling you. You must not listen to him or look into his face. And tomorrow you must follow your journey as quickly as you can.'

That night the children slept under the caravan in a stretch of bogland. They saw the great sky above the bog change from grey-blue to dark blue and then violet, and then the stars came out. A curlew cried in the twilight. They had dined on bread and cheese with a bit of onion and drank buttermilk and now they were sleepy and full of peace. The wood smoke from the dying fire was heady in their nostrils. They were clean, too, because the old woman had made them bathe in the stream and had washed their clothes. She had scrubbed Ossie's hair with soap and when Tito had gone in after him to bathe she had warned him to wash his hair or she'd come and do it for him. Tito washed his hair very quickly.

'Maybe we can travel a bit with this ould one,' Tito whispered, glad that his tummy was full and that he felt safe. Nearby Tir na n-Og was nibbling the sparse grass and young bracken that grew among the heather.

'She might eat us,' Ossie said doubtfully, remembering a story Grandpa had told them about a witch who ate children who got lost in a wood.

Tito groaned. 'She hasn't got enough teeth to eat us!'

Ossie went to sleep and Tito did likewise. But as sleep drew him down and away he remembered what she had said when he had asked her her name again while they sat round the fire over their supper.

'Some call me Brede, some Caithlin Ni Houlihan. There's a great welter of names.'

'Are you very old, missus?' Ossie asked.

She laughed. 'Old enough.'

'How old? Are you as old as Grandpa?' He looked at her with large eyes and nodded his head confidingly. 'Grandpa is very old.'

She smiled gravely, clearly impressed. 'In some ways I am not as old as Grandpa. I am the same age as Time. Approximately.'

Ossie was interested in further interrogation, but Tito gave him a dig in the ribs and suggested he shut his trap.

'Thanks for the food, missus. And thanks for getting us over that bridge.'

She nodded and looked into the fire and the children crept away to their blankets under the caravan.

The morning dawned chilly; there was a mist lying on the bog, a white fog which reduced visibility to a few yards. Tito and Ossie woke and looked around. Their clothes were beside them, dry and clean. Tir na n-Og was close by; all the blacking was gone and he was like a white ghost in the mist. He was wearing his bridle and they could hear him chewing the bit. But the caravan and the skewbald and the old woman with the long silver hair had disappeared.

Tito had had a dream, the same dream which had

come to him for years. He had walked with his mother along a beach. The beach was strewn with bits of seaweed and was covered in small round pebbles and different kinds of shells. She found him a special shell, one that was twisted into a cone and that you could put to your ear to hear the ocean. She was laughing; the wind picked up her hair and whipped it across her face. He examined the whelk and then raised his arm and flung it into the sea. It disappeared with a plop and the waves ran up onto the beach and receded heedlessly.

'Oh Tito, why did you do that? It's hard to find those shells! You've thrown away good luck!' his mother cried. He looked around, saw that there were millions of small white shells like fans, and millions of thin blue shells which crunched under his feet, but he did not see any like the one his mother had given him. He burst into tears.

'It's all right, *a chroí*. There'll be others.'

'I don't want others; I want that one!'

'We'll come back sometime and find it. The sea will bring it back.'

And then she had suddenly begun to move away from him, as though she were drawn by some invisible and irresistible force. She had her arms out to him, but she receded down the beach while he ran towards her crying. She became paler and fainter until he could see through her and she faded into the wind like a ghost.

It was an old dream, but it was based on reality. He remembered it clearly; being very small and with his mother on the shore and how she had found the special shell for him which, in a heedless moment, he had thrown away. But they had never come back to find it as she had promised. She had died a few weeks later. If he had not thrown the shell away, would she have died? This was the question that had haunted his childhood, that woke him at night.

Ossie looked at the lonely bog and the mist. 'Where's the caravan? Why did she leave us?'

Tito was silent, suffering. The dream was still with him and he was hardly aware of what Ossie was talking about.

'Why, Tito, why did she go?'

'I don't know.'

'Why are you crying, Tito?'

Tito just looked at his small brother and wiped his eyes. 'Come on,' he said, shakily. 'We'd better move.'

They mounted Tir na n-Og and gave the horse his head. By the time the sun came up and the mist lifted, they had made good progress. The countryside came out of the haze, smiling, glad to feel the warmth of the new day.

'I'm hungry,' Ossie announced.

Tito felt the pressure of his small brother's hands on his back. In the name of God, he thought, echoing his father's turn of phrase, when are you not hungry?

'We haven't got anything to eat,' he said. He felt the pressure of the small hands work their way down towards his pockets.

'What's this, Tito?'

Tito held the reins with one hand and felt for his pockets. There was something in them; he put a hand gingerly into one of them and extracted a lump of cheese. The other pocket had a similar surprise, a big lump of bread.

'Where did you get this, Tito?'

'I don't know,' the elder boy said in wonder. 'The ould one must have left it.'

Tito reined in Tir na n-Og and the boys dismounted to eat their meal. Tito remembered the old woman's warning to hurry on their journey, but, now that she was gone, he dismissed her as an ould one with a screw loose. The countryside was seductive now that their tummies were full and they'd slept warm and dry. They put the blanket on the ground and lay back on it among the furze bushes, watching the clouds high overhead, listening to the birds and smelling the wild perfume of the gorse. A hare came bounding by in the field, stood up to look at them with its front paws raised, and then dashed away to tell the other animals about them. Some cattle saw them and came towards them, all curiosity. There were a few cows and Tito asked Ossie sarcastically if he wanted some milk.

'No,' Ossie whispered nervously. He scanned the edges of the field, fearful that another bull might present itself. But all was quiet.

When the children remounted Tir na n-Og, they moved away quickly across country. They saw a wooded area and headed towards it. They would be safe for another while; no one would be able to find them in the woods.

'They must think we've disappeared,' Ossie said triumphantly.

'Yeah,' Tito echoed. 'It looks like we've given them the slip.'

'When will we be in the Wild West?' Ossie asked and Tito said he didn't know, but that it would surely be soon.

They did not expect the helicopter. It came later in the day, when they had come into higher country. It came clucking overhead, and Tir na n-Og threw back his head and surged immediately for the forest which was not far off. He pushed his way into the undergrowth, the children crouching to avoid being torn off his back by low branches or scratched by the long thin spurs low down on the tree trunks. After a while the white horse stopped. The boys sat on his back in silence, listening to the whirr of the helicopter get louder and louder, until the tree tops began to sway around them in the wind from the whirling blades. They stared up with terror at this great mechanical insect which had come to find them. After a while it left and the wind died and the noise of the whirling blades faded into the distance. The children dismounted shakily and inspected Tir na n-Og who was quivering from head to toe.

'Look at his face,' Ossie cried. 'It's all scratched!'

'He's got thorns all over him,' Tito responded in dismay.

'Take them out.'

The boys began to pick the thorns from the horse's coat and Tir na n-Og looked round at them and whinnied softly.

'Did they see us?' Ossie demanded.

Tito answered tersely, 'They must have.'

They stopped long enough only to extract the thorns bothering Tir na n-Og. They traversed the forest and as they came out the other side, the runaways heard a sound which made the white horse prick up his ears: the furious barking of dogs. The sound came from within the forest itself; it echoed through the trees like the howling of the hounds of hell. The children immediately left the shadow of the trees and galloped away, down the hill and into the glen. The dogs pursued them with frantic ululations, encouraged by men on horseback who shouted orders and gesticulated, not huntsmen this time but man-hunters. Then there was another wedge of forest. The boys huddled down, no longer aware where they were going, and too frightened anyway to direct Tir na n-Og. But their mount was surefooted and followed his own course as though he knew the lie of the land.

When they came through the second section of forest, the boys found themselves by a river. The horse splashed his way into it, following it upwards to a long white waterfall. Tito looked back at the countryside behind him, heard the dogs. He looked at the torrent roaring ahead of them.

'We're done for now,' he wailed.

But Tir na n-Og did not hesitate at the curtain of water; he walked round behind it and stopped under the overhanging rock. The two boys sat on his back in wonder as the cataract fell in a continuous sheet a few feet in front of their faces.

When the dogs arrived at the waterfall some time later they howled and barked, but there was no sign of their quarry. Their handlers looked around in

perplexity; some of the men climbed the nearby hill
and searched the countryside with binoculars. But to
no avail. 'It's as though they had disappeared from
the face of the earth,' someone muttered.

'They must have gone in a different direction,' someone else said, roaring to be heard above the noise of
the crashing water. 'They've given us the slip.'

'Take the dogs back to the forest again,' directed
another man, who spoke urgently into a walkie-
talkie. And after a while men and dogs moved away.

Behind the cascading waterfall, the boys waited on
Tir na n-Og's back for a long time. The barking of the
dogs had long faded into the distance before the white
horse carried them out into the barren countryside
where the shadows were lengthening.

'Tito?'

'Yes?'

'How did Tir na n-Og know about the waterfall?'

Tito shook his head. 'I dunno. Maybe he was in
there before.'

'Are we safe now?'

Tito sighed and crossed his fingers. 'We're safe
now.'

The children looked across the landscape before
them, saw the stony ground, a grey limestone plain
cut into various slab-like pieces by the work of wind
and weather. It was an inhospitable sight. But there
could be no turning back now, not if they wanted to
stay with Tir na n-Og. And without Tir na n-Og they
did not know how they would get out of the hole they
found themselves in. Behind them were men with
dogs who wanted them so they could claim the

reward. It had occurred to Ossie that maybe the reward was for their capture dead or alive, like real cowboys. But he was too frightened and too tired to mention this to Tito. Before them was a rocky wilderness where nothing moved except the wind, which came howling at them across the stony plateau, full of sleet. The weather had changed. Is it because we've come up high or what? Tito wondered.

'Tir na n-Og,' Tito said, his teeth chattering. 'We have to find some shelter. If we don't, we will die out here.' He took the remains of the cheese from his pocket and handed half of it to Ossie.

'Thanks, Tito.' Then he quavered, 'What are we going to do now?'

Tito, at a loss, just shook his head.

Superintendent O'Mara inspected the contents of the file which Inspector Bolger had recently given him. He picked out a handwritten sheet of paper which recited the terms of sale. The horse was to be sold to defray the damage caused in the fracas at the Towers. O'Mara studied it for a moment. 'What sort of old rubbish is this?' he asked, turning to Sergeant Brophy. 'There's nothing legal about this. It's up to the Corporation to sue for damage to the flats. No one except the City Sheriff is entitled to take the horse in compensation, and then only with a court order. Was there any court order?'

Brophy did not move a muscle. 'No sir.'

O'Mara waved the piece of paper. 'And this signature, this X. This means nothing on its own. How do I know he made it? It's not even witnessed!'

Brophy coughed discreetly.

'Did he make it or didn't he?' O'Mara demanded dangerously.

'I'm afraid, sir, that he did not. You might say Inspector Bolger made it for him.'

O'Mara went very red in the face. His voice became very cold. 'You'd better explain yourself, Sergeant.'

Brophy was happy to oblige.

'So this X was placed here under duress?'

'Yes, sir.'

'And Bolger forced him to do it?'

Brophy nodded.

O'Mara stared out of the window, only his heightened colour betraying his state of mind.

'I've given too much of my life to the police force in this country to see it reduced to the level of an Al Capone operation,' he said through clenched teeth. 'The gardai are being made fools of!' He turned to Brophy. 'And what is more, I'm being made a fool of!'

'What about the children?' the sergeant asked when he felt that it was safe to do so.

'We have to find the children, for their own safety, and then restore the horse to its proper owner,' O'Mara said. 'I will deal with Inspector Bolger, personally, at a later date!'

He left the room and Sergeant Brophy permitted himself the ghost of a smile. 'Got you, Bolger, you bastard,' he whispered. 'A hole in one!'

In a field about half a mile from the road on which Grandpa was travelling, there was a rath, otherwise known as a fairy fort. The fort, a circular area of about half an acre, was a hillock enclosed by stone fortifications. This was one of the dwelling places of the Sidhe, whose good side it was better for everyone to stay on. Grandpa had often laid snares near it, although, of course, he had never interfered with the fort itself, which, like all of its kind, was avoided by the country people. No farmer would plough a fairy fort or knowingly allow any interference with it. This would be to court disaster. The Little People were famed for their vindictiveness. Not that a modern farmer would admit that he believed in fairies; most did not, but they hedged their bets.

Folklore had it that one fairy fort was connected with the next by means of an underground passage, with the result that the Sidhe had the run of the length and breadth of the country without ever having to step above ground. The Sidhe were immortal; they had powers which human beings could only guess at, and, due no doubt to their immortality, a biting ennui which made them capable of anything. They were great lovers of the beautiful, and would spirit away a child or a young woman, leaving a facsimile in their place, a Changeling. They had hypnotic powers, and their music was so entrancing that you would willingly swap your mortal life in exchange for seven years with them. They were regal entertainers, but the intruder got short shrift and would be lucky to leave with all his faculties.

So when Grandpa realised that the only place he could get help was a location where his wits and his life might be in jeopardy, he was understandably fearful. How was he to approach the Little People so that they would know he came in good faith and not as an enemy? That he came as supplicant and as friend? He would have to give them a gift in earnest of his bona fides, although he knew that no material gift would interest them for very long. His mind scanned his possessions: he had a horse and a caravan, a small sum of money, his clothes, a few sticks of furniture, some bread, a hunk of cheese and a bottle of whiskey.

He started. Of course. The whiskey! This was the same bottle the travellers had given him as a present, a reward for entertaining them with stories, and it was still sitting there in his small cupboard against a rainy day.

He climbed into the caravan, found the bottle and carried it outside. He examined it in the fading light; the foil had been removed and the cork stopper had been tampered with, for the bottle was not even full. Someone had helped himself to a slug before he handed the bottle over. This didn't surprise Grandpa, for it was good whiskey, fifteen year old.

He sighed. He crossed the stile into the fields and walked towards the fairy fort, holding the bottle by the neck. As he approached it, his courage failed. The sun was going down and the last of its glory was in the west, but the shadows of night were coming in from the east. Soon it would be dark.

He sat on the grass near the fort and put his head in his hands. What was he going to do? His legs were weak at the prospect of proceeding any further. Maybe the Sidhe could hear him already, maybe they were preparing to repel the intruder.

'You have nothing to fear from me,' Grandpa whispered. 'I have come to beg your help.'

There was silence. Then, from a field nearby, came the lowing of a cow, a long drawn out 'moo-oo', lonely on the night air.

Grandpa waited, but nothing stirred around the fairy fort.

'They won't hurt you either,' he told himself. 'They've never yet harmed a fool!' But the longer he waited, the more he needed moral support. He drew the cork from the bottle, smelt the contents. The powerful perfume went up his nose, activated memory cells in his brain. He had been a drinking man in his youth and whiskey had been his god. But he had seldom had good whiskey. Good whiskey was expensive. Now he thought, what if I take one little sip – just to see what the flavour is? The Sidhe won't miss one little sip and it will give me courage to go on. It's not as though I'm broaching the bottle myself . . .

He raised the bottle to his lips and slowly tipped it. The spirit poured into his mouth and down his gullet. He coughed, spluttered, breathing in deeply; when he could, to savour what had been done to his palate and the back of his throat. He felt fire kindle in his stomach. He hadn't had anything to eat all day and the fire spread easily.

Grandpa put down the bottle. He thought of Tito and Ossie; he thought of the dark forces arraigned against them. He felt the hopelessness of it all. He felt silly sitting beside a fairy fort in the gathering night. Everything around him was normal; the cattle were settling down to ruminate, the last of the rooks had gone home. Somewhere in the distance a dog was barking. Dew was forming; he could feel the wetness on the grass.

'I'm a foolish ould man,' he said aloud, addressing the Sidhe if any of them were listening. 'I'm afraid to come any closer to your fort, but I'm willing to give you my immortal soul if you will save my grandsons, Tito and Ossie; I'll let you have that as the price. My soul is no use to me if anything happens to them.' He raised the bottle to his lips once again, drank, felt the fire mount to his brain, laughed suddenly. 'And you can have what's left of the whiskey too!' But he took another slug. Soon it became apparent that there would not be much left of the whiskey. Grandpa had had more than a drop too much and he eventually emptied the bottle.

After a while the moon rose. It looked out over the countryside from behind thick, dark clouds which were coming in with tomorrow's showers. It saw that Grandpa had keeled over and that he slept.

Afterwards the old man was not sure whether he had dreamed or not, because the clarity of his experience would be with him for the rest of his life.

He dreamed that he stood up and walked round the rath. He walked round it three times, seeking an entrance, and on the third occasion he tripped, tumbled forward and found himself falling down a tunnel. He heard music, faint at first and then louder, music so sweet that it seemed to permeate his flesh, to make him young, to satisfy every yearning of his soul.

The cavern he landed in was made of crystal, with gilded floors and silver columns. It was brightly lit and filled with tiny people of such perfect proportions that Grandpa knew that he was indeed in the land of the Sidhe. These people turned to stare at him. Some had wings, some not; their faces, although beautiful, were cold and their eyes glittered in the silver light.

'You have made a foolish journey,' one of them said. He was a young man, dressed in green, with a golden cap on his head, and his hauteur was in inverse proportion to his size. 'The Sidhe do not make bargains with mortals.'

Grandpa did not move. 'Please,' he said, 'will you not save my grandsons from their destroyer? You sent them a horse and, because of it, they are in danger. Do the Sidhe have no responsibility for their actions?'

'There is always danger,' the young man said. 'Mortals live by it and die by it.'

Grandpa shook his head. 'I am an old foolish creature, but this is no ordinary danger. There is a man called Catspaw who seeks my grandsons. I live in dread of him. I will give you everything I have, myself, anything!'

There was silence in the cavern. Eventually the young man spoke again.

'Old man, would you give your soul for this?'

Grandpa nodded. 'If I had ten souls I would give them all!'

The hush deepened. The youth looked around.

'That is the silence of awe,' he said. 'We cannot conceive of such sacrifice. With us there is no death and therefore no love as you know it. Go back. We will look out for the man called Catspaw. We know him well!' He smiled. 'Keep your soul; it is no use to us, but if, some evening, you want to leave a bottle of that whiskey you drank beside the rath, we would regard it kindly!'

Grandpa woke up with a start on the grass where he had fallen asleep. He picked up the bottle, saw that it was indeed empty and carried it back to the caravan. He was singing; old Dan was asleep, but he woke and nuzzled Grandpa when he caressed him.

Chapter Fifteen

Noel Harnett stood in his hotel room and stared out of the window at the storm. The rain lashed against the glass, peppered it with hailstones, and the wind cried and wailed down the street of the little town like a banshee on a rampage.

Harnett had not seen a storm its like in years and he ground his teeth in a fury of frustration. Behind him in the room was his secretary, Morrissey, who had just come off the phone and was nervously consulting some notes he had taken as he gave his boss the benefit of their content. Downstairs, the hotel dining room was filled with the riders, dog handlers and the helicopter crew who were munching lamb chops, quaffing pots of tea and awaiting further orders.

'Tell them I don't give a damn what the regulations are,' Harnett said coldly to Morrissey. 'Take the chopper up!'

Morrissey oiled his way towards the window and looked out at the raging elements. 'Control says no. They're estimating two hours before the storm breaks.'

Harnett turned to stare at him. 'We don't have a couple of hours!' He looked back at the street, saw the water wash over it as though it were the deck of a ship in a typhoon. 'Those tinkers must have the devil on their side!'

Even as he said this his eyes alighted on the figure at the end of the street, the slight figure of the man the travellers called 'Catspaw', slinking through the downpour, his head bent as though he could detect a trail through the worst the elements could throw at him. Harnett shivered involuntarily; the man gave him the creeps. He was too taciturn, too thin, too prone to perpetual movement, too wary of eye contact. And Harnett did not like the man's eyes; there was something in them that was not human.

But he had been glad enough to hire him as a tracker; he had dismissed whispers that the fellow was the best because he employed unorthodox means peculiar to himself. What those means were, Harnett had not enquired and did not wish to know. He ignored the shiver climbing his backbone at the sight of him. He could not afford to be squeamish. He had told Catspaw to get out and track the horse and let his performance be his credentials. If he found the horse, he found the horse. End of story.

Catspaw had already shown results; it was his tip that had led to the dogs and the helicopter being sent out, but the man himself had not accompanied them. He had indicated that, using his own methods, he would be with the children before the others got there. Harnett had told him that if he were successful he would reward him handsomely, but the man had smiled and said again in a very soft voice that he sought only the reward already on offer and that he be given charge of the children when the horse was found. Harnett had promised him this. He was not interested in what became of the damn children.

Harnett was tired and he was desperate with frustration. This chase was making a fool of him; two kids on a white horse and neither the police nor his own considerable task force could run them to earth. And now the storm! It was as though the elements were conspiring with the children against him. He wasn't seeking much; the horse was his. He knew there were irregularities in the manner of its sale, but that wasn't his problem. The vendor was an Inspector of Police and had procured, or so he had assured him, the appropriate signature to make the thing legal and had received a sizeable down payment.

Harnett went through all the reasons why the appropriation of the horse was above board. He lived by greed, but he had perfected a patina of reason. Never in his life had he yielded to the whisper of his conscience, to the promptings of any kind of generosity, or to compassion. He had a contempt for all kinds of weakness. In his book, emotions were weaknesses and therefore he did not indulge in them. He possessed passion all right, but it lay in his hunger for position and power. Without them, he did not really exist. And because his very sense of identity revolved round his power, he could not bear to be crossed in anything.

His earliest memory was being placed on a mantelpiece by his father at the age of four. His father had stood in front of him, put out his hands and said, 'Jump!' The boy had jumped, but instead of the parental arms receiving him safely, which the child had expected, he had been allowed instead to crash to the hearth. While he wept, his unrepentant parent bent over him and said, 'Remember that. Trust no one!' It was a lesson he never forgot.

He often congratulated himself privately on how well he had succeeded in life. Looking back, he was proud of his acumen and his success. The use of insider information did not trouble him. After all, he had paid for the information which created his empire. You got on whatever way you could and didn't bother yourself with idiotic scruples.

But there was one shadow at the bottom of Harnett's mind which he did not dwell on. It had to do with an unfortunate episode some seven years earlier when a bunch of travellers had been moved on. The land had been bought by his company and he would not tolerate trespassers, not even while the commencement of development was pending; at that point, the start of work was still months away. But one of the traveller women had been about to give birth and had done so prematurely in some Godforsaken spot after the tribe had been sent packing. He had heard later that she had died. Unfortunate; but it was a harsh world and if people wanted to get pregnant while they wandered the roads, it was none of his business. However, rationalise as he might, it haunted him still.

Harnett had married twice. His first wife was a

pretty, feminine woman, a girl he had first seen as a plump teenager, a sister of a friend. He had courted and married her as soon as he started his business. They had had two children, both girls. But her growing complaints that he spent all his time on his work, that he had no time for his family, grated on him and when she ran away with one of his employees, a bookkeeper, he had blotted her out of his mind. He had procured an English divorce and remarried in England a younger woman of French extraction, a dark-eyed beauty called Simone, who was as avid for wealth and position as he was.

Harnett felt that his life was on course. But to be damned and thwarted by two tinker brats was something he had not bargained for and it was not something he was prepared to tolerate. He would find them, he knew, and get back the horse. He would find them in time for the final of the World Cup and the horse would win. It had become a matter of principle.

Inspector Bolger, who was sitting on the far side of the room nursing a roaring headache, stood up and joined Harnett and Morrissey at the window, blocking out what was left of the watery light.

'Jesus,' he muttered, as he stared at the rain cascading down the street, 'it's enough to make you believe in the powers of darkness.'

Harnett laughed harshly. 'The powers of darkness! What do we have to do, Inspector, to get them on our side?'

Bolger glanced at him sourly. 'Well, if it's the kids' guardian angel that's responsible, he must be trying to take them to the next world in an awful hurry.' He gestured at the elements howling outside. 'There's not too many kids would be improved by being out in that.'

As if in agreement, a sudden squall of rain hit the window and hail danced against the glass. The men pulled back instinctively.

'If I get my way,' Harnett said, drawing his heavy brows together, 'those children will pay for this, one way or the other. And if they've damaged my horse . . .'

My horse! Bolger looked at him, but kept his peace. The throbbing in his head made him want to lie down. He had taken two aspirin but it was no better. He was desperate. Cathy was on his mind and his debts were on his mind and the obvious solution to the whole frigging mess was on his mind; but they were stuck here while the horse was somewhere not a thousand miles away and two little knackers were thumbing their noses at the lot of them. Also on his mind was his file on the subject back in Dublin. He wondered if O'Mara had read it yet. Bolger berated himself over the file. He could easily have fudged the matter; he could have mislaid the thing, suffered a lapse of memory, forged a signature. The super had obviously forgotten about the file by the time he gave it to him. Bolger knew that O'Mara had been trying to reach him recently and he would have to answer for being incommunicado. Trouble. There was trouble ahead.

He looked at Harnett with dislike and frustration.

He looked at Morrissey, whom he privately thought resembled a snake. He thought of the million he might have if the horse were recovered in one piece. He thought of a honeymoon with Cathy in the Seychelles, palm trees, wine, soft warm nights, the whisper of a tropical sea, his honey-skinned bride beside him. God, but it wasn't fair.

Morrissey moved back from the window. He maintained the inscrutable silence which was his wont, except when his boss posed him a direct question. But a question of his own kept repeating itself inside his head, a question to which there did not appear to be any sensible answer: 'Wouldn't you think a spirited animal like that would have been able to shake off a couple of brats if it wanted to?'

Morrissey knew a few things about horses, having seen plenty of them at close quarters. He knew that a spirited, high-bred horse would no more put up with two opportunistic kids than it would endure any close presence, human or animal, that it did not find empathic.

He shrugged. He wished the episode were over one way or another. The thought of two more hours in this dump in the rain was more than he could tolerate.

The children sheltered in a cave. Tir na n-Og had found it, almost as though he knew it was there, a big cave with a small entrance. But inside, it opened out in other caves and the plink, plonk of water dripping from stalactites, or plopping into ready-made pools, echoed eerily through the underground system in the darkness, making the children huddle closer together. Tir na n-Og lay on the ground and the boys curled up against him, and were reassured by his calm. They could hear his great heart beating, smell the warm pungent, horsey scent of him.

The night descended. The cave became completely dark, a darkness so intense that you could not see your hand in front of your face, a darkness so complete that the children could not even make out the pale presence of Tir na n-Og. They knew he was there because of his warmth and his breathing and because they could feel the coarse satin of his coat. The boys slept, wrapped in the brown blanket and another one belonging to the old woman, in which they had been wrapped on the night following their flight across the Shannon.

Afterwards Tito could not remember just what had wakened him or, indeed, whether he had been fully awake. It seemed to him that he woke with a start, every sense alert, and that his heart stopped with fear as he listened. Below the steady dripping from the deeper caves and the echoing of the water splashing was another sound, like someone creeping across a wet floor. It was a soft, nondescript sound, quite different from the crisp plopping of the water, and in the darkness and isolation and mystery of the subterranean system, it was inexplicable and therefore terrifying.

Tito was afraid to move, afraid to speak. He heard the slithering sound come nearer, tried to convince himself that he was imagining things, but something within him recognised jeopardy and he yelled before he had consciously formulated the words, 'Tir na n-Og, there's something in the cave!'

Tir na n-Og rose with a clatter of hooves. Tito grabbed Ossie, who was still asleep. The horse snorted and surged away from them, as though giving chase. The slithering noise stopped, but then a sibilant whisper came almost directly behind them, from the wall of the cave where the roof was too low to allow a horse access.

'Tito, Ossie, come over here. Come to me. I have food for you, chocolate. Come to me . . .'

The voice was unhurried, soft and silken, rising and falling in a gently hypnotic monotone, a whisper but not a whisper, a voice the boys heard in their hearts as much as in their ears. To Tito it sounded like his mother's voice; to Ossie it sounded like a voice he had never known and yet wanted more than anything to hear. Were they still dreaming? Or was it a nightmare? It was seductive; there was a promise in it of peace and journey's end.

Ossie, half awake and half in trance, moved blindly towards the voice; Tir na n-Og neighed in a high, urgent horse scream and Tito, who had been about to follow his small brother, reached out and grabbed Ossie by the heel, pulling him to his knees and dragging him back. It all happened in the pitch darkness. The noise Tir na n-Og made echoed through the caves, sending the sound from one cavern to another until the whole underground network seemed to reverberate.

There was a shimmer then in the darkness; a light appeared at the mouth of the cavern they were in, followed by a sudden tinkling laughter. The laughter seemed to be taken up by other voices and the light grew brighter. There was a sudden sound, a pattering like tiny footsteps flitting across the cave, and in the strange light the boys saw a dark figure emerge from beneath a low-slung rock mass, stare at them hungrily for a moment like a cat disappointed of its prey, and then make for the opening into another cavern.

Tir na n-Og screamed again, frightening Ossie who called for his mammy and grabbed Tito's shaking arm, and again the tunnels and caverns rang and began to rumble. The rumbling grew and the horse nudged the children into running towards the mouth of the cave. Inside, a rock fall thundered, sealing off the very cavern they had inhabited. The ground shook. They heard a sound like a human howl and then the rumbling settled and all was quiet.

They followed Tir na n-Og outside in terrified silence. The downpour had stopped but the night sky was murky with dark cloud. The air was cool and fresh after the rain. The horse led them to a sheltered cleft in the rock, out of the wind, and lay beside them. Tito and Ossie shivered together in shock and fear and it was a long time before they were able to sleep again.

'What was that in the cave?' Ossie asked, his teeth chattering, his heart beating much too fast.

'It was probably ghosts,' Tito said, not sure now whether he'd dreamed it all, 'but we're all right now.'

The morning dawned chill and fresh. The boys woke and found that Tir na n-Og was gone. They were cold;

their feet felt like ice; they were hungrier than they had ever been. But they raced into the raw morning calling for the horse and saw him eventually, down by the ruins of an old cottage, kneeling on the ground.

Tito looked at Tir na n-Og for a moment. 'What's he doing?' He raised his voice, 'Come on, Tir na n-Og.' The horse ignored him.

'Are you okay, Tir na n-Og?' Ossie yelled. 'Are you okay?'

'Tir na n-Og, get up please!' they both wailed.

The white horse whinnied, rose to his feet and trotted away. Tito and Ossie stared after him, aghast.

'Tir na n-Og, come back!'

'If we lose him,' Tito shouted, looking across the barren limestone of the Burren, 'we're done for!' But the horse followed his self-appointed course only for a few yards. And then he stopped.

The children picked their way across the stony ground to join him and when they saw that he did not try to run away they followed the direction of the horse's gaze and stared at the hewn stone set into the earth. It bore the legend, 'MARY RILEY, born 22.9.1960, died 12.11.1984.'

The children knelt to look at the stone. Tito started in shock and Ossie's small hungry face creased in perplexity. He turned to look at his brother.

'Why is my birthday on that stone?' he demanded.

Tito set his face and answered carefully. 'Because that's the day Mammy died.'

Ossie continued to stare. In his mind a host of suspicions he had never before considered began to crowd.

'Why did she die on my birthday?' he whispered.

Tito struggled with the emotion which was beginning to choke him. He made no reply.

'Tito?'

'Yes?'

'Did Mammy see me?'

'I don't know,' Tito whispered.

'Did I ever see Mammy?'

Tito could not help him; he could not trust himself to speak.

'She's not in my head; there are no pictures, Tito.'

Tito's memory filled with the face of his mother on a windswept beach and he thought of the shell he had thrown away. He groaned. He did not speak, but the words came unbidden into his head: 'It's all my fault. I killed her! I threw her luck away when I flung away the shell!' He began to cry inconsolably. Ossie tried to comfort him, stroking his arm nervously.

'Why are you crying, Tito?'

Tito wiped his eyes. 'Everyone has something to cry about, Ossie,' he said. 'Everyone carries something sore inside them.' He looked wearily into his little brother's eyes. 'Did you think you were the only one?' Before Ossie could interrogate him he moved away to pick a small flower, the intense blue of which caught his eye. He brought the gentian back and placed it carefully on his mother's grave.

It was in a very subdued mood that the two boys remounted the white horse.

'Where are we going to now?' Ossie asked in a small child's voice, from which all bravado had disappeared. 'Can we go home to Papa?'

Tito sighed. He thought of Papa, of his laugh when he was in good form, of the strength of him and the safety of him when he was not at the drink. He wished with all his heart that he could go straight to Papa. But he knew that Tir na n-Og would only go towards the sunset and they had no strength left to leave him, even had they wanted to.

'I don't know,' he said.

Tir na n-Og moved slowly over the broken land and the children took one last look behind them.

'Tito,' Ossie cried, 'it's that crow again!'

Tito followed the direction of his brother's pointing finger and saw the crow with the white wing tip alighting on the outcrop of rock which led to the cave of the night before. The bird cocked its head on one side and fixed its eye on the departing horse and riders, and then it began to flap as though something beneath the fissures of the limestone communicated with him.

Some hours later Papa, Kathleen and Barreller arrived at the ruined cottage. They had had a hard journey, short nights and long days. They had sheltered against yesterday's downpour in a caravan in a travellers' camp at the edge of the burren. There had been an old woman there, with a crystal ball, which she had shown to Kathleen out of a sense of hospitality when the latter questioned her about the fortune-telling business. She had laughed, said that the ball was for the fair-day customers with more money than sense.

'Do you tell them their real fortune?' Kathleen asked and the woman smiled, showing only three teeth.

'*Aroo*, no. There's few would pay for that! Anyway, their real fortune would kill me with the exhaustion of it.' She picked up Kathleen's right hand and stared at it with a cursory interest which changed to something else as she inspected it. She let the hand drop.

'Aren't you going to tell my fortune?' Kathleen asked with a smile. The old woman gave a short laugh.

'Is it coddin' me you are? And you with the Rings of Solomon on your index fingers – me tell your fortune? It's you who should be telling mine, who could tell all of our fortunes! There's the gift in your hand as plain as ever I saw it, more strongly marked than ever I saw it! You're the one here who should have a crystal ball!' She became aware that her voice had risen in the excitement of her discovery and she added in a low voice, 'Are you telling me you've never read fortunes?'

Kathleen turned her head away, but Papa had heard the exchange and came forward.

'What's this I hear, Kathleen?'

'I gave it up, John,' she said quietly. 'I don't have any truck with it. Sometimes I read the cards, but only for myself. I don't like looking into the crystal.'

'Why not?'

Kathleen didn't answer at once. 'Because it tells me the truth, John Riley,' she said truculently after a moment when she saw that Papa was not going to let the subject drop. 'Because once, if you must know, I looked into it full of hope, searching for the face of the boy I loved.'

Papa did not look at her. 'Did you find it, Kathleen?' he asked quietly.

'I found it all right, but it was turned towards another woman. She was there beside him in the crystal before he ever met her. I saw my own tears before I shed them.' She gave him a wry smile. 'Therefore, John Riley, I do not look into the crystal any more.'

'Will you look into it now?' he asked. 'For me?'

She shook her head. So like a man, she thought. Will you do it for me? All *plamás*. Do it for me and never mind what it costs! Aloud she said, 'Why should I do it for you, John Riley?'

'Because I ask you, Kathleen. Because my boys are gone and you know that I'm desperate!' He lowered his voice. 'Because we will never fail each other again.'

Kathleen motioned to the woman, who rose and took the crystal ball from its box and put it carefully on the table with a black cloth under it. The caravan became silent. Kathleen drew up a chair and seated herself, throwing her long red hair back over her shoulders. Then she cupped her face with her hands and stared into the crystal sphere.

She let her mind become still; she stilled it slowly, emptied it of thought, saw only silence. The crystal ball was clear and full of nothingness; light reflected from the window showed up the teapot on the table, showed the figures clustered behind her, bent them into unreal shapes. She waited. There was nothing. I have lost the gift, she thought, with a curious sense of relief. But still she waited.

She heard the squall of rain on the window, heard the wind buffeting the caravan as though these were events which were taking place somewhere far away. The crystal sphere ceased to be a distorting mirror; it clouded, became black and then, as though a curtain had been lifted, it became a window she could see through. She travelled through this space, entered the window, moved within it, watching and trusting. And then, in a moment, she knew. The tarot had not lied Papa watched Kathleen's face, saw her eyes glaze in trance. He stood watching for what seemed a long time and still she stared, sitting rigid. Alarmed, he put a hand on her shoulder, shook her gently, felt her start.

'Come back, Kathleen!'

She looked up at him, rubbed her forehead with her hand.

'What did you see?'

Her eyes were unfocused as though she were blind, the pupils dilated into black pools.

'I saw a mother who listens for her children,' she whispered when she had collected herself.

'Is that all?'

'I saw a woman grieving for her husband's grief. I saw a soul who wants to be free.' She paused. Her voice became stronger as she saw Papa, head bent, turn away from her. 'I also saw a neglected, yearning child screaming his mother's name to the changing wind.' Papa turned back to her abruptly and she challenged him with her eyes. 'And you know what that can mean as well as I.'

He started, seemed visibly upset. 'Did she hear him? Did the mother hear him?'

'She heard him. He called her and she heard him.'

Papa was breathing heavily. He stared at Kathleen, locking his eyes with hers as though in response to her challenge. Then he turned away.

'Superstition,' he said. 'More bloody superstition!'

Barreller was looking out at the rain. He turned uncomfortably to Papa. 'That pub down the road is open. What are we doing here?'

But Papa did not seem to hear him. He just stared out at the deluge.

'Are the children safe?' he demanded suddenly, his voice very low and hoarse. Kathleen bent her head.

'I think they are in more danger now,' she whispered, 'than they have ever been in their lives. There is a man who's looking for them.'

Papa turned to her. 'Bolger?' he said. 'It's Bolger who's looking for them. If he harms them—'

'No,' Kathleen said. 'The man I'm talking about is not Bolger.' She paused, frowned in recollection. 'He has strange yellow eyes, with a slit in them that opens and closes like a cat's.'

Papa shivered. Did Bolger have strange eyes? he wondered. Well, he was no beauty, but as far as he could remember he had the same eyes as anyone else.

The old traveller woman who was putting away her crystal ball froze in mid-movement. She turned to Papa and Kathleen.

'Watch out for that fellow,' she said in a hoarse voice. 'Him with the cat's eyes. There was people had dealings with him in the old days. They say he sold himself to the devil.'

The travellers listened in silence.

'He used to have a crow, with a white marking. If you see it, kill it!'

Papa shook his head. 'Old wives' tales,' he muttered, but he could see that the woman's eyes were wide with horror. He turned to Barreller with a gesture of disgust.

'Was that all you saw?' the woman whispered conspiratorially to Kathleen. She nodded. Her face was white with fatigue.

'I came back too soon,' she said simply.

Now they were at the ruins of the old cottage, probably built hundreds of years earlier, before the Great Famine when the western seaboard was densely populated. They stood at the stone, Papa bareheaded, his face a set study of pain.

Kathleen turned to Barreller. 'Stop him, Barreller; he mustn't dwell on it.'

But Barreller shook his head. 'It's where she died, for God's sake. She took his life away when she died.'

Papa bent his head over the simple stone. He stood very still, and did not respond immediately when Kathleen put a hand on his arm.

'John, John,' she whispered urgently. 'You have something you must do.'

He turned to her in a brusque gesture. 'What do I have to do?'

Kathleen took a deep breath. 'Make no sudden move, John Riley. Behind you on a rock is a crow with a white wing tip.'

Into Papa's mind flooded the traveller woman's warning: 'If you see it, kill it!'

For a moment he wanted to shout out that he wouldn't stand for any more ridiculous bloody superstitious nonsense, but instead, as though the matter had been decided for him, he felt in his pocket for the catapult, bent slowly and picked some stones from his wife's grave, fitted one slowly to his homemade weapon. Then he turned round without hurry, lifted the catapult and aimed at the only crow he saw. He did not wait to see if it had a white marking. It stood, apparently agitated, some hundred yards away, at the entrance of what had been a cave, and it cried out with a strange raucous caw as the stone impacted. Then it fell over and stuck its thin black feet in the air. Papa and Kathleen were about to go to examine it, but they were distracted by the arrival of Grandpa.

Every year, at some point in the year, Grandpa made the journey to honour his daughter at the place where she had died. She was as fresh in his mind as though her death had taken place yesterday. He saw her skipping and jumping as a child, laughing at him from the caravan, playing with the tin pots and pans and, later, sitting smilingly astride old Dan when he was a young horse and she a young woman about to be married.

'God, Da, I'm that excited,' she told him after the marriage had been arranged. 'I feel as though I could fly.' And she had bent down to embrace Dan's neck in a rush of happiness.

He brushed away a tear. Well, she had flown sure enough.

He had not expected to see his son-in-law here and he stared at him in surprise. The cards had told him that they would meet on the journey, but he did not know where. He had seen the sudden sure action with which he had dispatched the crow, and as he looked at him, his surprise became astonishment. Papa had changed. Not only was his frame sparer and fitter than formerly, but his face had shed its puffiness and putty-like colour and his mouth had lost its bitter twist.

Maybe he's learning at last, Grandpa thought in wonder, learning acceptance, the knowledge that John Riley's will is not paramount in the order of things, that the purpose of life is written somewhere outside of his reach. Maybe he's coming to terms with death and vulnerability. Maybe he's finding peace.

Papa gazed at Grandpa. 'How did you get here?'

'How do you think?'

Papa looked straight into his father-in-law's eyes. 'Where is that horse bringing me, Grandpa?' he asked. 'Why is it taking me back to all the old places?'

Grandpa grunted, allowed his eyes to move over the person before him. He was seeking the right answer to the question. He had debated it with himself so often that he felt he should be able to give a reply that had meaning. But he had nothing to say that would matter in the least. In his journey westwards he had begun to doubt himself, his life, what he had ever seen in cards or trances; he had begun to doubt the basis of his very existence. He remembered his dream by the fairy fort, dared not place too much hope in it. Too much was at stake. He had thought himself a seer of sorts, but now he knew that the currents of fate were too complex for any human skill to encompass or predict. All he had ever had, at best, was an oblique glimpse of something he had not even understood.

'Well, by God,' he replied cheerfully, playing for time, 'but it's not doing you any harm!'

Papa's eyes narrowed. He was disappointed in the response. It was the trite reply of someone who had no answers. He wanted words of wisdom and Grandpa had given him stones.

'If it harms my boys,' Papa said in a voice cold with fury, 'I'll never forgive you. I'll curse your grave!' He saw the sudden sorrow in the old man's face, remembered what Kathleen had said to him after looking into the crystal, and he paused and glanced at her. He knew that he was being unfair. His boys would be with him still if he had looked after them. What were an old man's stories compared to a father's love? He made a brusque gesture of apology.

Grandpa accepted it with pleasure. 'What was that crow you killed?' he demanded suddenly, turning to the spot where he had seen the bird fall.

Barreller moved to find it. But in a moment he threw up his hands in perplexity. He could not see it.

'I know it was here,' Papa said. 'You saw it, didn't

you, Kathleen, didn't you, Barreller?'

They all nodded. But the bird was gone.

He turned to Grandpa. 'Is it a good horse or a bad horse that got my boys?' he asked quietly without rancour.

'I don't know,' Grandpa admitted. 'But I do know, or think I know, where it is going.'

The travellers left, heading westwards across the stony uplands. When they had gone, a dark figure, like a shadow, crept from a fissure in an underground cavern and disappeared across the limestone waste of the burren.

The breakers were roaring onto the beach, crashing with curling crests of foam, flinging salty spume up onto the land. The noise crescendoed as each great roller broke on the shore and receded.

Tito and Ossie were high above the ocean on the cliff. Tir na n-Og was galloping furiously towards the cliff edge and the children held on for grim life, unable to check his headlong flight towards the sea. Behind and above them a helicopter hovered. The boys closed their eyes. But Tir na n-Og stopped on the brink of disaster, dislodging a rock which fell over the edge of the precipice and landed far below with a distant thud. The boys opened their eyes, stared across the hungry sea to the grey clouds on the horizon.

'What's out there, Tito?' Ossie whispered.

'America!'

Tir na n-Og turned sideways, raced along the top of the cliff and then down a natural embankment to the beach as though the devil were after him. He had returned to the place where Grandpa had found him.

Grandpa was there before him. With him were Papa, Kathleen and Barreller. The white horse continued his flight, kicking sand, slowing only as he neared the group by the breakers. Papa stood transfixed to see his sons come towards him like this. He was on the verge of tears. There was something magnificent about the scene, the white animal with flowing mane and tail, the toss of its head, and the two children it carried towards their father. Then he moved forward. Tir na n-Og came to a standstill, allowed himself to be stroked and then embraced.

Ossie whispered in agitation, 'They'll take you away, Tir na n-Og. They'll make us go back to the Towers.'

Papa studied his two sons, saw that they were thin and pale, but unhurt. He put his big arms up to them, but they did not move.

'Don't worry, boys,' he said. 'We are never going back to the Towers!'

Tito smiled and turned back to Ossie to share his delight.

'I missed you, boys,' Papa said, aware of the utter understatement of the remark. He said it humbly; he had had plenty of time to appraise his life. He knew only too well what the loss of his sons would have meant.

'We missed you too, Papa,' said Tito. Tito really wanted to weep with relief at the sight of his father and grandfather, at the familiar faces who would take charge again, relieve him of the burden of interpreting the Wild West, of being the tough guy when all he felt was small and frightened.

Papa knew this. He looked at his twelve-year-old with love and then at seven-year-old Ossie, who was still sitting perfectly still on Tir na n-Og. He wanted to take him and cradle him, but that would be to trespass on a dignity which was much too great for its owner.

'Ossie?' he said gently.

Ossie did not respond.

'Ossie?' he said again.

Ossie set his mouth in the petulant grimace he adopted for matters of great moment. The terror of the last few hours had given place to a new fear. His delight and relief at seeing his father and grandfather had been displaced by the pressing certainty that they would take the horse from him.

'I won't go anywhere without Tir na n-Og,' he said in high piping tones of desperation. 'I won't!'

Kathleen turned to Papa. She had been watching the approaches to the beach. She knew they could not expect simply to walk away. But Papa had brought her back to the waking world before she had seen it all, before she could interpret all the symbols or commit them to memory.

'John Riley!' she said suddenly in tones of warning.

Papa turned and saw the horsemen coming towards them down the beach. They were carrying something, which was passed between the two horsemen, thrown from one to the other like a rope.

'Don't let them take him, Papa!' Ossie screamed. 'Stop them, Papa!'

The horsemen urged their mounts to a gallop. The rope blossomed into a huge net.

Kathleen shouted and pointed and from the other end of the beach came two more horsemen, with another great black net, big enough to catch Jonah himself.

Ossie began to tremble. '*Papa!*' he screamed.

Papa, Barreller and Kathleen went for the first pair of horsemen who were now almost upon them, their net open and ready. But behind them came the second mounted duo, who threw their net over Tito and Ossie. The boys struggled frantically. Ossie, being small, slipped outside the net, but it pulled his brother to the ground. 'Tito,' Ossie shouted, 'are you all right?' But his voice was lost in the thunder of the sea and the sudden turn that Tir na n-Og made into the wind, springing forward down the beach into the tide.

The horsemen followed him at a gallop but were intercepted by Papa and Barreller, who grabbed the net and pulled the two men down onto the sand. Kathleen, too, had been knocked to the ground. She looked at the white horse, with Ossie still astride him, as he raced, backwards and forwards, in the surf. She saw Papa and Barreller trussed up in the nets like Sunday joints. She saw Tir na n-Og run towards Papa, stare at him for a moment, make as if to nuzzle him, before he wheeled round and made straight for the ocean. She heard Ossie's high-pitched screams, 'Save me, Papa, save me!' and Papa's shout, 'I can't! Get off the horse!'

Then Barreller roared, 'Papa, he's going into the

sea!' Barreller's huge fists tore the net, making a hole big enough for a man to crawl through. Papa went through it and jumped up, only to come face to face with Inspector Bolger who suddenly appeared before him wielding a broken branch. He aimed a kick at Papa who ducked, lunged back and grabbed the branch, striking out with it. The branch connected with Bolger's face and he fell back dazed on the sand.

Grandpa watched. Nothing in all his years, none of his stories, had prepared him for this.

He saw the child on the back of the white horse, saw the horse gallop into the crashing waves. He saw Papa run after them, like a demented spirit pitting himself against the wind and the tide. He saw the sea lash the shore and the white horse swim out and out, and he saw the waves come dancing shoreward and slap the child, who threw up his small arms as he fell from the back of the horse. He saw the child disappear and Papa dive after him.

Grandpa ran to the sea, calling, 'Come back, Ossie! Come back, Ossie!' even when he knew it was already too late and that Ossie could not possibly hear him above the din of the breakers.

Tito heard his grandfather's voice beside him, rising in a moaning, keening sound.

'He's in the water! Can he swim, Tito? Can he swim?'

Tito stared blankly into his grandfather's face. 'No.'

Grandpa knelt on the shore with his head in his hands. Kathleen raced after Tito who was tearing into the surf after his brother. She dragged him back to the shore. 'You can't save him, Tito,' she shouted. 'You can't fight the sea!'

'Tir na n-Og will save him,' Tito wept. 'Won't he save him, Grandpa?'

Grandpa, knowing betrayal, kept his head bowed. 'My stories,' he wailed, 'oh, my stupid stories!'

When he raised his head he saw that Papa was swimming, surging through the water with a powerful butterfly stroke. He searched with his eyes through the valleys and crests of the waves, but there was no sign of Ossie. The head of a white horse appeared for a moment, almost indistinguishable from the foam on the waves, and then was gone.

Chapter Sixteen

Superintendent O'Mara, followed by Sergeant Brophy, got out of the jeep and hurried to the edge of the cliff.

'Make your way down to the beach, Sergeant,' O'Mara instructed, 'and find out what's going on.' Then he surveyed the scene below him through a pair of binoculars. He saw the two groups, the travellers who stood, soaked, at the edge of the breakers, staring into the sea, and close beside them Noel Harnett with his men who were also staring into the sea. There were a number of human forms lying or sitting on the sand, among whom was Inspector Bolger. He had regained consciousness and was sitting up nursing his head. His face had been slightly rearranged when he had tackled Papa with the branch, so, although he was in uniform, it took the superintendent a moment to recognise him.

O'Mara was tired. He had driven cross-country in person to gain control over the shenanigans being orchestrated by Harnett and Bolger, and to rescue the good name of the force with as much discretion as possible. Bolger had been incommunicado for the past two days, ever since his men had been ordered off the case. Now O'Mara wanted to confront him in person and bring him back for disciplinary measures and whatever charges were appropriate – larceny of a valuable horse being among them. No one was going to make a fool of him and get away with it.

As for Harnett, O'Mara had made certain investigations about him and would have no compunction at all in flinging the book at him. He had wasted police time, he had received stolen goods in the shape of a valuable horse, he had conspired to defraud the Rileys, he had beset and terrorised two small children, he had engaged in conduct leading to a breach of the peace and, judging by what he saw on the beach, there was also a question of aggravated assault.

The superintendent was very angry. He was a cold, pragmatic man, but he lived by a sense of justice. It incensed him that he could have been fooled, that he had allowed the force to become involved in a private scam; his pride was outraged that he had not seen through the deception at the outset; it was intolerable to him that he should have been taken for a ride. All his professional life he had prided himself on the acuity of his judgement. Now Bolger and Harnett, by involving him in their circus, had shown him, in his own eyes, to be no better than any gullible new recruit still wet around the ears.

From his vantage point on the cliff, he examined the group of travellers, searching for the children and their father. He saw one child, the older child, but there was no sign of the other boy or of John Riley himself. Then Brophy came back to inform him that the horse had gone into the sea with the younger child on its back and that the boy's father had gone in after it.

O'Mara scanned the waves, saw how they churned and reared and flung themselves onto the beach but, although he looked far out, he saw no horse among their scudding crests nor any sign of life. The din from the breakers, still churning in fury after the storm of the day before, was deafening. The wind was cold and whipped against his face, making his ears sting. He thought of two children of tender years driven across the country by the old forces of greed and imposture; he thought of how they had survived and given their hunters the slip, only to end like this. The horse lost, a child lost and the father lost. If that were really the case, Bolger and the other beauty would end up behind bars. He would see to it himself.

Suddenly Brophy pointed. 'Look!'

O'Mara followed the direction indicated with his eyes. He saw the figure of a big man in a black coat stumbling out of the sea against the breakers. He was holding a child in his arms.

'It's Riley!' Brophy whispered.

O'Mara studied the form of the child in its father's arms, saw that he lay very still.

'Oh no,' he whispered. 'Oh no! Not the little fellow!'

The police watched while Papa put Ossie down on the sand. They saw him kneel beside him, bend over his child and give him the kiss of life.

* * *

Tito saw his father emerge from the sea with Ossie in his arms. He had a feeling in his heart that it might burst. He watched, afraid to breathe, while Papa strained against the waves; he was terrified that the surging water would suck him back into the sea. He saw Ossie, lying in his father's arms like a wet rag, so limp and lifeless that Tito felt it was a dream; everything was happening so slowly, like when they played something in slow motion on the telly, that it had to be a dream.

Papa put Ossie on the beach and began to squeeze his chest; then he blew into his mouth and pressed on his chest. 'Breathe,' he roared at him, in between the mighty blasts he blew into him, 'breathe!'

Water came out of Ossie's mouth but he did not breathe. Tito saw his father take the child by the shoulders and shake him, but still Ossie lay inert, his head lolling when his father moved him.

Tito heard the sea and felt the wind and while the tears ran unchecked down his cheeks his mind searched frantically for reasons, tried to make sense of why Ossie was silent and lifeless on the sand. Only a few minutes before he had been on the back of Tir na n-Og. But Tir na n-Og had failed him, had led him to his death.

Why had everything turned out so bad? Why was the Wild West not the way they thought it would be? Cowboys died on television all the time and it didn't matter. But if Ossie died it would turn the world inside out. If Ossie died he would die too. He might go on breathing but he would be dead.

He turned to look at Kathleen. She was weeping, staring at the inert body on the sand. 'Don't let him die. Jesus, don't let him die,' she was saying through her teeth, while she struggled for control.

Barreller, who had been watching his friend's furious attempts to restore life to his son, eventually approached Papa, took his arms gently.

'He's gone,' he whispered. 'Let him go.'

Papa moved back; he was shivering all over and his face was white and dazed. The grown-ups, except Grandpa who was hunched in anguish on the ground, stood looking down, as though all direction had deserted them.

'You can't die,' Tito said silently to his brother. 'Not after all this.' His mind churned with regrets. 'I'm sorry for shouting at you; I didn't mean it when I said you were an eejit . . . I love you, Ossie.' The tears were choking him. 'I wish you'd open your little squeaky gob right now!'

As though he had heard him, Ossie twitched. His eyelids trembled. There was the whistling sound of air being sucked into starved lungs. The boy's eyes flew open. He coughed water. He looked up at his family, perfectly oblivious of their consternation, and announced triumphantly, 'I saw her. Papa. I saw her!'

Papa, overwhelmed, reached down to cradle him. 'Easy son, easy!'

Afterwards Ossie remembered the silence. That was the strangest part of it. He had been so frightened, screaming in terror as the water rose around Tir na n-Og and the noise of the sea and the wind roared in his ears. He had seen the big wave coming, saw it rear over him slowly, very slowly, as though it wanted to have a good look at him first before it hit him. Then he had felt it sweep him up like a cork and the coldness had taken him down to the silence.

The water closed over his head. From the dreadful crashing of the sea he was suddenly surrounded by the glug-glug of water in his ears and, after a little while, by peace. He thrashed around for a bit, but soon he found that the panic left him; it was replaced by a feeling of being immensely tired and by a dreamlike serenity. The silence was gentle, and after a while he didn't mind that when he tried to breathe the water came in instead. It filled his lungs. He didn't mind the cold. Nothing mattered. It was like sleep. Like sleep after a long day.

He felt her hair first, silken and strong. It brushed his face. He knew she was there and he opened his eyes. He saw her hand. It was stretched out to him. He reached towards it and then she was all around him, and he felt the love. It was a great love. It was warm, so warm and strong that the cold went away. He put his hand to her face and she smiled. She covered him with her long hair, holding him in her arms, telling him things about himself, and Tito and Papa. He had never felt like this; he had never known that he was wonderful and beautiful and beloved; he had not known that it was good to be a child. He had never felt so safe. He knew now that he belonged to her, to Papa and Grandpa and Tito, to himself. He was no longer a waif in the emptiness; instead he knew that Ossie Riley was important, that he was loved beyond his understanding and that he had roots which stretched through the veins of Time and beyond all the boundaries he could possibly imagine.

He had thought that he slept then, but here he was on the beach and Papa, wet from head to foot, was standing there with the others and they were all crying.

Tito, torn with his own emotions, turned his face away. For the first time he noticed the length of the beach; he saw the promontory at the end where the cliff went out into the sea; he saw the rocks standing like sentries while the waves battered them. A memory tugged at his consciousness. He realised, with sudden certainty, what beach this was; he had been here once before and since then he had returned in countless dreams. If he closed his eyes he knew that he would hear her laugh.

O'Mara moved down onto the beach, walked to Bolger and looked him in the eye. He looked into one eye, because the other was closed. The inspector's face was bruised and bloody. But he understood the look on his superior's face. He knew he could forget Cathy and a honeymoon in the Seychelles and any immediate plans for rapid advancement in the world.

O'Mara gestured to his men and they escorted Bolger and Harnett away. Harnett had aged in the last half-hour. His face was grey. Not only had he lost the most incredible horse he had ever come across, but there was every likelihood that he would be dragged into a public scandal. His eyes, full of vengeance, swivelled to Bolger, but Bolger did not meet them.

Sergeant Brophy brought Papa some rugs from the jeep – the result of his own foresight – to wrap the children in. He looked back once more at the ocean, scanned the waves as far as the horizon.

'The horse has disappeared,' he called to the superintendent in tones of regret. 'It looks like he's had it.'

O'Mara nodded. He added another item to his mental tally.

'Get them off the beach,' he directed, indicating Harnett's men who were standing looking at each other and wondering why the sport had gone so sour. 'And give these people some peace. Keep a vehicle standing by to take them home.' Brophy nodded and moved away.

Ossie sat up. They were wrapping him in a big red and black rug.

'The horse has not disappeared,' he announced indignantly. 'He's just gone back to Tir na n-Og.' He sought Grandpa's eyes and Grandpa smiled. Then the child reached out and thrust his hand into the pocket of the wet coat which Kathleen had just removed from him, and pulled out a shell. It was a whelk, which he handed to Tito.

'Mammy said to give you this.'

Tito froze.

Ossie frowned in concentration. 'She said you would know.'

The adults looked on, uncomprehending. Tito did not speak. He pushed the proffered rug to one side, took the shell and walked away with it down the beach. The wind blew through his wet clothes. But he was warm, hugging the shell and speaking to the figure he had seen laughing, here on this same beach, seven years before. 'You didn't forget me, Mammy, after all!'

Chapter Seventeen

O'Mara interviewed Harnett personally. Since the episode on the beach he had reflected further on the best course of action. He knew that prosecutions would blow the whole business sky high, the media would have a field day and he would probably have to resign his position in the force. He had talked to the Rileys who did not want to press any charges. The child was alive and well and they were making no claims about the horse.

'Sure the horse came after me,' old man Riley had told him. 'He came out of the sea and now he's gone back to it!'

The superintendent sighed. Moonshine, he thought. Did you ever hear such moonshine. The travellers were great ones for superstition.

O'Mara's investigations had turned up a strange coincidence: it had been Harnett's company that had forced the same tribe of travellers away from their halting ground some seven years earlier. Mary Riley's death had followed. This could be ascribed to anything, poor health, bad luck, lack of medical attention. But it was a coincidence all the same and he didn't believe too much in coincidence. So he put the matter squarely to Harnett. Compensate them for the loss of the horse and the trauma he had subjected them to, or face charges in a public court of law.

Harnett did not dwell for too long on his options. He couldn't believe his luck and agreed with alacrity. What did they want as compensation? A hundred? Two hundred?

O'Mara assumed a thoughtful expression, drummed his fingers on the desk and looked out of the window at the clouds and then back at the man before him.

'I thought you estimated that the horse was worth a million,' he said conversationally.

Harnett's face lost its co-operative expression. His jaw dropped and he glared at the superintendent in outrage. But caution prevented him from making the response he wanted. He knew that he could not wheel and deal his way out of this dilemma. O'Mara could not be bought and this fact made negotiation impossible. His mind began to assess what the situation was worth to him. Was avoiding a scandal worth that kind of money? Would Simone stay with him if he was branded a criminal? How badly would his business interests be affected? What about his social position, his political contacts? What about his daughters? He remembered his arduous climb and looked with horror at the prospect of his easy fall.

O'Mara watched him and did not move a muscle. When the silence had lasted for a full half-minute he added, 'I dare say they would settle for half that . . . plus a donation of, say, fifty thousand to the Garda Benevolent Fund.'

Harnett capitulated.

Later O'Mara dealt with Bolger, a different Bolger. The inspector's formidable get-up-and-go seemed to have got up and gone. He still had bruises on his face, but he was basically recognisable, and he didn't put up too much of a fight when the superintendent gave him the option of facing a disciplinary hearing or accepting demotion to sergeant and a posting to the Aran Islands.

Papa went back to the camp site for his old caravan. He stood and contemplated it for a while, with its blue door and its weathered top and the old tea caddy in the cupboard with the photograph hidden inside. But the burning pain of loss inside him had changed into something different, into a recognition of reality, recognition of the ephemeral nature of all experience and, finally, into acceptance.

Ossie was alive. Every day Papa looked at him he was reminded of how nearly he had lost him. Tito had lost the worn, anxious expression which had marked his face when he had found the two boys. Papa realised that his elder son had been turning into an old man, an adult before his time, a child haunted by the requirements of survival, trying desperately to access wisdom and experience beyond his years. Now he had reverted to childhood, to the first stirrings of adolescence. He was happy. He laughed like a child for the first time in years.

Tito had a great talk to Birdie when the Rileys returned to the flat to remove their belongings. The flat seemed incredibly small and cramped; the hole in the wall was still there. Tito addressed Birdie through the hole, saw that she looked the same, that the little breasts under the jumper were the same. He thought she was wonderful. He thought her funny teeth were wonderful. He thought she looked nicer than any girl he had ever seen.

Birdie was embarrassed to find Tito looking in on her. She had washed her hair and was watching television. Her parents were out at the pub and she was ruling the other children with an iron fist. She had not managed to get rid of her breasts; she had rubbed in the vanishing cream but it hadn't worked, and she was beginning to think nothing would make them shrink. In a sneaking kind of way she was becoming proud of them.

Tito told her they were leaving, that they were saying goodbye to the Towers.

'It'll be bloody boring without you,' Birdie said, tears welling in her eyes. 'It was awful when you were gone. When me ma and da were out I used to look in at your place and wish I could talk to you . . .' She stopped, reddened and changed the subject. 'But Jesus, didn't you have great crack with that horse! We heard all about you on the telly!'

Tito smiled. 'I'll come back to see you, Birdie. And you can come and stay with us and we can go riding.'

Birdie wiped her eyes and said she would like that. 'Where are you going to anyway?'

'To the west,' Tito said. 'Papa's bought a big piece of land near the sea. We're going to live there a lot; it'll be great!'

Birdie's eyes widened at the mention of a commercial transaction. 'Where'd your da get the money for that?'

Tito shrugged. 'I dunno. The fellow who was chasing us had to give him something to make up for the way Tir na n-Og disappeared.' He grinned. 'It's a gas, isn't it? Tir na n-Og would have gone anyway. He only went back where he belonged.' He saw the furrow of incomprehension in Birdie's face and knew she was about to question him and there was so much he could not answer or explain. 'Tell us,' he said, quickly changing the subject, 'what have you been doing with yourself since we went away?'

Birdie raised a finger to indicate that he should wait. She disappeared for a moment and then brought a newspaper to the hole in the wall. She opened it, folded the paper so that Tito could see it. She pointed to a photograph of a young girl.

'Jaypurs, that's a picture of you, Birdie! Give us a look!'

She pushed the folded newspaper through the hole. Tito haltingly read the caption: 'Birdie Murphy the winner of the under-thirteens short story competition, with her entry entitled "The True Story of My Life".'

'My teacher entered it in the competition,' Birdie explained. 'I won fifty quid!' She glanced over her shoulder, lowered her voice to a whisper. 'I have it in the Post Office where my ould ones can't get at it!'

'You're going to be a writer?' Tito crowed. 'You'll write loads of stories and books and poems and make a fortune?'

Birdie nodded modestly.

They brought the caravan to the west, to the heather-covered acres which Papa had bought within sound and sight of the sea.

They waited until spring and then they went back to the place where Mary had died, and they took the caravan to the beach where the white horse had first appeared and had later left their lives. Grandpa and old Dan were there, in their usual halting place.

The beach was unchanged. But the evening was calm and the Atlantic breakers were muted as they crawled up the beach and frothed at the children's feet. Both Tito and Ossie stood for a while, looking westward, watching the sun set over the horizon. Tito was bigger; he had grown and had begun to acquire angles. Ossie was breathing normally. He had a new robustness and confidence. He remembered this sea and how he had found Mammy and what she had told him. He knew who he was now and nothing in life would really frighten him again.

Kathleen lit a torch for Papa. He took the fire from her and stood beside her for a moment before moving towards the caravan. He had decided to burn it.

He hesitated, staring straight ahead at the barrel-topped caravan which had once been his home. Barreller came and stood beside his old friend.

'Time to let her go, Papa. Time to let the woman go free.'

Ossie glanced at Kathleen's face. It was very still. She smiled down at the child, moved to grasp his hand. 'Everything will be okay now,' she whispered.

Papa threw the torch. The caravan, which had been sodden with paraffin, burst into flame. The fire burnt fiercely, devouring the canvas, exposing the frame, feeding on the wooden floor. The light was reflected in the sea. Through the hot haze of the fire, Ossie thought he saw shapes in the water, a white horse, then a young woman with long silken hair. He stared and pointed with his hand, unable to speak.

'It was Mammy, wasn't it?' he whispered after a moment to Kathleen who bent down to hear him. 'And now she's going home!'

Kathleen squeezed his hand.

'It was Mammy all right!' Tito whispered, smiling to himself and turning over the whelk in his pocket.

Grandpa stood in tears. But he nodded and smiled through them at his grandchildren, at his son-in-law, at their friends. Tito approached his father, watched his face become tender as he gazed into the flames. He stood beside him for a moment and when the fire began to die, he asked quietly, 'Are the travellers cowboys or Indians, Papa?'

Papa didn't answer for a moment. He seemed like a man in a trance. Then he turned to his son.

'There's bit of the traveller in everybody, Tito,' he said in a low voice. 'Very few of us know where we're going.' He moved back to Kathleen, stood beside her and reached for her hand.

Ossie watched the shadowy shapes in the water until he turned to his grandfather who had put a hand on his shoulder. And when he looked back, the shapes were gone.

* * *

More Fiction from Headline:

MALCOLM ROSS

The compelling Cornish saga from the bestselling author of A NOTORIOUS WOMAN

An Innocent Woman

Brought up by her unconventional mother amid the *crème de la crème* of Paris, Jane Hervey is in for a shock when she and her widowed father go to live in Cornwall. Polite Victorian society is a minefield of petty restrictions and Jane's wings are further clipped by the tyrannical behaviour of Mr Hervey, who, though fond of his daughter, treats her like a recalcitrant child.

Being a young woman with a substantial fortune, Jane soon finds herself courted by many of the district's eligible bachelors. Richard Vyvyan has her family's approval; lawyer Vosper Scawen makes no secret of his admiration; but it is the brooding good looks and devil-may-care reputation of Daniel Jago that hold most appeal for Jane. On the other hand, as she observes how the ladies of her acquaintance endure the "burdens of married life", she wonders whether she might not be better off a spinster. There is also a growing mystery about her mother – and about Jane's own true parentage.

Her attempt to unravel the truth and to fathom the eternal enigma of relations between the sexes leads Jane on a voyage of self-discovery that is to overturn her entire world and all its values. At the end she can no longer count herself . . . an innocent woman.

Malcolm Ross's other West Country sagas, ON A FAR WILD SHORE and A NOTORIOUS WOMAN, are also available from Headline.

FICTION/SAGA   0 7472 3347 0

More Compelling Fiction from Headline:

FRANCES BROWN

THE HARESFOOT LEGACY

Turned out by her bigoted preacher father when he
discovers she is pregnant, Liddy Nolan throws in her
lot with Jem Granger, a gypsy prize-fighter who offers
to be a father to her unborn child. Running away to the
gypsies turns out to be no romantic adventure, and at
first Liddy finds it hard to adapt to life on the road and
a host of unfamiliar customs and laws. She also
encounters hostility from the other Romany folk, who
see her as an outsider, and this hostility increases
when she inherits the haresfoot brooch that is a
Granger family heirloom.

Despite these obstacles, Liddy retains her spirit and
independence. Over the years, she and Jem raise a
family together and follow the age-old gypsy routes,
pitching their tent upon the common land and selling
their wares at country fairs, and in time Liddy shows
herself a true Romany at heart, earning herself an
honoured place in the community.

But the happiness of the couple is marred by the past:
Jem is haunted by the spectre of the unknown father of
Liddy's firstborn, while Liddy herself fears that Jem
feels pity rather than love for her. These
misunderstandings come to a head against the
tumultuous events of the Crimean War, and it is only
through almost unbearable tragedy that Jem and Liddy
finally acknowledge their love for each other and are
united at last.

'A wonderful tale – (with) a good helping of romance
and tragedy to give it true Romany charm' *Prima*

FICTION/SAGA   0 7472 3461 2

More Compelling Fiction from Headline:

HELL HATH NO FURY

M.R.O'DONNELL

When Lady Lyndon-Fury snubs Daisy O'Lindon on the
station platform at Simonstown that soft, rain-soaked day,
she has no idea of the whirlwind she is unleashing. For
Daisy – a spirited girl – resolves at once that she will
have her revenge by setting her cap at Her Ladyship's
youngest son, and goes to Dublin in pursuit of her plan.

Enrolling as an artist's model at the Dublin Academy,
where Napier is one of the most promising students, she
has no difficulty at all in catching his eye – for Daisy has
the body of a sylph and the face of Venus – but to her
surprise, she finds herself growing fonder of her victim
than she intends. And when her family – outraged that
their daughter is posing in the nude – throws her out,
Daisy moves in with Napier and quickly becomes
pregnant.

Together, the young people set out for Coolderg Castle to
break the news of their engagement, but Lady Lyndon-
Fury has other ideas, and Napier proves a man of straw
when it comes to opposing his formidable mother.

Now, as Daisy often points out, she is not the sort to bear
a grudge, but the role of a woman scorned does not come
naturally to her. Besides, the animosity between
O'Lindons and Lyndon-Furys (which, to be sure, goes
back over two hundred years) deserves some sort of a
response. So she sets up house not a stone's throw away
from the castle, and starts to make plans to get her own
back. But of course, this being Ireland, Fate ensures that
nothing turns out quite as she has planned . . .

FICTION/SAGA 0 7472 3481 7

More Compelling Fiction from Headline:

M. R. O'DONNELL
WHO ALSO WRITES AS MALCOLM ROSS

A WOMAN SCORNED

Five years after the tragedy that ruined her fifteenth birthday, Judith
Carty returns to Castle Moore and her flirtation with its heir, Rick
Bellingham. The past forms a special bond between the two, but some
of their friends would rather the romance didn't prosper. Rick's best
friend, Fergal, carries a torch for Judith himself, while Fergal's sister
Sally determines *she* will be the next Mrs Bellingham.

These gilded children of the Anglo-Irish aristocracy fall out of love as
easily as into it, and thoroughly enjoy the activity. But their rivalry
adds a touch of piquancy to the gay whirl of Dublin society and the
more leisurely country pursuits of those late summer days. They learn,
too, of a darker side of love: Rick's sister Henrietta risks all in an illicit
affair; Lord Vigo's eccentric sisters determine to resist family efforts to
marry them off; and Rick and Judith are thoroughly confused by the
conflict between their own desires and society's expectations.

True love never does run smooth, and none of the young women
relish the role of woman scorned. But the confirmation of an old
injustice finally upsets the romantic applecart and provokes a dramatic
and unexpected conclusion...

Don't miss M. R. O'Donnell's first romantic novel of nineteenth-
century Irish life, *Hell Hath No Fury*, also from Headline. And writing
as Malcolm Ross, his Cornish sagas, *On a Far Wild Shore*, *A Notorious
Woman*, *An Innocent Woman* and *A Woman Alone*.

FICTION/SAGA   0 7472 3756 5

A selection of bestsellers from Headline

FICTION

STUDPOKER	John Francome	£4.99 □
DANGEROUS LADY	Martina Cole	£4.99 □
TIME OFF FROM GOOD BEHAVIOUR	Susan Sussman	£4.99 □
THE KEY TO MIDNIGHT	Dean Koontz	£4.99 □
LEGAL TENDER	Richard Smitten	£5.99 □
BLESSINGS AND SORROWS	Christine Thomas	£4.99 □
VAGABONDS	Josephine Cox	£4.99 □
DAUGHTER OF TINTAGEL	Fay Sampson	£5.99 □
HAPPY ENDINGS	Sally Quinn	£5.99 □
BLOOD GAMES	Richard Laymon	£4.99 □
EXCEPTIONAL CLEARANCE	William J Caunitz	£4.99 □
QUILLER BAMBOO	Adam Hall	£4.99 □

NON-FICTION

RICHARD BRANSON: The Inside Story	Mick Brown	£6.99 □
PLAYFAIR FOOTBALL ANNUAL 1992-93	Jack Rollin	£3.99 □
DEBRETT'S ETIQUETTE & MODERN MANNERS	Elsie Burch Donald	£7.99 □
PLAYFIELD NON-LEAGUE FOOTBALL ANNUAL 1992-93	Bruce Smith	£3.99 □

SCIENCE FICTION AND FANTASY

THE CINEVERSE CYCLE OMNIBUS	Craig Shaw Gardner	£5.99 □
BURYING THE SHADOW	Storm Constantine	£4.99 □
THE LOST PRINCE	Bridget Wood	£5.99 □
KING OF THE DEAD	R A MacAvoy	£4.50 □
THE ULTIMATE WEREWOLF	Byron Preiss	£4.99 □

All Headline books are available at your local bookshop or newsagent, or can be ordered direct from the publisher. Just tick the titles you want and fill in the form below. Prices and availability subject to change without notice.

Headline Book Publishing PLC, Cash Sales Department, PO Box 11, Falmouth, Cornwall, TR10 9EN, England.

Please enclose a cheque or postal order to the value of the cover price and allow the following for postage and packing:
UK & BFPO: £1.00 for the first book, 50p for the second book and 30p for each additional book ordered up to a maximum charge of £3.00.
OVERSEAS & EIRE: £2.00 for the first book, £1.00 for the second book and 50p for each additional book.

Name ....

Address ....

....